THE BETTER MAN

A SILVER-BUCKLE BRIDES ROMANCE

BOOK TWO

LAURIE LEWIS

COPYRIGHT

BOOKS AND AUDIO BOOKS
BY LAURIE (L.C.) LEWIS:

Unspoken
Free Men and Dreamers:
Vol. 1: Dark Sky at Dawn
Vol. 2: Twilight's Last Gleaming
Vol. 3: Dawn's Early Light
Vol. 4: Dawn's Early Light
Vol. 5: In God Is Our Trust
Awakening Avery
The Dragons of Alsace Farm
Sweet Water
Love on a Limb
Love on the Line
Secrets Never Die
Revenge Never Rests
The Letter Carrier
Books in Silver-Buckle Romances Series
Cross-Country Christmas
The Better Man

This book is dedicated
to my precious baker's dozen of grandchildren:

Tommy, Keira, Christian, Brady, Avery,
Desmond, Chase, Wesley, Noah, Kenzie, Brooks, Mila, and Taika,

Love you without limits and forever,
Grandma

ACKNOWLEDGMENTS

I began writing a second Silver Buckle Brides book soon after sending *Cross-Country Christmas* off to the publisher. I was also up to my elbows in everything needed to get *The Letter Carrier* launched and we were just coming out of the Covid nightmare. My story revolved around a couple who ended up being quarantined together on a ranch during a feared second Pandemic, but my publisher wisely recognized that the manuscript was not what readers wanted or needed at that time, and it was put on hold.

A lot of events in my life and in the publishing house's business plan would have delayed the book's launch further, so my wonderful publisher not only offered me the right to publish the story on my own, they offered me the right to continue the Silver Buckle Brides Series independently as well. So, my first and greatest thanks go to Covenant Publishing for being so kind and generous with me regarding this project.

Beth Bentley, my wonderful friend and longtime editor, pulled off another five-star edit on this manuscript. She's a grammar and punctuation guru with a knowledge base in almost every area. These characteristics make her an excellent editor and they make me a better writer. Her praise for the greatly overhauled story gave me the gumption to carry on with the project. Thanks, Beth. I love the great stories we've created together.

Sheri McGathy, my talented cover artist, stepped into a second pair of shoes and also handled the formatting on this book. That she endures my artistically challenged feedback on the covers is remarkable, but her willingness to put up with me during the formatting truly makes her a martyr for her art. Thanks tons, Sheri. So glad you're my sweet friend.

So many willing, wonderful beta readers read this book as it evolved over three years. Sadly, it was more than I can remember. My grateful thanks go to all of you, including—Cyndy Packer, Cathy Morgan, Gail Ostheller, Cheri Frazier, and Bruce Morse. Your comments guided the edit helped get the finished version clean and ready for launch.

The countless hours required to produce a book are hours pulled from other priorities, so endless thanks go to my husband, Tom, and my family, for understanding their crazy wife and mom, and for all the support you've given me. I couldn't do this without your love.

The Better Man is based on real life experiences. I had a chance meeting with a father whose teen son was under arrest for criminal acts performed under the influence of alcohol and drugs. The father teared up as he told me that no alcohol was ever allowed in their home, and that neither he nor his wife ever drank. Their son had been introduced to alcohol by the "cool" parents of his friends who allowed kids to drink in their home. That "privilege" had not only violated this young man's parents' wishes without their knowledge, but it had also created a teen alcoholic, and ruined this young man's life.

I headed to the Internet to research similar stories and there were many. This research made me consider the prospects of forgiveness and change, how that might look to young people whose lives had been sidelined by teen alcoholism, and the journeys that might be required to reclaim their lives. These were the seeds behind *The Better Man.*

Lastly, I want to thank you, my readers, for your support, for your encouragement, and for giving me a reason to tell these stories. I hope they touch you as writing them has touched me.

Warmly,
Laurie L.C. Lewis

THE
Better Man

A SILVER-BUCKLE BRIDES ROMANCE
BOOK TWO

AWARD-WINNING AUTHOR
LAURIE LEWIS

CHAPTER 1

Friday, March 24, 2023

Four wheels and a tank of gas can change your life.

Laramee Stone had a bit of experience on the matter. Her battered old truck had been what she needed in the hour of her need—an express train to adventure, an impromptu flight to freedom, an escape from loss. All from the seat of this old truck. Her battered Ford was still a time machine of sorts, transporting her from the Arizona desert back to a time when the future looked as endless as a snow-swept Colorado prairie. But she was different now. A hard-edged square peg that no longer fit in the promising round world of her youth.

She twisted the cracked leather on her steering wheel. Her mom's early-morning phone call had been the catalyst, the rocket fuel that sent Laramie tossing essentials into her suitcase and shooting her boss a text with the news that she was taking a few weeks off without notice.

She groaned at her foolishness. "That was brilliant."

No matter. It was the slow season when fewer people booked guided horseback vacations, so work was scarce, and if her boss fired her, oh well...The sad truth was that in the post-pandemic world where people ate out more than in, she could make a better wage flipping burgers.

She took a deep breath as she surveyed the Alpine Peak Ski Resort sign. She'd only come here a few times. Once on a school-sponsored ski trip, and once when her rodeo-queen prize package included a week's stay at the posh resort. *Posh*...She tittered. That was a word she hadn't used since she was fifteen. This place and the past were creeping up on her.

The thought forced Laramee to consider her current appearance. She'd left in such a hurry that she hadn't concerned herself with grooming. Glancing down at her grungy work jeans and then into the rearview mirror confirmed her worst fears. She looked as bad as she thought. Tattered jeans, her long brown hair shoved under and falling out of a knitted cap, and nails that looked like they were manicured by a rabid badger. She wasn't embarrassed or ashamed of what hard work had done to her, but she momentarily reconsidered her last-minute plan to pop by the resort's bakery to grab a box of their world-famous ginger cookies for her mom. Then again, what did she care about the establishment's spandex-clad ski clientele's opinions of her? She was buying her mom a box of her favorite cookies.

As she feared, there were no empty spaces in the guest parking lot. New snow and lots of it sent ski people into a frenzy to hit the slopes. There was, however, an empty spot in the check-in lane between two shiny, pricey SUV's. She would be in the place for just a few minutes, she told herself, so whispering her father's shopping mantra under her breath—"Get in, get out, get going"—she drove into the empty spot and entered the resort's lobby.

The beauty and elegance of The Alpine's elegantly rustic interior left her awed again. She breathed in the scents of woodsmoke, and some musky aromatic infused into the air as her eyes were drawn to the fire blazing in the massive stone fireplace. Comfy sofas and chairs surrounded the fire, where she once sat in the company of young men vying for the chance to teach a pretty rodeo queen how to ski.

She pulled back from those memories and others it stirred as she turned to scan the rest of the grand lobby. A silver placard advertised the day's primary events—a retirement party in Ballroom 1, a meeting in Ballroom 2, and the Smithfield/Westerly wedding in Ballrooms 3–5. It sounded like a grand affair.

She walked on and looked for the bakery. It was where she remembered, except its sought-for sign now appeared over a sparkling bright window painted with cupcakes and cookies in pinks and browns and greens. An unexpected face appeared in the doorway. The young man did a double take and beamed an excited smile her way as he waved her over.

Laramee recognized him immediately. "Duncan?"

"Yep! Except I hope I'm not a brat anymore." He swept her up in a bear hug. "Even so, you were my favorite babysitter. I've missed you."

She suddenly felt much older than her twenty-five years. Preferring a quick change of subject, she broke free of his hug and slid onto a stool. "When did you start working here?"

"October. Employees get big discounts on lift tickets and I'm a bit of a ski bum when I'm not in class." He placed a mug before her and filled it with steaming cocoa. "It's so good to see you, Laramee. Man… how long has it been?" He added an extra-large swirl of whipped cream and handed her a spoon. She began to stir, ignoring the question.

"Thanks for the cocoa. I forgot how cold a Colorado March can be. But I can't stay long. I'm parked in the check-in line."

Duncan swept her worry away along with the sweep of his dishrag across a chocolate slosh on the counter. "No one will notice your car parked out there if you sit a few minutes to catch up.

She begged to differ, knowing that her ramshackle Ford was likely generating considerable attention. "I'm in a bit of a hurry to get home."

"Oh, it'll be nice to have you close again. We've all missed you. It's been years since I've seen you at any of the big family gatherings."

Laramee felt the walls closing in on her. "Listen…I'd love to get together with you sometime, but just the two of us, okay? I don't like crowds."

He laughed as his brow wrinkled in protest. "Since when, Your Majesty?"

Laramee dipped her head and took a sip to evade answering, and then mercy, in the form of a timer beep, caught Duncan's attention. "I need to check the next batch of cookies."

"Speaking of which," she said, "I need two dozen of your famous ginger cookies."

"They're my dad's favorite."

Her mom's too, probably because boxes of the delicious treats were Duncan's father's gift to his four siblings each Christmas. "Two dozen will do it."

An attractive man with brown, wavy hair entered the bakery and stood back as if waiting for Laramee to be served. He was tall and muscled, with the most captivating eyes. Their ice-blue coloring gave them a vulnerability that drew Laramee in until she had to force herself not to stare. He had a good face with features and irregularities that needed to be studied more than simply seen, beginning with a few scars and a nose which was slightly crooked as if it had been broken at some point. She thought it actually added to his character.

"Welcome," Duncan said to the man. "What can I get for you?"

The man stepped back farther and pointed to Laramee. "The lady was here first."

Laramee glanced the man's way, acknowledging his kindness with a muted smile while Duncan completely dismissed her presence.

"She's my cousin. We're just catching up. What will you have?"

"In that case, just an herbal tea and a bear claw, please. To go."

Laramee glared at Duncan, but she hid her frustration from the man. He looked her way, and she faced the opposite direction so he didn't get the false impression that she was checking him out, which she told herself she was most assuredly not doing. The last thing she wanted or needed was another guy in her life, well-intentioned or not.

Duncan's dismissal of her and her urgent parking situation ramped up Laramee's stress. She peered past the tall glass windows of the lobby to make sure no tow truck was pulling in to take her truck away. No truck was visible, but her glance caught and held on another interesting sight. A stunning couple entered the lobby looking as if they were modeling for a cover shoot. Two bellmen followed behind with two luggage carts. One held four large suitcases and the other carried two bulging garment bags. The black bag had *Armani* written across it along with the name of an L.A. men's store. The white garment bag bore the name Monique Lhuillier, a high-end designer of gorgeous wedding gowns. The couple was evidently the bride and groom mentioned on The Alpine's event placard.

A woman in a red suit arrived to greet the couple. Laramee's heart broke a little when she saw the tender way the bride leaned into the groom and how his arm slid behind her as they spoke. They were a love match. Not a couple just falling into marriage or two people marrying out of convenience. She wondered if she ever looked as smitten and happy as they did, but before she went too far down that road, she reminded herself that men were the cause of most of the chaos in her life.

After a few moments, the bear claw man came up behind her saying, "Excuse me."

She shifted left to allow him to pass, but he stopped suddenly, and did a double take before stepping back inside again. His abrupt retreat surprised her. She assumed he'd forgotten part of his order, but she was too focused on the handsome loving couple to care. They were being escorted down the hall toward the Alpine's elegant, magical reception hall where they would celebrate the beginning of their life together.

When they were beyond her sight, she scoffed at her silliness, only to find Bear Claw Man still in the doorway, huddled behind her, also watching the couple's exit. She blushed at the thought that he'd noticed her mooning over someone else's happy moment, but before she could come up with a suitably indignant response, he proceeded out The Alpine's door, and another sight caught her attention.

The two bellman who had attended to the Smithfield/Westerly's luggage were now quite obsessed over her truck. One stayed with it while the other hurried back into the lobby to search for the owner. When he moved to the front desk to make inquiries about the owner, Laramee spun back into the bakery.

"Forget the cookies, Duncan. I've got to go right now."

"All ready," he said, handing her a pink box tied in brown string.

"What do I owe you?"

"Nothing. It's on the house. I get a dozen free somethings every week so I'm passing my benefit on to you."

"Thanks, but you don't—"

He waved her concern away. "Just keep your promise and call me for lunch sometime."

She gave him a quick hug and darted for the door, getting past the first bellman and making it through the resort's main door before finding her truck blocked by the other uniformed bellman. Standing to her left was Bear Claw Man. He handed his ticket to the valet who ran off to fetch the man's vehicle. Laramee prayed the car would arrive and take him away before she suffered another humiliation.

Her prayer was in vain. The bellman approached her, pointing to the truck. "Is this your *vehicle?*"

She heard the derogatory tone to his voice. Pulling herself up straight to look as Alpine-worthy as possible, she said, "Yes, but my plans have changed and I'm leaving now."

The bellman looked at her cookie box and pointed to the sign that said, *Parking available for registering guests only.* He kept his finger aimed at the sign and said, "The only people allowed to park here are registering guests. Not bakery customers."

"I see. I'm very sorry. I'll be leaving."

The man did not immediately move from her path, and Laramee wondered if he might be intending to hold her car hostage until a tow truck arrived. A showdown began while she schemed to find a way around the man. Laramee was prepared to squeeze him out of the way if need be, but Bear Claw Man stepped to her side while addressing the bellman.

"She made a mistake and said she's sorry. I think you've made your point. Why don't you let her pass."

Laramee felt smaller with every word he spoke. Another man's face flashed before her. He too wanted to help her. To save her. *Look how that turned out,* she told herself. She swallowed down her pride, and began to offer a meek, "Thank you," when saw Bear Claw man extend his hand to the bellman with a twenty exposed. As the bellman reached for the money Laramee groaned, "No!" as she pushed Bear Claw Man's hand back and away.

Startled, he explained, "I'm trying to help."

His voice sounded sincere, and his expression didn't show superiority or condescension, but this man had already seen her in an earlier vulnerable moment. The idea that he was now attempting to save her by paying off the bellman made her feel naïve, childish, incapable. "Thank you," she said, biting each word, "but I don't need your help." She saw a Range Rover pull up and pointed to it. "You can go. I've got this."

"Okay then," said Bear Claw Man as he turned and left, but the stubborn bellman was still there, shaking his head slowly as if she were all the things the other man made her feel. She remembered the twenty she'd expected to pay for the cookies. Pulling it out, she offered it to the man along with an apology. "I saw the sign. I thought I could be in and out so quickly that I wouldn't be a bother. I was wrong. I'm sorry."

The man bowed and refused her money, "Next time..."

"There won't be a next time."

Anxious to get away and put as many miles as possible between herself and that place, Laramee jumped in her truck, moved tools off the passenger seat to make room for the cookies, and put the vehicle in reverse without looking in her rearview mirror.

She'd barely moved four feet when she felt a bump. Her stomach flipped, and she slumped against her seat when she saw the two bellmen shaking their heads at her as if she, once again, was a disappointment.

She found the will to open the door, but before she took a step down, Bear Claw Man was there, offering her his hand and smiling sympathetically at her.

"There isn't any damage to my vehicle. My bumpers have bumpers."

Laramee stiffened her back and took his hand, allowing him to help her down. He walked her to the front of his car and pointed to thick rubber pads attached to his bumper. As he said, they had protected his metal bumper from hers. She took a breath and fell against her truck.

The man continued. "I didn't inspect your vehicle for damage."

Laramee eyed him, unsure if he was being friendly, or making sarcastic comments about her junker. She knew it was time for another bitter swallow of pride. "I'm so sorry. I-I-I was so upset that I—"

"—No need. I understand. Neither of us is having a particularly great day."

The regret-filled tone in his voice mirrored the ache in her heart. This guy had his own troubles. Maybe he did know how she felt. "Well…thanks for understanding."

He nodded and lifted a quick hand in goodbye. Laramee waited until his vehicle disappeared down the lane before she started the truck and drove away. She thought going home would be the hardest part of this trip. After the past hour at The Alpine, facing her parents looked better and better. At least things couldn't get any worse.

CHAPTER 2

*J*ames Marston Cannon's head was spinning as he drove away from The Alpine. The situation in front of the resort had provided a much-needed temporary distraction, but he was alone now, with only his thoughts and his regrets as companions.

He picked up his cup, hoping a warm swallow of lemony tea would soothe his rattled nerves, but the cup had grown tepid, so he set it back down and pulled into a fast food joint off to his right to pick up a Coke. It wasn't warm but he hoped the caffeine might do the trick. He pulled into a parking spot to dump the cold tea and settle his mind, and then the phone rang.

He checked the caller ID. It was someone he'd actually like to talk to right now, and he clicked into the call.

"Hey, Mikie."

"What's up, Dog?"

"No one says that anymore, especially married dads from Yale."

"No one but you still calls me Mikie anymore, either, but you're probably right."

"So, what's up?"

"I was thinking about you and thought I'd give my little brother a call."

Jamie offered a thoughtful laugh. "Thanks, man. I could use a brotherly chat today. You are not going to believe who I walked into."

"Well...Dad called and told me you took a few days off to grab some R&R by skiing at The Alpine, so I can make an educated guess. Did you run into Victoria?"

"How did you...Wait...are you saying she sent Mom and Dad a wedding invitation?"

"Yep."

"Unbelievable."

"I know, right? Now that's cold."

"Did she send you and Lillith one too?"

"Yes, but I bet you can imagine what Lillith did with it." Mike laughed in that high-pitched hyena laugh he gave when he thought something was ridiculously funny. Jamie wasn't amused. "I'm glad you're enjoying this."

"I'm sorry." Mikie's laugh slowly skidded to a halt. "But I'm glad she's marrying someone else. I never thought she was a good fit for you. Just when it seemed you had things figured out, she came along and tried to reinvent you. And that's probably why you ran away from her."

"I didn't *run* from her. Not exactly, anyway. She's seriously beautiful, intelligent, and witty. She knows exactly what she wants, and she doesn't let anything get in her way. I wish I had a fraction of her clarity."

"I didn't hear anything about loving her."

"That...that was a given." Jamie knew he'd backed himself into a corner. "I love so much about her. Things just changed as time moved on."

"How many times have you two taken a break from your relationship? Four?"

"Three. And they were mutually agreed upon."

"Listen to yourself. That's still an alarming stat. No one wants to begin a marriage where leaving is a possibility going in."

"I suppose not, but I invested years in that relationship."

"You're twenty-nine, Jamie, not ninety. You've got time. A good marriage is worth taking it slow and getting it right."

"Marriage has made you quite passionate about the institution."

"It's the best, brother. It'll come to you. But no rebound romances, okay? Whatever emotions you're feeling today, throw them into work. What's on today's list?"

Jamie shuffled papers on the passenger seat to see the options before him. "Dad sent me three properties to look at. Two are in Denver—"

"—Hard pass on those. You don't want to be in Denver right now. Denver holds too many Victoria memories. What else do you have?"

"There's an old ranch about three hours east. Dad thought it might be a good fit for several of our clients."

"That one. Go there. Getting a little dirt under your nails would be good for you."

He'd been excited about that property from the first moment he'd seen it. "Maybe you're right. Thanks."

"You know I love you, and I'll always have your back."

"I know. Love you too, Mikie."

"Hey, and here's a heads up. Expect a call from Mom and Dad."

"Oh, gosh, no. Please tell me it's work stuff and not personal."

"I wish I could, but you know how it is with them. Sorry, Buddy."

"Is this ever going to end?"

"They still ask if my knee hurts from that surgery I had in eighth grade, so probably not. Just tell them you love them and that you're okay."

Jamie sucked in a fifty-gallon breath and slowly let it out, ending with. "Will do."

"See ya."

"You, too."

Jamie ended the call and picked up the documents for the ranch property—an old dude ranch in the Colorado plains. Just the thought of an old ranch setting stirred some of his sweetest memories. He set the GPS for the ranch property and pulled onto the access road that led to the highway.

There had barely been time to process the route when the phone rang again. The caller ID assured him that this conversation was going to get awkward. He hit the exit for the highway, answering the call on the ninth ring. "Hey, Dad."

"How are you doing, son? I was just thinking about you."

He could hear his mother in the background posing questions to his father about The Alpine.

"So…you said you were going skiing. Did you stay at one of the resorts or did you just grab a day pass?"

Jamie knew the least painful way to end this was to avoid the agonizing dance around the subject and lay it right out. "I stayed at The Alpine, Dad, and imagine this. I ran into Victoria and her intended. They looked good together. And don't worry about me. I'm fine. Happy for all of us, in fact."

He regretted adding that last bit. He'd overplayed his hand. It was a common coping technique he'd used in the past, and he waited to see how his parents reacted to it. Their elongated silence told him he was right about his error. When they responded to him, worry and fear tinged their voices.

"You know son, the company has plenty on its plate right now. We don't need another real estate deal straining our resources at this time. Why don't you set those properties aside, come home to Boise, and relax for a while? We could pack into the Boise River and go fly fishing for a few days. Doesn't that sound nice?"

Jamie felt sweat break on his skin. They still saw him as broken. If not completely lost, at least fractured and too fragile to navigate a simple disappointment without a crutch. He weaved through traffic, pulled onto the shoulder, and set his car to park, while he dealt with the blow their lost confidence meant to his worth.

The silence went on too long, and his mother's worried voice chimed in. "Jamie? Jamie?!"

He bit down on his knuckle as he figured out how to respond without hurting his folks. "I'm here, Mom," he said in an annoyed singsong. "And I'm fine. Do you hear me. I'm really, truly, fine. Running into Victoria like that was a shocker, but I know we weren't right for each other. I'm really okay."

"Are you sure? I'd love to have you home for a few days. Mike is so busy with his new house and the family. We'd love some one-on-one time with you."

He knew it was true, and maybe that was part of the initial problem. Once Mike married Lillith, his parents' hold on Jamie tightened, until he rebelled…in a big way. "Soon, Mom. I promise. But not today. I'm actually heading east to an old dude ranch. Working this place up will be fun. But it snowed up here and traffic's bad on these winding mountain roads, so I've gotta go and focus on my driving. I'll call you tonight, okay? Bye-bye."

He hung up and held his breath, expecting them to call back more worried than before, to note his hasty exit from the call. When neither happened, he pulled into the traffic and wrangled through the never-ending stream of ski-toting cars carrying arriving and departing skiers. He also knew that some of those cars were carrying Victoria's wedding guests.

The going was slow, and as each mile put him farther away from Victoria, he considered that he might never see her again. It was a strange concept. As Mike pointed out, their breakups never felt final —more like timeouts where they'd argue, declare they weren't right for each other, and then through a text or a call, meet as "friends" and fall back into their old patterns. But this was different. She was getting married to another man. And, interestingly enough, he realized he really was okay with that.

About thirty minutes later, he reached the exit for the freeway. Traffic was heavy there as well, and he was grateful when he reached the turnoff for the state highway that would be his route for the next hundred miles.

He pushed the accelerator a little harder than suggested, but traffic was light, and he became more relaxed as snowy cityscapes and suburbs gave way to miles of flatlands, bluffs, and buttes. The wind carried the dry snow, depositing some along the way in snow-dusted valleys while blowing the bulk of it to the mountains where it piled up in deep banks.

Jamie could see for miles and miles, and the sight of the sprawling, unencumbered terrain freed his spirit as well. These acres were nothing like the lands of the Anasazi, but the feelings they stirred were very similar. He grew more excited as each mile passed, and happily called the owners of the ranch to tell them he was on his way.

Committed to this plan now, he passed most vehicles as he hurried along, anxious to reach his destination. And then, up ahead, he saw an unmistakable sight—a battered green Ford truck.

&.

*L*aramee tried focusing on the ride home rather than on what she'd face when she arrived there. She had missed the beautiful snow-covered mountains during her years in Arizona, and she regretted not hitting the slopes for a few hours before heading home, but that pleasure would have to wait for another day. Perhaps a day far away.

She headed northeast and set her sights on the snowy plains ahead. Bedroom communities had sprung up on the previously open prairie east of Denver, and in a curious homage to the past, the developers dotted the fringes of the communities with metal artwork that resembled the silhouettes of buffalo. Out on the eastern plains where she was headed, the land still looked much as it had two hundred years ago, sparsely populated big spreads of several thousand acres each, far from organized towns. Shopping was a big event that required planning. She didn't mind that, but community hospitals and state-of-the-art medical attention were equally sparse. That, along with the danger that accompanied ranching, made this lifestyle one for the brave and the few.

She looked in her rearview mirror and about died. There, reflected in her mirror, was a black Range Rover. She tried to convince herself that it couldn't be the same one driven by Bear Claw Man, but as the vehicle drew near her, and then slowly drew up beside her, the driver was the same man, and his expression seemed as dumbfounded as her own. She wound her window down and he did the same.

"Are you following me?" she shouted with obvious accusations attached.

"No!" he shouted back as the wind grabbed and muffled his message.

She purposely twisted her face into an expression of utter disbelief and signaled toward the shoulder of the road. She pulled off and the man followed suit. Just in case he was some sort of highwayman or murderer, she grabbed her horseshoe nail puller out of her farrier bag. It weighed a few pounds and would deliver a good whack if one was needed.

The man's eyebrows looked like they were doing pushups as he watched her stomp his way. Before his door opened, Laramee was tapping on his window, her nail puller tucked behind, ready with her speech.

He exited his car and gasped as the cold wind hit him, prompting him to reach back into his car. Guessing that foul play was his motive, Laramee pulled her "weapon" out and backed up several feet, assuming a wide battle stance. When she realized he was only reaching for his coat, she hid the puller and struck her earlier, defiant pose.

He wrapped his arms around himself and asked, "What's the problem now?"

"You say you're not following me, but I find it very strange that you're on this particular road at this particular time, especially when you left before me. You should be miles ahead of me."

"My delay at the resort left my tea cold." He pointed inside to his soda. "So, I pulled off at a drive-through to grab a Coke."

Laramee felt her cheeks flush warm. "Oh." It was her third humiliation in an hour. The man's explanation still didn't sit well, and she challenged him again. "Even so, that only takes a minute."

"Well…if you must know, I parked in the parking lot for approximately three minutes during which time I received a call from my brother Mike, and then I spent another few minutes talking to my folks, Darlene and Bill. I could check my phone log and give you actual phone length data, or would you like their numbers? You could also interrogate them if you'd like."

She jutted her chin forward. She was batting zero, and she felt like a fool. "It just seems very strange that you'd be traveling this very road at this very time."

He waved his arm east and west, several times, as if blazing the road's trail. "It's the only road to where I'm going."

"It runs through small towns and ranches." She looked at his Range Rover as if that alone should negate his argument.

"I'm a real estate investment broker." He reached into his pocket and pulled out a business card which he handed over to her. The embossed lettering read—

James (Jamie) Marston Cannon,
Associate Broker,
Cannon Capital.

"I find properties my clients are looking for. Today I happen to be headed to a small ranch about eighty miles from here."

Eighty miles ahead was where her family ranch lay, as well as those of her family's friends. He had her full attention again. "Which ranch? Who owns it?"

Jamie blew on his hands to warm them, but Laramee stood resolute until he opened the car door and grabbed the papers.

"The owner's name is…Stone. Sterling and Cathy Stone."

The blood drained so quickly from Laramee's head that the pullers slipped from her hands. She fell against the Range Rover and Jamie Cannon rushed in to support her, dropping his papers which flew yards away on the prairie wind.

"Are you okay?" His hands gently held her until her strength and balance returned.

"Yes," she said as she pulled away and beyond his reach. "That's my ranch. My family's ranch," she corrected, as she regained her strength. "And it's not for sale."

Jamie rushed into the tall grass after his now damp papers. When he returned with them in hand, Laramee had her arms crossed in front. "You can just turn around and go back to wherever you're from."

"The owner of the property is Sterling Stone. Since I just spoke to Sterling I assume you're not him."

"No, but I'm his daughter, Laramee." She hated the pleading tone in her voice.

"Then I can't turn back. I'm sorry. Your parents are expecting me."

Betrayal hit Laramee like a rock in the gut. She was angry at her father, but this man before her was a suitable proxy. She fisted her hands and leaned forward, unleashing her anger on him.

"You're wasting your time. My mother called me home from Arizona to talk about the ranch's future. She promised me Dad wouldn't sell the ranch if I wanted to take it over, and that's why I'm here."

"To claim the ranch?"

She hesitated before answering, "Yes."

Jamie's face softened, and his chin dropped to his chest for a moment before he met her eyes again. "I'm sorry. I feel how much you love your ranch, but your parents are expecting me—"

"It's my home," she cried out, letting a piece of her heart slip out with the words.

His ice-blue eyes looked beyond her face and into her pain, until her ache was as visible on his face as it was in her heart. The timbre of his voice was caring and mellow and filled with his own pleading as he echoed, "I can't turn back, but I make you this promise. I won't do or say anything to convince your father or mother to sell. I'll test the soil and assess the property's value and potential, but once I turn that information over to your parents, the decision is totally theirs."

She bought into the caring he exuded, but his words *assess the property's value* pushed her right back again. How could anyone place a value on her home? Or what it was worth to *her*?

She'd never been ashamed of her family home, but it certainly wasn't what this guy was used to. He didn't appear snobbish or judgmental, but Laramee was certain she'd lose it if he rolled his eyes at their rustic little ranch or cringed at a little bunkhouse dust. If her opinion of the ranch was tainted in any way by his *valuation*, she'd never get over that.

"I'll set a value for you. It's priceless. My parents may have forgotten that, but I'll remind them, so as you can see, going there is pointless. Go back to The Alpine, or home, or go assess the value of someone else's life, but you're not welcome at our place."

Laramee expected him to get in his vehicle, rev his engine, and take off. She was not prepared to explain herself further, so she shifted onto one hip and scrambled for a reply. "You seem like a decent person. You don't want to do this. So, please…go." She turned for her truck, waiting for his tires to peel out, but all she heard was the purr of his idling vehicle. She turned back to him. "Why are you still here?"

"I could give you three or four professional reasons, but most importantly, because I gave my word to your father."

She cocked her head to the side and studied this honor-bound intruder. Under other circumstances, she probably would have appreciated his integrity. Perhaps she would have even respected him, but he was discussing the sale of her home, and that changed everything. "I'm leaving. Don't follow me."

Jamie bent down and picked her pullers off the ground. "Or what?" He extended them to her and raised one eyebrow. Those previously tender blue eyes hardened. She tried to hold her angry glare, but once again, an embarrassed blush burned her cheeks. "Just don't come. Please. You don't know my family or what we need."

She returned to her truck and drove away, staring back at the rearview mirror, hoping that if reasoning with him had failed, compassion might succeed.

CHAPTER 3

*I*f Laramee Stone's tirade had been the only side of the story he'd heard, Jamie might have changed his plans, but after speaking to Sterling Stone, he knew there was a giant familial disconnect about the property. Sterling wanted desperately to sell. And Jamie had told him he'd come. Laramee would be livid when she heard the rest of the arrangements.

The woman lived up to her surname—Stone. She was stubborn and principled, which he would normally see as positive qualities, but she pushed back hard and stood her ground like a rock, which he now realized was not unlike Victoria. But Victoria's beauty and persuasiveness made people bend to her will, whereas Laramee simply bulldozed anyone in her way.

As far as he could see, the biggest differences between the two were style and appearance. Victoria was a lady…well…except for her temper which he'd witnessed more times than he cared to remember. On the other hand, Laramee was an adult version of a tomboy, from her unkempt hair to her rough and calloused hands. She was going to make this assignment difficult, but he'd done difficult things many times. He'd honor Sterling's wishes and then they'd be done.

He could do this.

He waited until a small sedan and a farm truck drove past before he put the vehicle in gear and pulled out behind the farm truck. He still felt her fury burning into him from her taillights.

The highway ahead was nearly straight for the next forty minutes until Laramee turned north onto a narrow, bumpy state road. Jamie tried to enjoy the scenery, but something Laramee said kept running through his mind.

You don't know my family or what we need.

After thirty jarring minutes, Laramee signaled a left turn as she came upon a rise where a narrow, potholed road broke to the left off the state road. Jamie made the turn when he reached the rise, providing him with an unobstructed view that allowed him to see for miles, and what he saw were a few clusters of buildings surrounded by broad, occasionally fenced acreage. He assumed the Stones ranch was one of these properties. Sure enough, Laramee's truck lumbered a few miles before turning on to a dirt lane marked with iconic western décor—rusted wagon wheels and an ancient plow to the left, and a decrepit old wagon bearing sun-bleached cattle skulls to the right. A weathered sign was nailed to the wagon's side. It read, "Welcome to The Stone's Throw Ranch."

There was a certain romance to the entrance of the Stone's place that reminded Jamie of his time in southern Utah. The artifacts were real western items, not the manufactured stuff people ordered from catalogs to adorn their multimillion-dollar homes so they blended into the western landscape.

Laramee's truck followed the ruts in the lane, and as he followed Laramee he saw the less romantic and more practical hardships of ranching. Their approach revealed a two-story frame house in sore need of paint. Two badly weathered gray barns, one large and one smaller, were situated in the back. One long ranch-style structure was set nearest the house. He assumed this was the bunkhouse. It looked as if a coat of whitewash had been slapped across it every now and then, more then, than now. Structurally, it looked sound, and he almost wondered if the lack of paint was intended to make it look rustic and authentic.

A few goats and chickens ran loose on the place, and five horses grazed in the overgrown paddock. Laramee parked her truck ahead of the last hundred yards to the house and stood in the open space between the truck's body and its open door, just glaring at Jamie's vehicle as it rolled close and came to a stop. With the sun rays beaming behind her, she looked friendly, and even attractive, with her freckled cheeks and nose, but when she slammed the door and walked his way, she was all business again.

"You surprised me, Pretty Boy. I can't believe you came where you aren't wanted. How long does this assessment of yours take? A few hours? All day?"

"*Several* days."

"What?" Jamie watched her eyes bulge. "What do you plan to do here? Tear the place apart?"

"I need soil samples, water studies, and an examination of the structures. I need to ride or drive the entire perimeter and photograph what I see. It takes time."

Laramee's hands moved to her hips. "And where do you plan to stay? There isn't a hotel within fifty miles."

He glanced at what he assumed was the bunkhouse.

"No, no, no."

"Your father offered it to me."

"You're not going to be comfortable there."

He scoffed at the comment. "I've camped on frozen ground, basement floors, solid rocks, and in a cave. I'll be just fine."

"How you sleep isn't my worry."

She got in her truck and drove down the lane, parking close to the house. Jamie followed and parked a few yards behind. She exited her vehicle and Jamie exited his. Pointing to the bunkhouse, she announced, "There you go. Your own personal five-star resort. The men's dorm is to the left. The kitchen and commons area are in the center. And grab a key off the rack by the door. You'll need to keep it handy because the dorm room doors lock behind you when you close them. Also, the place has been empty for a while, so you ought to begin your *assessment* of the property by cleaning out the cobwebs and sweeping the place. Any questions?"

She stood like a sergeant looking at a recruit she'd love to break. Well, he wouldn't give her the satisfaction. "Fine."

"Fine then. There should be a broom inside. Good luck."

He felt as if he'd been conscripted into Laramee's army. "I'd like to meet your parents first, since they're the ones who requested I come here." Panic flashed in her eyes and her entire visage tightened at the mention of him meeting her parents. A moment later, her features softened to match the pleading tone in her voice, and he could see he'd touched a nerve in the unwavering woman.

"I need...I'd like to spend a few minutes with them first, if you don't mind. I haven't been home in a while and..."

Visible nervousness, even pain, surfaced when Laramee mentioned seeing her parents for the first time in a while. Her response opened an ache in Jamie. He understood those feelings. "All right. Call me up when they're ready to talk."

As he turned around, he caught a goat pawing his rear bumper. He set off in a run, waving his hands wildly at the beast and yelling, "Hey! Hey! Hey, you! Get off my truck!" The goat initially ignored him and his flailing and hollering until Jamie drew close, lunging for the animal who bleated and broke left in a mad dash. The beast outpaced him, and Jamie knew if he caught the thing he'd be more inclined to give it a toss than to merely set the goat aside.

Laramee saw the event and tore after him, yelling, "Hey! What do you think you're doing?"

Jamie was certain he was on the side of right, especially after having forgiven Laramee Stone of her own earlier assault on his truck. And trusting that he and the woman had just achieved a temporary understanding, he slipped into one hip, pointed to the animal, and argued, "That stupid goat tried to climb my SUV like it's his personal mountain."

The woman's wall flew back up. "Cut him a little slack. He works for his keep, eating the tall weeds and keeping the snakes back. Show him a little respect."

Jamie didn't bother arguing further. His phone rang and his father's number showed on the screen. Jamie groaned and considered getting in the SUV and driving away. His father would understand.

Worse, he probably would have expected it from his youngest son because there was a time when the easy road was the only one Jamie wanted. But that was then. *Wasn't it?*

Laramee clearly had issues also. They weren't his concern. He'd given his word to Sterling Stone, plus he'd told his father and his brother that this was the assignment he'd chosen. He wasn't backing down. Not this time. Not even to save his Range Rover. He grabbed his bags and turned for the bunkhouse.

§♣

*L*aramee grabbed the box of cookies off the seat when she heard the door open from behind. She turned to see her mother in the doorway, wearing a tearful smile as she rushed upon her daughter.

"Hi, Mom," Laramee said sheepishly as she surveyed the toll the past few years had written on her mother's face. Her once-dark hair was almost steel-gray, and lines spread from the corners of her once bright and happy eyes. A few tears traced down her mother's plump cheek as her padded arms pulled Laramee close. "My girl is home."

The feel of her mother's arms around her was both sweet and painful. She hugged her back for several long, tender seconds, remembering how those arms held her when she was little, and after every rodeo competition, heartbreak, and happiness. And then she remembered a change in the feel of those arms. Laramee wasn't sure if the cause was hers or her mom's, but the stinging memory led her to break the embrace sooner than her mother expected. Cathy Stone's disappointment over the move was apparent. She pulled her sweater around her, and Laramee pushed her consolation prize forward. "I brought these for you. I know ginger cookies from the bakery at The Alpine are your favorite."

"Oh…they are. They surely are. Thank you for remembering how much I love them." She hugged the box tightly. "That means a lot."

Laramee noticed how Cathy Stone hugged the box but didn't open it or taste one. "Go ahead and try one. Duncan works there now, and he packed them special for you."

"Duncan? Really? How nice."

"Yeah. He packed them special for you. Try one."

Her mom hesitated again. "I shouldn't just now…but I will…later. It's just that my sugar tested high this morning."

"Your sugar?" The health implications struck a nerve in Laramee. She rushed back and took her mother by the arms. "Are you diabetic now?"

"No. Don't worry about me. The doctor and I are working to prevent problems. I'm on a special diet. Reduced sugar. You understand."

"Why didn't you tell me?"

"What could you do from Arizona?"

Laramee detected a hint of reproach in the comment. "I call you every Friday. You should have told me." She moved on to the next topic of worry. "How's Dad?"

Her mother bobbed her head left and right. "He's sleeping."

"Is that code for 'he doesn't want to come to the door to talk to me?'"

"No!" her mother scolded. "You've got to stop assuming things like that and move past old hurts, Laramee. Your father loves you, he's just not well. He hasn't left the house in over a week."

The news got Laramee's attention. "What? What's wrong with him?"

"It's his heart. He's got A-fib and a murmur. Dr. Mathers put him on blood thinners. He's tired all the time."

"There must be a better answer than that."

"The doctor referred him to a specialist in Denver, but he refuses to go. He said he just needs a little more rest."

Laramee pulled her cap off and slapped it against her thigh. "Perfect. More silent suffering. We all know how well that's worked out in the past. Is Dad's health the reason you're considering selling the ranch?"

"Mostly. Look around you, Laramee. We can't keep the place up anymore, and we can't afford to hire help. I do my best to feed and water what few animals we still have, but it's still too much. We called

Max, and he votes for selling the place, but we're all willing to give you a chance if you want to try taking it on."

"Except you already hired a realtor." She pointed to the Range Rover from which Jamie was hauling his bags. Evidently noticing that he was the object of the women's attention, he raised a hand in a wave, which Cathy Stone returned.

"We didn't ask his company to list it. They're—"

"I know, I know. They're assessing it to determine what a buyer can do with it and what it's worth, but it's priceless to me!"

"The memories *are* priceless, Laramee, but we can hold on to them no matter what you decide." Cathy leaned against the truck. "The drag of caring for this land with so little return makes it harder to remember how wonderful it once was. Ranching is a hard, 24/7 job. One we didn't want to saddle you kids with unless you really want it."

Laramee crumpled the hat in her hands. "The truth is, I don't know what I want." She moved beside her mother and leaned back against the truck. "I hope to figure that out while I'm here. What's Cannon Capital's grand plan for the place?"

Cathy Stone stared out at the broad vista of Stone's Throw Ranch. "Keep in mind that Mr. Cannon hadn't seen the place yet—"

"Jamie Cannon? The man who's here now?"

"No. William Cannon. I assume it's young Mr. Cannon's father. Anyway, when we called him and asked him to tell us what our options might be, he said the obvious buyer would be someone who wanted to start his own ranch. But then again, depending on the quality of the soil and the water access, he might recommend it to a big hotel firm that's looking for a spread like ours to turn into a fancy dude ranch excursion adventure for their vacation club."

Laramee straightened and laughed softly. "Oh, wouldn't Dad just love that?" There was no humor in her comment. "And what about the ridge?"

"We'd try to keep that small plot to protect it."

"But what if the buyer insists it be included?"

"I suppose we'd make them promise to protect it."

"And you'd trust them?"

Her mother threw her hands in the air and said, "I don't know, Laramee. I guess we'd put it in the contract."

Laramee knew she had pushed her mother too far on a topic that was also painful for her. She slipped her arm around her mother. "I'm sorry. I know this is hard for you too."

Cathy Stone wiped her tears away and pulled herself together. "Before we finalize anything, we'll let you and Max read the contract and tell us what you think. The one option we're trying to avoid is to have our only offer be from a mining company that'll turn the whole place into a big ugly hole. None of us want that."

Laramee was at least glad they agreed on one point. She noticed her mother shivering. "You're freezing in that thin sweater. You need to get inside."

"Come with me."

Laramee wasn't ready to cross that threshold and see her father. Her mother noticed her reluctance and offered a second option. "Let me grab a heavier sweater so we can sit out here and watch the animals graze." While she ran to get her sweater, Laramee glanced back at the smoke rising from the bunkhouse chimney. She bit her lip, wondering if Jamie Cannon was trying to keep from freezing, or if he had decided to burn the place down.

Cathy Stone returned and said, "You're mighty interested in whatever's going on in the bunkhouse. I assume you've spoken with young Mr. Cannon."

"Yep. He said you two offered to let him stay in the bunkhouse while he was conducting his assessment."

"Your father did, except I didn't get in there to clean it up for him."

Laramee heard the worry in her mother's voice. "If he doesn't like it, he can drive his sorry backside back to Denver and get a fancy room."

"Laramee!" her mother scolded.

"I don't feel sorry for him. He's working for us, so we don't owe him anything." This was the part of Jamie Cannon's presence that tore at her. She couldn't bear the thought of his criticizing the place she loved, but at the same time, part of her hoped he hated the place, so he'd leave without recommending it to any buyers. But that would mean her parents would be stuck here, or that she'd be. She didn't know what to hope for anymore.

"You might as well know that when your dad heard you were coming home, he called Sutton."

She leaned back against the rail and groaned. "Why on earth would he do that without asking me first?"

"Probably because when Sutton makes his weekly visit here to check on us, he always asks your father to be sure and let him know when you're coming for a visit."

Laramee closed her eyes to black out the flood of memories washing over her. "He still visits you every week?"

"Most always on Friday nights."

"When I call home?"

"Mostly after."

"Is he dating anyone? He's a good catch."

"That's why we were so happy when you two got engaged. He still feels like part of the family. He does whatever chores we need help with, and then I feed him supper from whatever we ate that night. But most of his questions are about you."

"The thing I'm least proud of is the way I handled things with him. I owe him a personal apology."

"I'm sure he'll be stopping by."

Laramee shot to her feet. "It's Friday, isn't it?"

Her mother nodded and smiled. "Don't make yourself ill fretting about it. You've got a lot of worries on your plate."

"I can handle it." She noticed a deep rose color on her mother's cheeks. "Promise to tell me when you feel chilled? The last thing I want is for you to get sick."

Her mom turned her head and gave Laramee a sideways glance lassoed to an ear-to-ear smile. "Of course. Anything for my girl."

Laramee ached from the hunger to feel those arms around her again. To feel loved and forgiven, and to give love to someone without expectations. She started to say, "I love you, Mom," but instead, she winked at her and nodded. "So, do you think you and I can make a list of all the repairs needed on this place?"

*J*amie carried his luggage inside the bunkhouse to settle in, but he stopped when he saw how dirty and cold the place was. The interior walls of the structure were made of logs chinked with plaster. Those walls and the single-pane windows left the summer dude ranch a poorly insulated building for winter habitation. He searched the house for a thermostat and quickly concluded that the giant fireplace and two kerosene heaters were the only potential sources of heat. Unfortunately, the heaters had no kerosene. Hoping he'd find some on the ranch, he moved one heater into the men's dorm, and one into the kitchen that anchored center of the sixty-foot bunkhouse.

He paced around the men's bedroom with its four sets of bunks, four dressers, and four posts, with hooks for coats and hats. After assessing the situation, he finally chose a bunk on the interior wall that was, if not warmer, at least less drafty.

The center commons area was split between a rustic kitchen/mess hall setup to the left, and the family room on the right. The kitchen sink, appliances, and cupboards were banked against the back and the men's dorm walls, leaving the rest of the kitchen space available for the long farmhouse table and sixteen chairs. The family room area boasted three leather sofas set in a U-shape that faced the large, brick fireplace on the back wall. Jamie found three dust-covered logs in the wood rack and a few long matches on the hearth. The wood caught so easily that Jamie guessed it had been drying there for years. That timeframe of neglect seemed to apply to the rest of the place.

Everything was covered in a thick layer of dirt, dust, and cobwebs so he kept his clothes in his suitcases and started in on his assignment. He'd learned to clean during his Anasazi days in Camp Sipapu. Everyone worked and mediocrity was unacceptable. His present project was so daunting that mediocrity would be an excellent goal. He had no tools to speak of, and no idea where to begin. Whatever dust he attempted to move with the rodent-gnarled broom simply went airborne, landing somewhere else. He needed a vacuum, or a bomb, and he really didn't care which presented itself first.

He opened the door and stepped outside to make his own demands of Ms. Stone, but she and her mother weren't talking by the truck anymore. After a quick search, he saw them walking around outside. The stress and sadness in their faces made it clear that while Laramee's homecoming was joyful, it had also stirred up old pain. Not wanting to intrude in their personal family business, he tried to back away quietly, but Laramee saw him, swiped her hands across her reddened eyes and came around the corner in a flash,.

"I'm having a private conversation with my mother, Paper Pusher. Do you mind?"

"No. And what did you call me?" he replied adamantly. "I have a name."

Mrs. Stone hurried into the fray. "Honestly, Laramee," she scolded. "He's our guest. Mr. Cannon, it was so kind of you to come and estimate our property's worth."

"Happy to help, Mrs. Stone. I look forward to sitting down with you and Mr. Stone." He sweetened his greeting with his best hundred-watt smile. "But I do have a little problem in the bunkhouse."

Fire flew from Laramee's eyes. "What problem do you have with our bunkhouse? Plenty of families came here for years to play and work together. A few wrote to tell us how that week on our dude ranch saved their family. Aren't our rustic little accommodations hotsy totsy enough for you?"

The fight in her took him back. His instincts went on defense, but he managed to cancel the barb his brain teed up, and reply in a calm, measured voice. "I'd say the bunkhouse has just the right amount of both hotsy and totsy. What it sorely needs, and lacks, however, is a vacuum and a mop."

Laramee's face shifted colors into bright red. He finally took a moment to process *what* she said instead of focusing on how she said it. She was defending her home. He felt ashamed of himself for condescendingly throwing her words back at her. While he scrambled to make a kinder point, her mother inserted herself into the conversation to end the spitting match.

"Oh, my, Laramee, he's right. You know how long it's been since someone's used the place. I saw how dusty it was when I took the linens over, but I assumed you and I would be the ones doing the cleaning. Not Mr. Cannon."

"Please call me Jamie, ma'am. And I don't mind straightening up if you can show me where I can find some cleaning supplies."

"Thank you, Jamie. I believe there's a wet/dry vacuum in the tool side of the barn, and I'll get you a bucket and mop from the house. Did you find the fresh pot of soup in the fridge?"

"No, ma'am, but thank you very much."

"My husband knows you've arrived. Settle in and we'll have a chat later on, all right?"

"That sounds great. Thank you."

When Mrs. Stone left to get the items, Jamie noticed how Laramee dug her toe into the moist earth, avoiding eye contact with him. "I'll get the vac," she said. "I know where to find it." She turned for the barn, then stopped, and spoke again, keeping her gaze set on the ground. "Sorry for jumping to conclusions a minute ago. I'll clean the bunkhouse. Maybe you could walk around the outbuildings and get familiar with the place."

He considered the option, but once her mood shifted from nuclear to contrite, Jamie's cooled down as well, and the little victory wasn't as satisfying as he expected.

"No," he said. "I'm not your guest. This is business. I'll clean the bunkhouse." He nodded toward the family home. "You spend time with your mom."

She glanced up at him and slowly spun on the heel of her cowboy boot until she'd done a one-eighty. "Thanks. I'll bring you the mop and bucket in a while."

Her gratitude was sincere, and when Jamie turned back for the bunkhouse, he found himself looking at it with new eyes. Laramee loved this place. It explained why she reacted like a tiger to anyone who slighted it. He could understand that. He could even respect her for it, but why did she have to turn everything into a fight? It was going to be a tense few days.

He found the vacuum and began cleaning the walls, corners, and floor in his room. He caught glimpses of Laramee and her mother through the windows, as they walked along outside. Their eyes met a few times, but he quickly glanced away so Laramee wouldn't accuse him of intruding again.

Once that room was cleaned, he moved into the commons area and began doing the same. Four strong posts supported the center beam that anchored the roof. After the cobwebs were removed, he noticed that the rough texture on the wood was actually caused by intricately burned images of cowboys tossing lassoes at cattle, and bucking broncs straining to throw off their riders. He traced the images with his finger, admiring the artist's beautiful work. Like rubbing a magic lamp, tracing the images opened his mind to what the place once was and could be again. Beneath the rough structure and cobwebs, this place represented the Stone family's dreams, and years spent preparing and sharing their home with others who came seeking adventure and a taste of the old West. He began to love the place.

When he finished vacuuming, he wiped down the table and every chair. He was grateful the mattresses were zipped into plastic sleeves that protected them and made wiping them down easy. Hunger gnawed at him, so he finally microwaved a bowl of the soup Mrs. Stone sent over and ate it standing up, admiring the art on the posts when Laramee entered.

She gave an approving nod to his housekeeping. "You did good. Very nice."

Jamie tipped his bowl to acknowledge the comment. "So is your mom's soup."

"I'll tell her. What were you looking at when I came in?"

"The poles," Jamie said between spoonfuls. "Whoever burned these images was an artist."

The slightest of smiles curled the corners of Laramee's mouth. "You'll find all kinds of artwork in here from our dude ranch days. Raising cattle was often a financially negative enterprise, so my father came up with this idea. Some weeks during the summer, we packed up to sixteen guests in here. Western art was one featured activity offered in our brochures. Mom taught the class to our guests. The cupboards are probably filled with her charcoal drawings and watercolor paintings." The tenderness of the memories colored her voice.

Jamie touched the art on one of the poles. "Did she do these?"

Laramee's eyes darted to the floor and then the hard edge returned to her face. She poked a list of some sort through one of the hooks on the pole. "My mom and I came up with this list of needed repairs. Would fixing these issues impact the market value of the ranch?"

"I thought you didn't want to sell?"

She rolled her lips and looked at the lengthy list. "I'm keeping my options open."

Jamie sensed he'd hit a nerve, and rather than pick at it, he sat on the edge of the table and said, "That's a rather long list."

Laramee's shoulders dropped, and she followed Jamie's lead, sitting on the table also, but on the other end. "That's just a drop in the bucket, I'm afraid, Pretty Boy. Still want to stick around and assess the place's worth?"

"First of all, I have a name. It's Jamie. I'd appreciate it if you'd use it."

She bit her upper lip and nodded nonchalantly. "Fair enough."

"Show me what you have on your list."

Laramee nodded again and rose, grabbing her list off the hook and pulling a pencil from her pocket. They walked around the exterior of the bunkhouse as Laramee pointed out loose boards, drooping gutters, and windows that sorely needed to be caulked. Then they moved on to the machine barn where the effect of neglect was obvious. Jamie sighed and scratched his head. "You need a contractor."

"All I have are these two hands, and they'll have to do."

Jamie reached for the list and the pencil. "May I?"

She handed the items over, but Jamie noticed how she fiddled with her hands as if she didn't know what to do with them when idle, so he handed the paper and pencil back to her and had her write down additional items he pointed out. They made it around the aged outbuildings and noticed a few issues of neglect on the main house itself. Jamie noticed how the weight of reality ground Laramee down. He stopped as if he were tired and leaned against a splinter-covered fencepost.

"This is a lot of responsibility for one person to bear. Do you have any siblings?" He knew the answer to the question before he asked, having overheard the women speaking earlier.

Laramee's cheeks paled. She looked at the ground, picked at a dead weed, and straightened. "An older brother named Max. He's married and in the Navy."

"Does he love this place as much as you?"

She shrugged and shredded the outer layers of the weed, avoiding eye contact. "He does, in his own way. He's content with the memories he made on the ranch." She tossed the remaining weed litter into the air and watched the frayed pieces float on the cold breeze until they landed on the ground. "He had a lot of good ones, and he has his career, so he doesn't care about saving this place, but he's giving me the chance to decide for myself."

"Your family must love you a lot to let the final decision be yours."

She smiled, but in resignation rather than in confirmation of Jamie's observation. "They want to get me back to being happy, whatever the heck that means anymore."

Jamie started to question the comment but stopped before he opened a wormhole neither of them wanted or needed to explore.

They heard the rumble of an engine coming down the lane. Laramee tensed and rubbed her hands along the front of her jeans to clean them.

"You've got company."

"That's Sutton's cruiser."

"He's a sheriff?"

"More than that, he's my ex-fiancé."

CHAPTER 4

*J*amie watched Laramee draw a deep breath. She seemed to shrink as she let it out, making it clear she was dreading this visit.

She seemed nervous as she said, "Do me a favor and head into the bunkhouse. Estimate the materials we'll need for the repairs or something, will you?"

"Sure, sure. I get it. You need some privacy. I'll just be inside."

Jamie heard the worry in her voice and stared at the car's window, trying to get a bead on whether her ex-fiancé was an ex because he was someone she feared, but when Jamie glanced from the cruiser, back to Laramee, he saw no fear on her face.

He reached the door of the bunkhouse and entered, leaving the door slightly ajar so he could observe how the initial greeting went. As soon as the deputy exited his car it was evident that he was no soft-bellied donut eater. He appeared to be of average height, but nothing else about his size was average. His broad shoulders, muscled biceps, and forearms strained the fabric of his shirt. Jamie waited to see if this guy intimidated Laramee. She was arrogant and rude and tough, but not pit-bull tough or confident. She reminded him more of a wounded pup who snapped and snarled as a defense, and Jamie wondered if this tough-guy-looking ex was the reason.

He kept observing, but as Laramee walked toward the officer's cruiser, *Sutton* leaned away from *her* as if he were the nervous party. Jamie gave him points for that, and points for being a good-looking dude who appeared not to act as if he were anything special, at least with Laramee.

The man's face twisted with worry as she drew within six feet, and his concern increased as he scanned her appearance from head to foot. Jamie assumed that the Laramee standing before Sutton was far different from the woman he saw last, and evidently, not for the better. Jamie wondered what had happened to her, and then he remembered her comment about her family wanting her to get back to being happy again. Life had dealt her some hard blows, and to his surprise, Jamie felt sympathy for her. So did Sutton, it appeared. The deputy straightened his arm to extend his hand to her. She likewise extended her arm and took his hand tentatively in an distant, awkward, friend-zone kind of welcome.

Jamie couldn't hear the conversation, and he scolded himself for wishing he could. *She's all right*, he told himself as he closed the door and sat at the table to attend to the task of estimating the materials the repairs would require—lumber, caulking, flashing, paint, nails, roofing shingles, tar paper, roofing nails…A sixth-grade shop student could do as good at assembling the list, but at least it would make him seem legit if the deputy questioned his presence on the property.

His pencil tip broke, and he got up to search for another pencil, stopping by the window on his way to the cupboard. He peeked through the curtain to see if his own interrogation was imminent and found Laramee and Sutton talking by the deputy's cruiser. Laramee seemed more at ease, even though Sutton continued to hold her hand. *Good for them*, Jamie told himself.

He thought about Victoria and how many times they'd broken up and reconciled. Maybe it would be the same for these two. He could give Laramee plenty of free advice on how not to repeat the same mistakes a dozen times, but then again, if he really knew how to avoid those mistakes, he would be the guy walking down the aisle with her instead of someone else.

Their last conversation replayed in his head. It was actually an argument, spurred by Victoria's callous treatment of a waiter. He just couldn't listen to one more cruel word from her, so he stepped between her and the poor man and told Victoria to stop.

She was livid, as he expected, but she hadn't expected Jamie to walk away from her and the ugly scene. She called him later that night, crying.

"You humiliated me."

"You did that to yourself."

"I was upset." The bite in her voice reached through the phone.

"I know what it feels like to be on the receiving end of your temper. Being upset isn't an excuse for being cruel."

Her tears began again.

"I'm sorry, Victoria. I'm trying to be honest with you. We've taken pauses in our relationship because you say I can't commit, and I argue that you're obsessed with work, but maybe those aren't the real issues that keep us apart."

"Which are?"

"We don't make each other happy."

"I can't believe this. Are you breaking up with me?"

"We each need to figure out what we really want. Maybe we're forcing something that doesn't work for either of us. Let's take a pause and talk in a few days, okay?"

"Maybe there are a few things I need to figure out about you as well." She ended the call.

Jamie wasn't sure how he felt about their relationship or if he cared whether it would continue when the call ended, and a few weeks later, it didn't matter. She had moved on. He hoped things would end better for Laramee and Sutton.

The door opened, and Laramee sent him a wide-eyed look he interpreted as a plea for help. "Jamie Cannon? This is Deputy Sutton Bryndall."

"Hello, Deputy." Jamie nodded and smiled at the massive man

entering the space. The two sized one another up and shared a tepid, uncomfortable greeting.

Laramee faced Jamie with her eyebrows arching and narrowing in a manic dance. "I mentioned to Deputy Bryndall that *we'd* be quite busy the next few days attending to repairs ahead of your final assessment of the property, and he offered his assistance if it would speed things up and help you be on your way more quickly."

Jamie wasn't exactly sure what the requested response might be. Was she trying to dismiss the deputy or get rid of *him*? And then her lips mimed, *"Please say no,"* and Jamie did his own mental gymnastics to determine what might be the correct response.

He leaned back into one of the posts, attempting to look thoughtful but nonchalant as he addressed Sutton Bryndall. "That's very kind of you." He glanced Laramee's way, and using the bulging of her eyes as a gauge, assessed that this was not the direction she wanted him to head. "But…you see, officer…"

Hope brightened her face a bit and he had his answer—d*issuade the good deputy.*

"It's the testing and data accumulation that takes the time. I could sit here for three days reading books by the fire while the tests run, so I might as well make myself useful and help my clients by making small repairs that could increase the value of their property."

Laramee's head was bobbing in tiny nods of assent that, if verbalized, appeared as repetitive shouts of "Yes! Yes! Yes!" Her gratitude, so evident on her face, touched a tender spot in Jamie's heart. Someone had similarly intervened for him once, and it changed the course of his life. This situation wasn't equal to that, perhaps, but it felt good to repay the favor to someone else who needed a break.

Officer Bryndall slipped into one hip. "I've got a few days of vacation saved up. It wouldn't be any problem at all. In fact, I'd love—"

Another flash of panic swept over Laramee's face, and Jamie prepared to close the deal.

"Clearly, a man in your profession understands obligation and service. Well…I'm obligated to do what best serves the interest of my company and my clients, and in this case, using my time here to help the Stones would be a more honest use of my time than allowing you to do the work while I sit on my keister. Wouldn't you agree?"

"But I—"

"I knew you'd understand. There's no need for you to change your plans." He stood up and grabbed his broom. "Now, my first order of business is to finish sweeping up in here, so if you two would excuse me, I'll finish this little chore before I head outside to take some soil samples."

Jamie glanced at Laramee, who smiled in relief. "Let's go, Sutton. We're in the man's way."

But Sutton held firm and turned to Laramee. "Would you give us men a minute alone? I just have a few questions for your *realtor*."

Laramee shot Jamie a worried glance, but he nodded her way, and she stepped outside. It was barely a moment past the close of the door when Sutton shook a finger Jamie's way.

"Just so we're clear, your help isn't needed here. Laramee knows I'd bend over backwards to help her and her family with anything they need."

Six feet apart or not, Jamie felt Sutton bearing down on him, egging him on, but to what end? Jamie wasn't sure. He ran his hand over his mouth as he fought old defenses bubbling inside him. *Stay cool*, he told himself. *He's a jealous ex. Don't give him cause to mistrust you.* "I'm sure she knows that, but as long as I have to be here, I might as well do what I can."

Sutton removed his hat and pointed it at Jamie' chest. "That's all you're here to do. Remember that. And don't get any ideas about Laramee. I saw your little glances and winks her way. Don't think you can sashay in here for a few days, flirt with her under the pretense of doing your job, and then just pull out as if it was just a little fun. She's been through enough, and she hasn't been home in a long while. She sure doesn't need some wannabe ranch hand complicating her life right now. I won't allow that."

"I have zero interest in her, and her only interest in me is what value I bring to her property. Period."

"And I'll be by regularly to check on your work. You can take that to the bank."

"Are we done here?" Jamie asked, not caring at all that his irritation was on full display.

Sutton slid his hat back on. "For now."

Jamie opened the door with more force than required and slammed it shut with equal zeal when the deputy left. He wondered what mess he'd just stepped into.

The deputy pulled out a few minutes later. Laramee entered the bunkhouse, crossed her arms in front of her and said sarcastically, "Well, that appears to have gone well."

"What got him all fired up?"

"I'm sorry. And thank you. Your performance saved me for the time being." She closed her eyes and bit the side of her mouth. "I apologized to Sutton for the awful way I broke things off with him, and unfortunately, he took my apology as an invitation to resume things. I told him you were here and said we'd be busy making repairs. I made it clear I didn't have time for anything but the ranch right now, so he offered to help."

"Which you clearly didn't want him to do. Why? He seems like a nice guy."

"He is. He's a really nice guy."

She left it there as if that explained anything that just happened. "It appears you're forgiven and I'm the new bullseye on his target."

"No, that's just his tough-guy way. He wasn't angry with you." She pressed her palm to her forehead as if a headache were coming on. "In fact, what you said about having *zero interest in me* probably encouraged Sutton, who hopes we'll get back together."

Jamie cringed over the callousness of the words he used to describe his business-only purpose in being there. He could only imagine how bitter they evidently sounded to Laramee. "What do *you* want?"

"To figure out whether I'm going to stay here or if I'm heading back to Arizona in two weeks. You don't need to worry about Sutton. You'll spend the next three days giving my parents a valuation on the ranch while I try to figure out what I want the rest of my life to look like. Easy-peasy, right? Did you work up those estimates?"

Once again, she was all business. "Here's what I have so far."

She gave the list a cursory glance. "Set the quantities and I'll phone it in for delivery tomorrow."

"And in the meantime?" Jamie asked, looking at the clock that read two-thirty. We have a lot of daylight left and I saw some horses in the paddock. How about we saddle up and ride the perimeter? We could check the fences."

She tilted her head to the side and eyed him.

"What?" he asked, bracing for another salvo of sarcasm.

"I appreciate what you said to Sutton about working on the ranch. I really do, but I'm not going to hold you to that. Do what you need to for the assessment. Take your pictures and test the soil. That's all you're obligated to do."

Jamie felt a challenge, one he was ready to accept. "You think I'm too citified and soft to be helpful here, don't you?"

"Do you actually think a paper pusher like you can pull his weight on a ranch?"

"Try me."

"Hah! I bet you work out at a gym with weights and machines?"

"Yes," he said with a certain smugness.

"Uh-huh. And do you run a mile or two on a treadmill from time to time?"

"Three miles, five times a week."

"Hmmm…" she replied thoughtfully. "I bet after an hour or two, you finish up with a soak in the hot tub or a steam shower in the sauna. Maybe a massage, followed by another shower, and then to the office or home to relax."

"And your point is?"

"That's how city boys work out. Odds are one in a hundred that you could last a week on our ranch. Do you actually believe you're up to pulling twelve-hour days twisting and pulling fencing, hauling posts, or riding a fence line on a horse you have to accordion-squeeze with your knees so hard you can count his ribs through your thighs, just so you don't fall off in rugged, untamed prairie or into a freezing stream or rocky hillside?" She chuckled and shook her head. "Stick to what you know, Paper Pusher. It's okay."

He felt his blood boil as she threw another insulting pet name his way. He spit on his hand and extended it her way. "I'll take that challenge."

"I wasn't—"

"I'll stay a week instead of three days and do the work of a ranch hand."

"You can't be serious."

"Are you backing down?"

"No chance. You're on. Mount up, City Boy. We're going for a trail ride, and we'll check the fences as we go." She handed the list back to Jamie for him to write down quantities by each needed item.

"Give me thirty minutes to unpack and change."

&

She grabbed her large duffel bag from the truck and hauled it up the porch stairs. Her mom was waiting by the door, and Laramee wondered if she was standing there as an emissary between two warring parties.

Entering the house was a milestone she'd considered with dread. Five years had passed since she'd lived in the house. She stayed a year after Tyler died, and when she thought she would suffocate if she stayed another day, she took off. Every good memory in her life began in this house where mornings started with bacon and hot biscuits, followed by chaos and laughter, packed schedules, hard work, and love. The whir of the old fridge felt like a murmured welcome home. Laramee also found a welcome in the familiar smells in the air—her mother's favorite pine cleaner and a simmering pot of spices on the stove. She breathed it all in, hoping it was a sign that more good things were ahead.

"Look at our girl, Sterling," her mother called out in the direction of the living room. Isn't it wonderful to have her home?"

Laramee set her bag down and slowly inched her way to the doorway. Her father looked up from his television show and said, "The Prodigal Daughter returns."

Laramee's first instinct was to turn for the door, but her mother's hands were on her shoulders in a flash, massaging them while she cooed gently in her ears. "He's a stubborn old goat who's missed you as much as I have. Trust me. Talk to him."

Laramee took a step forward and launched a second attempt at a civil conversation. "How are you feeling, Dad? Mom says you haven't been out of the house in a while."

"What's worth seeing out there? I'm too weak to work my own land, and I can't bear to watch it decay around me."

"Well...I'm here now. That guy from Cannon Capital and I are going to fix a few things up so the place looks her best."

His eyes never left the TV screen as he said, "If you'd stayed we might not be in this fix."

Laramee's fingers nervously tugged on the hem of her shirt. "I had to leave. I think you know why."

His head swung her way as his glassy eyes burned into her. "Yes...I know...I know exactly...why...you...left," he gasped as each breath became more labored. Laramee rushed to him, but his hand flung forward, pushing her back, as he coughed and gasped. Laramee stared in helpless horror as her mother raced over with medication that slowly calmed Sterling's spasms. His breathing slowly eased, and he eventually fell back into his chair weak, sweaty, and pale.

Laramee saw all of it, but what stuck in her mind was the accusation that preceded the attack—

"I know...I know exactly...why...you...left."

She picked up her bag and bolted for the door. Her mother cried out, "Laramee? Laramee! Don't leave. Please. Where are you going?"

"I can't stay here. I can't."

She headed for her truck, and then she saw Jamie, waiting on the bunkhouse porch dressed in sweatpants and sneakers, ready for their ride. If she left, her parents would surely sell the place. Maybe that was best for all concerned, she thought, but what would happen to the ledge? And would they get the best price for the ranch, enough to meet her parents' increasing medical needs? She stopped midway between the two buildings. Jamie stared at her, looking confused. A glance behind her revealed her mother standing on the porch, her hands clasped.

Laramee turned back to the bunkhouse. Jamie was coming now,

and instead of confusion, concern filled his face as he moved from a walk to a jog. It was only then that she realized she was crying. Rock-hard Laramee Stone was crying.

She didn't want Jamie's help. All she wanted was a private place to pull herself together. With a swing of her bag, she blew past Jamie and headed for the bunkhouse as his bootsteps followed behind. Inside, she beelined for the key rack and grabbed a particular set. Once the key was in hand, Laramee swung around to face Jamie Cannon.

She flashed the keys before him. "Two keys. Two locked doors. Two completely separate apartments. Think of us as North and South Korea, and this kitchen is the Demilitarized Zone. Got it?"

His brows pinched so tightly that his eyes nearly met.

She waited several seconds for some reply from the man staring at her as if she were crazy, and when none came, she said, "Good talk. I'll be ready in five and we'll take that ride."

CHAPTER 5

*R*eeling, Jamie sat at the table unsure what just happened or how to respond. He saw the list before him and kept himself occupied by adding a few more items to it. Laramee still hadn't reappeared from her vault in one of the Koreas, so he began estimating amounts of nails, wire, fence posts, and other items needed to get started. His heart wasn't in the work. He wasn't welcome here, and the repairs would be a farce—cosmetic fixes at best. What the place needed was a serious overhaul. After calculating the numbers, he slid the list under Laramee's door, and stood close by until the last corner of the paper completely disappeared.

He sat back at the table and heard a phone conversation ensue from behind the door. From what he overheard, delivery wasn't going to be as quick or smooth as she'd hoped.

"I understand there are supply and manpower shortages, but I'm desperate, Sam. What do you have on hand that you can deliver tomorrow morning? Yes, thanks. Bring what you can with your pickup. If your men will load it, we'll unload on this end. I promise. Thanks."

Jamie assumed he had been conscripted as part of "Team *We.*"

He wondered how she was managing in that dusty, dirty dorm. An idea came to him. When Laramee finally opened her door, she found Jamie standing in her self-proclaimed Demilitarized Zone sporting a broom in one hand and a mop in the other. Her reaction was the one he'd hoped for.

Laramee rolled her eyes at him, and then little by little, she started to chuckle. He thrust his tools forward and asked, "Are you North or South Korea?"

"Does it matter?"

"Very much. You see, if you're North Korea, I'm staying put because crossing that line could mean death. But if you're South Korea…well…they're an ally, someone to whom I could safely offer my help."

"All right, smart guy. I've probably felt like a dictator, but you're safe around me."

"So…are you saying we're allies?" Jamie winced and extended his hand to her.

Laramee fought the smile pulling at her mouth as if smiles and laughter were unfamiliar or uncomfortable to her. She finally surrendered with a snort and a head bob, reaching her own hand forward. "But I don't need your help cleaning. Fifteen or twenty spiders are guarding my gear. I'll dismiss them and clean the room when we come back."

They shared another brief chuckle and then Jamie broached the next sober topic. "I heard you talking to someone about supplies. You didn't sound happy."

Laramee moved into the kitchen and sat on the edge of the long dining table. "We'll be lucky if we can get half our order. Maybe this is a sign that it's time to surrender and sell the place."

"Still want to ride the fence lines?"

Her phone beeped, and she checked it. Whatever the message was, it brought another tear to her eyes, so she focused on her watch and then gazed out the window, as if she were looking for any place that prevented Jamie from seeing her cry.

"That was from Mom. She's making spaghetti. She'll leave a pot on the porch for us around six. It'll be dark before then, so let's head as far as we can before dusk, but first let's get you dressed in some suitable gear. What sizes do you wear?"

"Anything close to a seventeen and a half shirt with a thirty-two-inch arm."

"And the pants?"

"Something around a thirty-six-inch waist with a thirty-two-inch inseam."

The numbers made her visibly sad.

She headed to a footlocker in the men's dorm and opened the lid, releasing the scent of cedar, which wafted through the room. Laramee pulled clothes from the chest and checked the sizes, bringing certain pieces to her nose and holding them close to her body. Jamie watched the ritual. It spoke of loss and longing, and he worried that Laramee was breaking a sacred trust when she held out two pairs of jeans and two flannel shirts for him to borrow.

"Are you sure?" he asked before receiving the items.

Laramee nodded and turned for the door. "I'll start saddling the horses."

The pants were an inch short, and the shirt fit snugly, but Jamie could get by in them. When he finished dressing, he made his way to the barn, noticing Laramee's reaction when she glanced his way. She gasped and her breath held as she tightened her hold on the reins as if to steady herself.

"I remind you of someone, don't I?"

She nodded. "Just the clothes. He was shorter than you but all legs, and his hair was blonde."

"It's clear you loved him very much."

"Very much." She returned to cinching the strap on her paint pony's saddle.

Jamie turned back for the bunkhouse. "I'll just wear my own stuff. If it gets ruined, so be it."

"No. It's okay. He'd tell me I'm being silly."

Jamie wanted to ask more about the owner of the clothes, but he knew the time wasn't right. The woodsy, balsam scent of the cedar-lined chest had fully permeated the fabric, telling him the clothes had been stored in there for years, and yet the impact of seeing them again upset her visibly.

He headed for the stall of a tall gelding whose nametag read *Caruso*, but Laramee blocked his way and pointed to a smaller, older-looking horse.

"Saddle Nugget, the bay," Laramee said. "He'll take it easy with you."

"You don't have to baby me. I can handle a horse."

"We'll see, Pretty Boy. We'll see."

Jamie hoisted a saddle but stopped to see if she was teasing him in humor or in sarcasm. She wasn't smiling.

"I'm not moving until you call me by my name. Call me James or Jamie or Cannon, but don't call me Pretty Boy or City Boy or Paper Pusher again."

They had the stare-down equivalent of the showdown at O.K. Corral, and Jamie wasn't giving an inch. After ten long seconds, Laramee broke eye contact, mounted her black, brown, and white paint horse, and said, "Okay, Jamie...Patches and I'll wait for you outside."

He felt a moment's victory over getting her to use his family's nickname for him, but she drew it out with a sarcastic lilt as if it were the most ridiculous thing she'd ever heard. It wasn't worth arguing with her again, so he mounted Nugget and walked the horse to where Laramee waited.

She set the pace at a gentle trot and handed him a batch of yellow plastic ribbons with the instruction to tie them wherever he saw a problem on the fence line. They moved out together, leapfrogging around one another. When Laramee stopped to mark a problem spot, Jamie would pass her and search for the next one. When she finished identifying one problem, she'd move past Jamie to the next troubled area. This went on for nearly two hours, with him stopping to take photos every now and then as they made their way over flat, empty terrain that eventually butted up to the foothills of the Rockies. Mountain waters converged in a stream that flowed along those hills into a corner of the property where the land and water appeared to drop off suddenly. As Jamie and Laramee turned the corner on one fence line, they began moving toward that area.

Laramee's eyes fixed on that spot, and her face took on a sorrowful longing that increased the closer they drew to it. Jamie attempted to maintain the appearance of being fully occupied photographing the property and identifying damaged spots in the fencing, but his attention was riveted on Laramee and the magnetic pull that area had on her.

A dozen yards before the drop off, Laramee slid from Patches and walked him toward the spot. Jamie rode his horse up behind her and dismounted as well. He heard the splashing water before he saw it. The stream's flow continued west, along the base of the foothills, but a small dam, created from fallen trees and debris at the hill's edge, impeded the stream. The dammed waters overflowed, forming a small rivulet that broke off and went rogue, travelling downhill to the north, where a ledge ended in a thirty-foot drop. The flow that reached the ledge fell like laughing water that settled in a pool at the bottom. The overlook was stunning, and Jamie hoped to follow the paths that led down to the pool.

"This spot is beautiful," he said with genuine awe.

Laramee just stared down at the pool of water until she broke her silence saying, "It's sacred to me."

"I can see why. It has a reverent feel to it. But that drop off is a killer. I get a little case of vertigo just from looking over the edge."

"Be careful!" she said with alarm in her voice as she reached for his arm and pulled him back and against her. He felt her body tremble and when he turned, he saw panic in her expression.

"I'm sorry. I didn't mean to worry you."

"It's beautiful but it's also dangerous. I don't think I could survive another…" She walked a few paces away. "We should be getting back."

"I see paths that lead to the bottom. Can't we ride down there?"

"It's getting late. By the time dusk sets in here, it's dark at the house. We should get back. I'll lead you down to the bottom tomorrow."

He heard the soft-sad tone in her voice and decided not to argue. "You're the boss," he said as he mounted Nugget for the ride to the bunkhouse. He waited quietly for Laramee who remained moments longer. His wait became a study of the area's impact on the woman. It was as if she required more time to disengage herself from the emotional pull of the place. Her eyes closed and her lips moved in a silent conversation with the place or with someone the place brought to her memory. She muttered a few words in parting and mounted her horse as if nothing out of the ordinary had happened at all. Melancholy seemed to surround her, so Jamie led out with her following close behind. He eventually slowed down to get their horses even, and then he attempted to make casual conversation.

"I think I counted one hundred and twelve fenceposts that need to be replaced, and we probably ought to get three rolls of wire."

The comment drew her from her reverie. "I'll phone that in and see if we can get them added to tomorrow's delivery." Almost as an afterthought, she added, "You worked hard today. Thank you."

The compliment left Jamie off-center, and he sat back in his saddle, eyeing her curiously. She blushed and then, out of the blue, she yelled, "Race you!" She dug her feet into her mount and slapped the reins across his flank yelling, "Ha! Ha!" causing her horse to bolt forward like a shot. Jamie was stunned for a second, and then he urged Nugget forward, pushing him to match Laramee's horse's pace, but Nugget had no high speed.

Jamie loped along on Nugget, destined for a losing finish. He didn't mind. The view from behind allowed him to admire the beautiful synchrony between Laramee and her mount. Whatever special bond the two of them shared had not been dimmed by Laramee's absence. She laid low against Patches who responded to her as if they were one being, flying across the frozen plains until they disappeared into the curtain of dusk. The sight was so mesmerizing that Jamie happily enjoyed the view from the loser's position. He and Nugget loped into the yard well after Team Laramee was back in the barn. He remembered Laramee's comments about how Nugget would go easy on him, and Jamie wondered if she purposely put him on the slowest horse on the ranch in case they raced, or if her choice of his mount was rooted in her concern for safety.

By the time Jamie cooled Nugget and settled him in for the night,

Laramee had his dinner waiting on the bunkhouse table, but she was nowhere to be found. All that was left behind was a note that said— *Enjoy your dinner. I'm going to have a chat with the cook. See you in the morning. Bon appétit.*

The emotional rollercoaster of working with Laramee was exhausting, and this confusing conclusion to a day that had some good moments left him whiplashed and frustrated. Ravenous and parched, he asked a blessing upon the food, prayed for patience, and devoured the spaghetti, bread, and salad left for him, washing it down with three glasses of water. His gorging left him sick and bloated. He walked around the bunkhouse's open space trying to ease his stomach, but as much as it pained him to admit it, he was also saddle sore, and while walking eased his gut, it aggravated the other region.

After a quick survey of the bunkhouse, he was drawn to the cupboard that supposedly contained artwork from the dude ranch. He also hoped the cabinet might contain a book he could read until he fell asleep. Opening the cupboard was adventure in and of itself. Instead of being stored in neatly organized shelves, the material in the space appeared to have been tossed in quickly to simply get it out of sight. He delicately searched through the unkempt piles and hit paydirt when he managed to pull three old western romance novels out without disturbing the chaotic paper towers.

A photo pasted on a scrapbook page caught his eye. It pictured a young girl with a woodburning iron standing beside a post. He pulled the page out carefully and found a pictorial history of the posts' evolution from ordinary wood poles to delicately created pieces of western art. He studied the face of the proud smiling artist. She seemed unfamiliar at first, until further study conjured memories of brief smiles and glimpses of Laramee in happy moments. She was the artist who transformed the poles.

Jamie thought about Sutton's worried expression as he surveyed Laramee's appearance today. He wondered if the happy-faced girl in the photo was the person who left Sutton, and who the deputy expected to see when she returned. Instead, Sutton seemed shocked by the changes he found in her.

The shelf where Jamie found the scrapbook held other pages as well. He removed a few more and Laramee's story played out before his eyes. Pages of age-progressive rodeo photos showcased her as a bedazzled young cowgirl dressed in brightly colored outfits and fringes as she raced her paint pony through barrel courses and posed with him beside ribbons and trophies. The horse was Patches, the mount she'd ridden that day.

He found photos of young boys riding sheep in a rodeo event Jamie knew well—the Mutton Buster. The larger of the two boys had dark hair. The smaller of the two had blonde. Jamie pulled on the front of his shirt, wondering if this blonde-haired young man was the owner of these very clothes.

The last page he grabbed interested him the most. It pictured a beautiful, confident woman of eighteen or twenty dressed in cowgirl glam—a studded black and silver blouse over black sequined jeans and boots. Another photo showed her in red-leather pants and a matching jacket that threw light from a thousand rhinestones. The banners that crossed her chest read Parkersburg Rodeo Queen 2017 and 2018. The girl was a glamorized clone of Laramee, but with full cheery cheeks and a rounded figure she wasn't afraid to show off. Her hair was long and shiny, curled to make it cover-girl gorgeous, but what captured Jamie's attention most was her attitude, as if she'd downed a six-pack of pure sass.

What happened to you, Laramee? Jamie asked himself. He'd seen milliseconds of that inner light and spunk escape her dour mood, but she hadn't been able or willing to sustain it. He replaced the pages and closed the cupboard door before turning his attention to washing his dishes and putting the food containers in the bunkhouse fridge. Still no Laramee. He carried the novels into his room and dressed for bed, listening for any sound of Laramee's return. He had a thousand questions, but he knew there was no assurance Laramee would offer any answers. A bigger worry was that his prying could just as easily drive her deeper into that dark, quiet place she preferred. He laid his questions aside and settled in to read about the Old West Laramee so obviously loved and about which his own love was deepening.

CHAPTER 6

Saturday, March 25, 2023

Laramee hoped the smell of sausage would be enough to entice Jamie Cannon from bed without requiring her to rap upon his door and order him about like a shrew. She knew that's how he saw her, and she added that to her list of regrets. She wasn't always tough and pushy. Running to Arizona hadn't opened the doors she hoped it would. When her dream career didn't manifest, she fell back on what she knew best—horses—but that world was hard and demanding for most men, and certainly for a woman trying to prove she was equal to her male peers. Three-and-a-half years of jockeying for respect had toughened her.

She turned the sausage patties over and stared at the old bunkhouse kitchen. Some of her best memories took place here, like making breakfast by her mom's side for a dozen or so hungry guests and hearing their excited chatter about the day's scheduled events—riding and roping and packing a horse to go fishing by the mountain-fed stream. The grand adventures the guests marveled over were everyday pleasures she took for granted. And they treated this cowgirl and rodeo queen like a celebrity. She loved those days.

When the sausage was cooked, she moved the pan off the fire and set the griddle over the burner for pancakes. She smeared butter over the cast iron and let it heat while she whipped up the box mix her mother set out and poured the first four cakes.

Sutton crossed her mind, and she wondered if he'd come by again today. Facing him hadn't been as awful as she expected. She forgot how easily they fit together, like puzzle pieces. Their conversation seemed to pick up exactly where they left off, as if nothing in his life had changed. It probably hadn't and likely never would. Facing a future of sameness was one of the reasons she'd left.

She flipped the cakes and heard a few thumps from behind the door, like boots hitting the floor. Jamie was awake. The thought made her happy, until she reminded herself that he was like the guests that had come. Each brought a special spark of fun and interest to her life, and then each one left. And so would Jamie Cannon. As he said. He had zero interest in her, and she needed to keep her position the same.

The door opened, and Jamie appeared in yesterday's clothes acting more like a wounded bear than himself. His hair was utterly disheveled. His eyes were squinty from the light, and he set his hands on either side of the doorframe and moaned, first at the light, and then again when he stretched left and then right, into the frame.

"Stiff and sore?" Laramee pressed her lips tightly together to restrain the smile she desperately wanted to release.

"Don't...just...please...don't say I told you so. I need compassion right now, not sarcasm."

Laramee raised her hands in surrender. "I'm not one to kick a man when he's hitting bottom, especially one whose help I need. And especially when that's where he's hurting."

Jamie groaned and rolled his eyes at the joke.

"Take a seat, cowboy. Breakfast is ready."

Jamie slowly made his way to his chair and was deliberate and careful as he sat. "Everything smells great, but you don't have to cook for me. I live alone, and I'm a fair cook if I do say so myself."

"Oohhh...a single man who cooks in his fancy bachelor pad."

"Only if a single guy's townhouse with a bed, a sofa, a big screen, and a Peloton meets the bar for a fancy bachelor pad."

Laramee set a plate before him and one in front of her seat. "Dig in."

"Mind if I ask a blessing on it for both of us?"

She felt her neck and face prickle over the request. She and God hadn't had a lot to say to one another in recent years, but memories flooded over her of family dinners that began with her father's strong resonant voice thanking God and petitioning His blessings on the food and the family. That voice made her feel so safe back then.

She didn't verbalize an answer to Jamie's request. Instead, she closed her eyes and inclined her head forward enough to acknowledge some reverence for God, but not so much that He'd think she'd forgotten how He'd let her down. As a child, she believed her father had a direct line to God and heaven. That all changed six years ago.

Jamie's prayer was short but personal, as if he were speaking to a God he knew well. His eyes opened wider as he fully awakened and the tight lines around his mouth and across his brow were easing. This was the first opportunity Laramee'd had to really study his face up close, and she found it as interesting as it was handsome. Several scars roughed the terrain of his face—a crooked one along his chin, a straight one along his hairline, and a patch of small scars, as if from a skid, across his right cheek. His nose was bent, starting and stopping where they should but breaking slightly right and then back left in the middle. His smile was somewhat shy and unpretentious, but his eyes were his greatest feature, like aquamarine gems, but soft and filled with gentleness. He was much more than a mere pretty boy and she felt bad for judging him so unfairly. She suddenly realized he'd caught her staring, and she jumped to a stand and blurted, "I could heat up the syrup if you like."

Jamie smiled and waved her off. "Thanks, but no need. This is great. Where are we getting the ingredients for this food? Your mom?"

"Not after today. Mom's heading into town and she's offered to pick up the foods you like. All we need to do is make a list." She pushed a pencil and piece of paper his way.

"I'm easy, but as I said, I like to cook, so I'll make dinner tonight." He added a few items to the list. "Sound good?"

Laramee grunted. "I'll tell you after I eat it." Jamie broke into a laugh, and she raised one eyebrow. "I'm not easy to please."

"No..." He slathered the word in sarcasm and drew the "o" out until he ran out of breath. As an added punctuation, Jamie offered a whistle that resembled the whir of a bomb dropping, complete with a little explosion at the end. Laramee did her best to withhold her laughter until it escaped in a snort. That victory was all Jamie seemed to need. His right eyebrow arched victoriously, and he doubled down like an arm wrestler who'd pushed past the midpoint and knew his opponent was weakening. Laramee forked in another bite to occupy her mouth muscles, but Jamie wriggled his eyebrows, daring her to smile. She pressed her fist to her mouth and coughed, and Jamie called her on it. "You can try to hide it, but you can't hold it in. You can't. You know you want to laugh."

She lifted her head and maintained her decorum, just to spite him.

Jamie set his fork down and cocked his head sideways. "You'd cut your head off to deny me this minor victory, wouldn't you?"

Her face slackened as if he'd hit a nerve. "It's not that."

"The world's hard enough, Laramee. Laughter, love, and joy are the best ways to push it back."

She nodded and toyed with her fork. "I'll try to remember that."

He cocked his head to the left and the right and then said, "Something's different with you today."

The comment caught her off guard and, assuming the worse, she snapped back, "Like what?" She touched her head to check her hair and surveyed her button-front shirt and jeans to see if she'd gotten pancake batter all over the front.

"It's not a bad thing. You just look nice. Very nice."

"All I did was shower and put on clean clothes."

"That's it!" he teased, finally earning that hard-won smile from Laramee. He sobered, realizing he owed her something as well—the compliment she deserved. "No, it's your hair. It looks really pretty straight like that."

"Thank you," she muttered. Compliments hadn't always made her feel awkward. In fact, back in her rodeo days, she'd primped and fussed to win as many as possible. But that was then, and few had come her way in the past few years. Flattering words had become prickly to her. They required a gracious reply that overtaxed her unease with such niceties.

The crunch of tires on gravel and a soft horn honk ended the moment. "That's probably Sam with the supplies. We need to unload."

"I'll do it."

She waited while Jamie stabbed another large bite and noticed that he rose with a little less of a groan as he turned for the door and opened it.

"Hey, Sam," Laramee called out to the young driver.

He waved at her and rolled the window down. "Good to see you, Laramee."

"Thanks for delivering this stuff."

"I'm sorry you have to unload. I threw my back out the other day, and I didn't have another driver to send, but I'm glad you have some help." He glanced Jamie's way as if hoping for some explanation about who the helper was.

"No problem," Laramee inserted quickly without offering anything more. "And the rest of the goods?"

"We have a shipment due in at the store. I'll try to get the other items on your list to you tomorrow."

"I'd appreciate it. How's Brenda?"

"Busy with the baby and all."

The news caught Laramee off guard. "A baby? I...I didn't know."

His mouth tightened into a thin line. "I assumed your mom told you. You should call Brenda. She'd love to tell you all about him."

Jamie walked up. "The delivery is missing more than half of what we ordered. I unloaded what was delivered."

"The rest should come tomorrow."

"Thanks, Sam. Tell Brenda I said hello and that I'll call her soon."

"Will do. Hopefully, I'll be back tomorrow with the rest of your order," Sam said as he pulled out.

Jamie looked at the pile of supplies. "Where shall we begin?" He moved his hands like pans on a scale as if he were weighing the options. "Mucking stalls? Replacing fencing? We could pick up where we left off yesterday."

She knew what Jamie was really hinting at was that he wanted to explore the falls. She promised him they would, but she wasn't ready to go there again. Not yet. And she didn't want to argue the point. "I'll muck," Laramee said. "Mom told me some tree limbs punctured small holes in the roof during a recent storm. Dad hasn't gotten around to fixing them yet. We've got tin, nails, and tar now. Why don't you start mending those holes?"

The lines between his eyebrows deepened and one side of his mouth pulled up. "Uh…I've never…I mean…I don't even know how to mend a roof."

"Well, the good thing is that you're not afraid to get your hands dirty, so you can do this. The pitch of the roof isn't steep, so you shouldn't be in danger of sliding off. Put on some rubber gloves, cut a tin patch bigger than the hole, slap some tar on it, and press it down. Then seal over it with more tar and 'voilà!' You've patched your first tin roof."

"Sounds easy enough. I can knock that out in no time."

"Wonderful." She pointed to the shed as she turned and walked the other way, toward the barn, putting distance between herself and Mr. Cannon. "You'll find the long ladder in the tool shed."

"Okay. So, once I knock the roof repairs out, I'll head to the corner by the falls and start mending the fence."

She'd hoped she'd put an end to this discussion, but he wasn't letting it go. "We don't have enough posts."

"We marked about fifty or sixty rotted posts between here and the falls. We have enough to get that far. It's a nice day to stop and visit it again."

She felt the panic rise in her once more. She turned around, hoping he'd see her dismay and just let it go, but when their eyes met, he was smiling, as if he believed a cute grin could change her mind and wash the old hurts away. She fought to keep her voice even, but the words that shot from her mouth? They were the harshest she knew, and she rolled them out in cold even tones. "Go or stay. I don't care. But if you stay here, you do what I say. Got it?"

Time stopped for a moment, leaving Jamie frozen where he stood, as if he were unsure he'd actually heard her correctly. His brow pinched slowly, and his jaw lowered by degrees until it gaped open. Confusion paled his face, then betrayal caused it to burn red. He gave her a lazy salute, turned on one heel, and beelined for the bunkhouse.

Laramee felt sure he was going there to pack and leave. All she knew was that his expression was one she knew well, one she herself had once worn, and seeing it on his face cut her as deeply as when she was the target of those very words.

She'd been leading a trail ride when a novice rider decided he was ready to take off at a gallop. Panic hit her then also. He was having the time of his life, but all she saw was potential danger and hazards she had to prevent. She told the rest of the group to stay put and she bolted after the daredevil before he injured himself or his horse by blindly riding into a hole or one of the ravines cut by old dry riverbeds. When she reached him, she grabbed his reins and pulled his horse to a stop, berating him so badly that he headed straight back to the office and filed a report against her with the manager. When she returned later that night, the manager called her into his office and said, "Go or stay. I don't care. But if you stay, you do things my way. Got it?"

She had nowhere else to go if she left there. Heading home was not an option. Knowing that made her feel as if she were standing on a cliff with no safety net. She managed her panic and complied from then on, opting out of trail rides unless there was no one else to lead them. She chose stable work and gave riding lessons to children, work that amounted to little more than leading ponies around the pen. Safe things. Things that didn't harrow up old hurts.

She walked to the barn, glancing out at the bunkhouse for some sign of Jamie. She picked up her pitchfork, but she didn't have the will to work, so she leaned on it and stared at the bunkhouse door through a hole in the barnwood. Jamie finally exited and headed for the toolshed.

She stepped outside and bit her lip, waiting for a moment and searching for the words to apologize. When he got close she lifted her head and started to speak, but his hand came up and he brushed her attempt to apologize aside.

"I heard you, loud and clear."

"I'm sorry."

"Me too, in more ways than you know."

He gives as good as he gets, she concluded, making it clear he was sorry he'd ever met Laramee or come to The Stone's Throw Ranch. She figured the only reason he was still here was because he was too proud to renege on his promise to help.

They were both stuck in a miserable situation she'd made worse. Much worse.

ॐ

Just thinking of you...

The text was from Jamie's mom. He wondered if she were checking to see if Victoria's wedding had sent him into a backslide, or whether she'd psychically heard his angry thoughts and knew he needed to remember her counsel. *Don't judge* she'd say whenever they came home from school or church or a sports game angry at someone's rude, hurtful behavior. *They may be having a very hard day, dealing with things you don't understand.* He eventually needed that grace himself, and he quickly sent his mom a heart emoji before stowing his phone.

Jamie knew Laramee was dealing with things, but he'd tried to be reasonable and patient, hadn't he? She was bossy, rude, snippy, and she flip-flopped on plans at will. *Her will...*Working down by the falls was the one thing he'd looked forward to on this godforsaken place, and she knew it. That's why she yanked it away from him. To prove who was boss.

Don't judge...

He wanted to pack his bag and head out, but to where? He couldn't return to The Alpine, and he couldn't go home. His mother would worry. His father would think he was fragile. And his brother would helicopter over him again. He was more worried about how his own heart would record his failure. As exactly that. A failure. Nine years of progress and success would evaporate. He would see himself as weak and flawed.

Laramee was a pain in his saddle area, which was already in pain, but he knew he struck a mortal blow to her when he said he was sorry about being there. The hurt in her eyes would pick at his peace all morning.

He grabbed the ladder and wrestled it off its hooks, nearly knocking paint cans and other hanging tools from their perches before he reached the door. By the time he reached the wall of the damaged roof with the blasted thing, he was sweaty and frustrated, and more of Laramee's *wisdom* played in his head, comments about him being *gym strong*, which meant *paper-pusher strong*, which had nothing to do with actually being able to perform hard work. She thought he was soft. "Hah!" he scoffed, even as his carpel tunnel syndrome acted up in his wrist. He set the ladder down and flexed the ache from his wrists and hands, and then he stopped. *Good grief. I am soft.* He did a quick scan of the area to be sure Laramee hadn't seen him nursing his aches, and then he picked up the ladder, determined to work through the discomfort.

He felt a twinge in his right shoulder as he hefted the unwieldy ladder up and to the roof. *Maybe Laramee had a point.*

After setting his tools along the base of the ladder, he organized his load in his hands and climbed to the roof. Once there, he realized he should have brought a broom to sweep what looked like a decade of dead leaves and broken limbs from the surface, and maybe have his tetanus shot checked because of all the bird poop he'd have to touch. He put on his gloves and swept the big debris away with his hands, gagging a little when a fresh smear of bird droppings stuck to his gloves. He'd been more manly when he was ten, when such a task would have been viewed as an adventure. He'd become a better man who learned to work hard and enjoy it during his time at Sipapu. The work relieved the boredom, but he also discovered the pride it brought. He now viewed such menial tasks as chores for day laborers. Shame hit him like a whip. Who had he become these past nine years? And worse, how?

He sat on the roof for a moment, considering the shift from the dirt-loving, explorer he once was to the boardroom sitter he'd become. He worked hard at what he did, and he did his assigned work well, but being on the ranch shone a light on previously undetected changes in his attitude about himself and others. He was proud to be known as a kind man and a gentleman, but inwardly, he did set himself apart, above certain things, where his wealth allowed him to pay others to do work he considered unworthy of his time. That realization made him feel small, inadequate, arrogant, and yes…*soft*.

He looked over the broad vista of The Stone's Throw Ranch. It was a hard land, relatively untouched and unimproved over the one hundred fifty years the Stone's ancestors reportedly owned it. The Cannon's owned land too, a vacation cabin sitting on seven acres of an Idaho mountain. An acre or two were in pastures that were fertile and constantly fed by snowmelt and regular rain. It was so unlike this land, whose harshness reminded him more of Camp Sipapu.

This land was much like Laramee herself, rocky and hard and impermeable. The arid acreage was vast, brown, beige, and thirsty, a sharp contrast to the snow-blessed mountains that ringed it. The winter snows that filled lakes and streams in the higher elevations passed over this land, bestowing but a dusting of windblown snow, except for small piles that caught and held in the tufts of wild grass. He saw hope off to the edge of the property, where the level plains reached greener bluffs that met the foothills. Water trickled there, but it didn't bring its life-giving moisture to the flatlands, leaving the prairie dry and poor, with nothing but those few tufts of wild grass popping up here and there. It could never support a large herd of cattle on its own.

Jamie knew resurrecting the dude ranch was Laramee's best hope of saving the place, so he abandoned the tasks of identifying the failings in himself and in the land and set about patching the holes in the roof.

The actual task was simple and relatively satisfying. He made square patches and set them with the tar. His patches weren't attractive, but the roof was so high, no one on the ground could see them anyway. So much tar accumulated on his gloves by the last patch that he played a game of grab-it with the tin square, pulling it loose from one hand and then getting it stuck on the other. He repeated this unnerving exercise four times before frustration overwhelmed him and he shook his hand wildly, hoping to fling the square loose with wilder and faster slings that shook his entire upper body. The wild flailing caused his foot to jerk right into the tar bucket, sending it sliding straight into the ladder, which tilted back until it was straight up and down for a moment. Jamie froze and prayed a silent prayer, all the while wriggling his tarred fingers in hope that a breeze, or good Karma would tilt the ladder back his way, but it was not to be. The ladder slowly, ever so slowly, continued its pathway backward, landing on the ground, and leaving Jamie stranded in tar and leaves and bird droppings, with the blasted tin square still attached to his fingers.

He closed his eyes and calculated his two choices, neither of which appealed to him. One involved possibly breaking his legs. The other would most assuredly break his pride. Pride seemed more affordable, so he drew in a deep breath and called out, "Laramee? Laramee! Help!"

She came out of the barn in a dead run, calling, "Jamie? Jamie!" searching the ground and breathing hard. When she looked up, Jamie noticed how pale and panic-stricken she was, and how she slumped in relief when she saw him sitting safely on the roof. Her legs seemed unable to bear her weight, so she dropped to the ground and rolled onto her back near the downed ladder and the slow ooze of tar from the bucket.

She stared up at him as she lay there. "I thought..." She gasped a few times. "I expected to find you broken on the ground."

The truth of her concern was evident, and it pierced Jamie to see her fear. "I'm sorry. I kicked the tar bucket trying to get this blasted piece of tin off my fingers. It was like a bad Rube Goldberg experience after that, where one thing pushed another, until..."

Laramee's breathing turned to curiosity, and then into shudders of laughter. Jamie saw her so differently in that moment. She was childlike and beautiful, with her hair spread out around her like a dark halo that framed a lovely face with playful eyes. A relaxed joy encompassed her, and he wondered about the curtain of pain or self-doubt she hid behind most of the time.

She caught him studying her and ended her laughter with a final sigh. "Oh, I like this," she said as she tapped her chin. "What to do… what to do…This gives me good leverage."

"Very funny. I'm more useful once rescued than I am as an ornament."

"I don't know about that. You do make a nice ornament."

He wriggled the fingers attached to the patch. "I still have this last patch to set."

"Okay, Pret…" she caught herself—"Jamie. I'll help you out." She stood and positioned the ladder with shameless ease, then climbed up with the tar bucket in hand. Once she reached the top, she sat and leaned back, enjoying the sun on her face and, apparently, the feel of the sun-warmed tin on her bottom.

Jamie swallowed his pride and said, "I take it you've done this before?"

"I love it up here. You can see forever."

The view was suddenly more beautiful than it had seemed a few moments ago when all he saw was an arid, beige spread. "How many acres does the ranch include?"

"Nearly a thousand, but about a third of them are too rocky and arid to be of much use."

Jamie was glad she was aware of the problem, but he'd have raised that percentage substantially. "What are your parents hoping to get for the ranch?"

She looked at him as if she were challenging him on the next point. "You'll get them the best price possible won't you…if they decide to sell?"

"Of course, I will. The very best price I can."

She nodded. "Thank you. It might not be much to some folks, but whatever the price turns out to be, it'll be more money than they've ever seen."

He knew she was referring to what she assumed was his own family's wealth. His father had been street savvy, building his successful business one piece at a time. He began fixing up old cars which he sold at a profit, spinning that profit into a few lucrative lots in his native Boise. He sold those lots for ten times the purchase price, and on and on, he bought and flipped bigger and bigger properties with an eye for where the next real estate hot spot might be. Others came to him for advice on where and what to buy, and he offered them his uncanny instincts for an advisory fee. He was teaching his sons to do the same. "What would you do with the land if you decide to run the place?"

She turned and bit her lip. "You're a businessman. What do you think I should do?"

Her eyes bore into him as if she were starving for some surety she believed he had the power to offer her. His first impulse was to tell her the truth, which he felt quite sure would crush her, but then again, he thought, maybe that hard truth was exactly what she needed to hear. Hard truth with a little spark of hope.

"Do you really want my honest opinion?"

She seemed to know in advance that the news would not bring her comfort, and yet, after several silent moments, she lifted her sagging chin and said, "Yes."

"I'm a businessman, so I see balance sheets and profit margins. The grass is poor on most of your land, and the cost of supplementing the cattle's feed is probably what killed your father's profit. We had another client who had that problem. He was able to save his ranch by leasing government land with green valleys. He and his partner found out that sweet natural grass produced fatter cattle at a better price."

"We have that mountain stream."

"It doesn't have enough flow to support irrigation. You'd need to drill wells, several of them, and install irrigation equipment. Truthfully, I see tons of hard work and cash outlay, with only a slim chance of profit." Sad resignation creased her brow. His own heart broke a little when her mouth turned downward and trembled. He added a little spark of hope.

"But I'm also the son of a man who sees value in land, the way you do. With that said, I did see hope in that corner with the ledge and the waterfall. That's exquisite. What more are you willing to tell me about that place?"

"I'm sorry about earlier." Laramee drew her knees up close to her chin and wrapped her arms around them. "I love this place but coming home has been harder than I expected...in many ways. I had no right to take it out on you."

"Apology accepted."

"Thanks. We'll work the fence line after lunch, and I'll take you down to the bottom."

He noticed how deftly she avoided his question. "I'd like that. And then I'll have a better idea of which, if any, of the current opportunities would be best for the ranch and for your family."

"I'd appreciate that."

"Great." He enjoyed this Laramee. She was reasonable and smart and open. He didn't want to risk all that by driving her back into the shadows again, but neither could he pretend there wasn't something odd going on about the falls. "Can I ask you another question?"

"I don't promise to answer it."

"Fair enough. Why does the falls make you so sad?"

Laramee stiffened and met Jamie's gaze. "My best and worst memories happened in that place." She held him like a tractor beam with a yearning in her eyes for him to accept her answer and ask nothing more. Jamie knew not to push further. Not to do anything to send her back into her dark place.

"I trust you can finish that last patch and safely get yourself back down?"

"Yes, ma'am."

She smiled and rolled her eyes. "I'll go check on my folks and warm up the leftover soup. After we eat, we'll head out? Sound good?"

CHAPTER 7

*J*amie finished the last patch with far less drama. Pleased with himself, he stood on the roof and studied the overall job. It wasn't attractive, but a coat of silver paint would make that entire roof look fresh and solid. He'd offer the suggestion to Laramee.

From that vantage point, he could see the main house clearly. An older man, who he assumed was Sterling Stone, came out to the back porch and looked his way. Jamie raised a hand of greeting to Sterling, who raised one in return. The man seemed nice enough, and having seen how kind Cathy Stone was, Jamie wondered about the difficulty Laramee had with being home.

He thought it was time he at least introduced himself to Sterling, so he gathered his supplies, climbed down the ladder, and set all the tools in the barn before heading the man's way.

Sterling was a tall, thick man who was bent forward from what Jamie assumed was severe back pain. Sitting was a slow and arduous process accompanied by groans and grimaces and then a long, slow rush of relief. Jamie stopped his approach when he saw Laramee appear in the sliding doorway. She moved to her father's side, keeping herself between him and the door as if she were giving herself an emergency exit. She initiated a conversation, and it appeared Sterling barely responded, causing Laramee to throw her hands in the air and take that quick exit through the door and into the house.

The timing seemed poor for an introduction, so Jamie turned and headed back to the barn when he heard the man call out to him.

"So Laramee's put you to work, has she?"

Jamie spun around and waved. "Yes, sir. Good morning. I'm Jamie Cannon. So nice to meet you."

"I figured that's who you were, the man who'll either save or sink us."

"No, sir. All the decisions are yours. I just present options."

Jamie reached the porch and looked up at the man whose perch was still several feet above Jamie's head, so he used his hand to shield his eyes from the sun and hollered, "Would you like me to come up there so we can talk?"

The man replied as if he hadn't heard a word Jamie said. "You're riding to the falls today."

"Uh...yes, sir. That's my understanding."

"Stay close to my girl."

It was an unexpectedly tender request from the man with whom Laramee had such a conflicted relationship. "Yes, sir."

Sterling leaned his head back and laid his arm across his eyes, both blocking the sun and any further attempts at conversation. Jamie took it as his sign to leave and did just that.

He arrived at the bunkhouse only seconds ahead of Laramee's tornadic arrival. Curses flew, doors slammed, and the day's agenda seemed lost. Not knowing when she might reappear, Jamie decided to take some initiative. He warmed the soup, served himself a bowl, and said a prayer, asking the Lord to bless both the soup and Laramee. As he started eating, Laramee appeared from her dorm flushed, but otherwise settled.

Jamie jumped from his chair. "I'm sorry. I wasn't sure if you were coming out to eat or not. I shouldn't have started without you."

"Don't apologize. I wasn't sure myself. Thanks for warming it up though. I think there's bread and butter in the fridge. I'll grab them."

Jamie weighed the risk of asking questions or discussing his brief but encouraging conversation with her father. He decided the best course of action was likely to lay low, play dumb, and follow Laramee's lead.

She steered the conversation away from herself and the unpleasant conversation with her father by conversing about safer topics—the food order her mom was picking up, and a change in the day's work plans.

"We'd need the truck to haul fenceposts around the acreage, and right now, I'd rather ride a horse than drive a truck. How about instead of mending fences, we finish inspecting the rest of the fence line and get some of those tests done that you need to assess the land."

"I'm always up for a horseback ride."

When they finished eating, they headed outside. Jamie went to his vehicle and pulled out a few tools—a hole borer for soil samples, some plastic bags, and a blue box that contained chemicals and vials. The horses were saddled in quick time, and this time, Jamie and his derriere happily agreed to stick with slower, easygoing Nugget when Laramee offered him a faster, stronger animal.

He stowed his equipment in a saddlebag, mounted up, and fell into a smooth rhythm beside Laramee. They stopped several times so he could grab soil samples and take photos in different locations. The bore screwed into the ground, collecting soil from depths up to eighteen inches. Each sample was placed in a bag and recorded by location.

"What will those samples tell you?" Laramee asked.

"The composition of soil tells the story of the land, how it formed, what it's made of. Lots of things. I can only test for simple things like how acidic or basic it is, and how deep the topsoil is. I have county people coming out tomorrow to do perk tests to see how quickly water drains through the soil."

"And how will that effect the value of the ranch?"

"We'll know whether it can support agriculture like crops and livestock, or if it can be used for industry and development."

"Like factories?"

He heard the disapproval in her voice. "Or a hospital or a school or homes."

Something in what he said appealed to her. "Are you a geologist?"

"No, not really. I just came to love and appreciate the land and the science that explains it."

"Were you a Boy Scout?"

He kicked at the ground and rolled his lips. "Something like that."

She set her sights on the fence ahead without pressing him further, and for that, he was grateful. They were learning one another's boundaries, that they each had topics they chose not to share, and a rough idea of where those lines lay. He completed his tasks, and then they mounted their horses and completed the fence inspection in a few hours, ending opposite the far corner where the stream and falls were situated.

Laramee dipped her chin and slipped her gaze his way. "Could you handle a little faster pace?"

Jamie sensed that her confidence in his abilities was increasing. He gave her a nod and said, "I'm game."

❧

*L*aramee admitted that despite his aches and pains, the man knew horses, and though his hands were soft, he gave his all to the work. She found the two to be a pleasing combo—a polished gentleman with a rancher's heart and sense. She looked back over her shoulder and watched Jamie lean into his stirrups and give Nugget his head. The little horse seemed to be enjoying the recent opportunities to run, and judging from Jamie's smile, so did he. Laramee and her mount beat them handily, but she didn't make a point of it. Jamie had proven that he was worth his salt. He was honest about what he was and what he was not, and more interestingly, he appeared to be comfortable with both. She envied that about him.

He and Nugget were both winded when they arrived in the snowy borders of the foothills. "That was fun," he said between breaths. "The view here is worth any potential heart attack risks."

Laramee dismounted and held her horse's reins. Jamie followed suit.

"The way down is pretty steep," she said. "How about we walk?"

"A walk sounds good. Lead the way."

The straight drop off from the cliff was about thirty feet, but the walk down was much longer as they followed a meandering trail cut around rocks and trees. In some places, the path was steep and shaded, with a covering of melting snow which made sliding a frequent threat. From time to time, they hit stable stretches of packed snow where they could dig in and relax a little. Laramee stopped at one point along the path but before she had a chance to point out her secret, Jamie's hands were rubbing the cliff wall where aqua patches and protrusions appeared.

He turned to Laramee with his mouth agape. "This is turquoise!"

She shivered over the awe in his voice. "Yes, it's beautiful, isn't it?"

"Incredibly. There are clusters all over the cliff face, and a vein that runs…" He tried to follow the broadening blue line around and down the wall.

"It gets wider as we go down, until it's almost three-feet wide at the bottom. We have no idea how deep it runs into the rock."

"Laramee, do you know what it could be worth?"

She closed her eyes and stiffened over the comment. She'd been wrong about him. She'd hoped he was someone who would appreciate the wonder of the stone and the grotto that surrounded it more than its financial worth, but he was a businessman first and foremost. A man who rated the value of things on dreaded balance sheets and profit and loss statements.

"It's priceless," she snapped. "No matter how much turquoise is here, it's priceless to our family."

Jamie leaned close to her. "I understand why you'd want to protect its beauty, but mining this could bring in enough money to build the ranch the way you want and support it for years. I could get a team up here to bore into the rock and test the vein's potential."

Her disappointment came out in an audible cry of, "No." She shook her head. "You don't get it."

She began heading down the path again, away from Jamie, but he followed behind her, stumbling along as he led Nugget. He reached her and grabbed her hand. "Don't run away. Stop for a moment and explain it to me."

Don't run away. His voice was soft but firm as he attempted to persuade her to stay. Running had become her strategy of choice the last few years. It was easier than facing the people and the pain they dredged up. *Don't run away.* The request was still there in his eyes. His hand continued to hold hers, more like the offer of an olive branch than an effort to restrain her. She felt sure he would stand there as long as it took to win her trust, and his patience paid off. Now she just needed to find the words to explain herself. "Forget that you're in real estate and that your job is to determine the monetary value of our land. I was trying to give you a special moment, like the one you talked about earlier."

His confusion was still apparent, and Laramee tried again, using some of the humor he relied on with her. "A wise man recently told me that laughter, love, and joy help us push back against the hard things in the world. I wanted to give you a moment like that, by bringing you here to a place I thought would give you joy. I wanted you to see beyond the vein's monetary value and just enjoy its beauty and the marvel of it."

"I get it." His shoulders eased and his eyes closed. "Forgive me. And thank you for trusting me enough to show me this place. I'm sorry I didn't understand."

"I shouldn't have gotten so frustrated with you."

He looked at her and offered a repentant smile. "I really am just trying to help."

"I believe that."

Jamie leaned back against Nugget. "So...you think I'm wise?"

She shook her head and teased, "Don't let it go to your head."

A burst of laughter rolled from Jamie, and then he sobered and gave her hand a squeeze. "Last night, you asked me what I thought you should do with the ranch. I was just offering you another option to save it."

"I understand, and I thank you, but it's one option I can't take."

"Okay. So long as we understand one another."

She looked into his beautiful eyes and trusted him. "I believe we do. Would you still like to see the bottom?"

"Very much." He looked at their joined hands.

Laramee followed his gaze and gave his hand a squeeze before letting go and leading the way down the path. They turned a corner on the path which opened their view to glimpses of the blue-green little grotto below, and each time she heard Jamie "ooh" or "ahh," the place that held both her best and worst memories once again became her magical place, and her heart felt lighter, happier than it had in a long time. She had Jamie's patience to thank for it.

The last few yards of the trail turned muddy as it opened to the pool which sat protectively in the curve of the cliff wall sheltering it on two sides. The waterfall splashed and danced as it hit the bottom, spraying the walls and turning the end of the trail into mud.

"It never fills," Jamie noted with wonder. "The bottom of the pool must contain cracks and fissures that drain the water into the earth." He turned around slowly, marveling, as Laramee had hoped, over the grandeur of the place.

She stood to the side in delight as he studied the three-foot-wide, blue/beige streak that began at the water level, spreading up and out like branches of a tree.

"I'm no expert, but the quality of the stone is really impressive, Laramee. This vein appears to run deep. Someone has mined stone here in the past."

"My mother's people found the vein soon after they settled the land. As the story goes, they mined enough turquoise to buy more land until their property spanned this thousand acres. Mom said their digging created the ledge and made it so steep and dangerous. We were warned not to come here without Dad, but we sneaked down here more times than we could count, especially on nights with a full moon. That was our favorite. We sat on the ledge with the moon hanging over us and told spooky stories and dreamed our dreams. It's a wonder we never fell and broke our necks here."

The sweet memories dispelled the sad ones for a moment, and

then the old dagger of a memory rushed back in, sweeping that brief solitude and peace away.

"Why did your parents never mine it? Their lives could have been so much easier."

"They felt they had all they needed, and rather than destroy this wonder, they decided to work the land and make the turquoise their legacy to us, our inheritance, to put us through college or to finance our dreams if we ever wanted a life away from the ranch."

Jamie leaned back against the rock wall, distancing himself from her as if giving her the space he knew she'd need when he asked her the next question. "If your ancestors sold some of the turquoise, they must have filed claims for it, which means its existence is a matter of public record."

"I suppose."

"Interesting…" He scanned the walls again and turned back to her. "I still can't imagine why this place you love so much is also the place that makes you so sad."

For the first time, Laramee didn't slam the door on the question or turn and run away. She picked her way along the edge of the pool like a nervous cat as she remembered that night, and weighed which details she was willing to share. "I love this place, but it was also my brother's favorite place."

"Max?"

"No. I had another brother. His name was Tyler. He died six years ago."

"I'm sorry. I didn't know. Was he younger than you?"

"Yes, by four years. When he came along…I don't know…maybe it happens this way for most girls when a new baby arrives in the family, but he was mine. Mom had to negotiate with me to hold her own baby."

The memory caused prickles to rise on her arms. She rubbed them and paced within a small spot of ground, needing a physical release of the nervous energy building inside her.

"Max was the oldest, but he was mechanically inclined. He loved tractors and equipment, but he didn't like dirt or the smells of animals and ranching. He and Dad would tinker together, but when it came to the animals, I was Dad's shadow. I milked the cow, fed the stock, and mucked the stalls. Dad said he had a perfect team in us."

"You two were close."

"Very. Once." She tipped her head, marking the change that had occurred between them. "When Tyler was old enough to come to the barn with us, it was clear he and I were cut from the same cloth. We loved the stock, especially the horses, but he was born brave, and he loved to ride. Oh, how that boy could ride."

She didn't realize she had stopped talking as images of Tyler on a horse crossed her mind, like frames from a movie. When she finally refocused, Jamie was looking at her patiently, as if he too were trying to see the images by studying their impact on her.

"I'm sorry," she said with a shake of her head as she tried to return to the moment. "It's…uh…I've never talked this openly about Tyler to anyone."

Jamie smiled at her, and his face was filled with pain, her pain, as if he knew beforehand where the story was headed. He kept his eye on her, but he seemed to know not to move or speak or attempt to comfort her. She appreciated how she felt his empathy and closeness from ten feet away, more than she likely would have if he were standing beside her, crowding her sacred space.

The cold seemed to settle into her, and she took a deep breath, letting it out in a ragged exhale before she continued. "Mom and Dad worked out the dude ranch schedule so Tyler and I could participate in the local rodeos. I was a barrel racer, and Tyler was a tie-down roper. He and I competed together in team roping, and when we kept winning our events, we were invited to more competitive events farther away from the ranch. Dad took us, but that put more responsibility on Mom and Max. We hired help to fill in, but the bulk of the burden fell on Max, which is probably why his affection for the place burned out. He enlisted in the Navy when he turned eighteen. When I think back on those days, I can't believe how selfish we were."

"You were just kids."

She glanced at Jamie's unshaven face and wondered what stories lay behind those scars and that broken nose, and whether they were the reason she found no judgment, just understanding and empathy there.

"Tyler set his heart on bronc riding when he was about fifteen. He begged Dad every week to let him just sit on a bronc in the gate. Dad insisted he was too young, but on the last Saturday night of the rodeo season, I threw my support in for Tyler to try, and after the spectators left the event, Dad gave in."

She closed her eyes to finish the tale. "He thought it would scare Tyler into waiting a few more years, but that horse slammed against the gate so hard that Tyler slid sideways, hitting his head against the wood." She wrapped her arms around her body.

"The doctor assigned to the event had left by then. Tyler said he was okay, and we thought he was, so we drove home. Dad told me to keep him awake, so I talked to him about anything I could think of to keep him from falling asleep. There was a full moon that night and Tyler kept telling me over and over that it was following us home, as if he'd forgotten that he'd already told me that a dozen times before. I should have known then that something wasn't quite right, but Mom and Dad settled him into bed when we got back, and he fell right to sleep. We all turned in for the night too."

She felt she might be sick, so she allowed her weakened knees to bend until she was able to drop onto the moist ground. Jamie pushed off the rock wall he was leaning into and made a step as if he were coming her way, but Laramee put her hand out, sending him back to the wall. She didn't want to be comforted or appeased. She just wanted to face the recurring pain square on, here in this place instead of in her nightmares.

"Laramee?"

She glanced at Jamie and caught the concern on his face, and the tension in his body as if he were prepared to override her wishes and come to her, but she held him off again as she weighed how much to share. Part of her wanted to throw it all out there so he'd have no questions that would require her to revisit the awful experience again with him, but part of her feared she'd see disappointment in his eyes, or worse, so she gave him the abbreviated medical conclusion.

"The official cause of death was an aneurysm."

"I'm so sorry. But surely you don't blame yourself for not—"

She shook her head and pushed back again. Pushing and running had become her go-to.

"Mom and Dad shut down. Their marriage seemed to die that night too, or at least it suffered an irrecoverable paralysis. Max only had a few days' leave. It was long enough to see the toll Tyler's death was taking on the family, so he called his good friend Sutton, who'd just graduated from the police academy, and asked him to check on us from time to time. I think Sutton took the sheriff's deputy post in this county to honor that request. He was the only person I could count on in the following months. The only person able to relieve some of my guilt, at least for the hours we were together. He asked me to marry him, and I said yes. He was a good, gentle man who'd sacrificed a lot for me and my family, and the person I was most comfortable with."

"Did you love him?"

The interruption of his voice startled her. She almost expected he'd sit there in silence until she permitted him to speak, but he wasn't having it anymore. He walked to her side of the pool and sat several feet away but close enough that she could not avoid him or his questions, so she asked him one in return. "Have you ever had a person fill a need so deep in you that the relief they brought felt as beautiful and sweet as you could imagine love being?

She knew she'd hit a nerve.

"Truthfully?" He sat silently, staring into the water for a time. He turned back to her. "Yes. I understand those feelings. Someone came into my life and brightened the darkness for a time. I thought it was love, until she was gone. Looking back, I don't know if it was ever really love at all."

Laramee stood and brushed the dirt from her clothes. "Then you'll have to accept that as my answer too."

"My indecision caused me to break things off with her. Why did you leave Sutton?"

"For reasons that aren't as clear anymore, but that's a talk for another day. We should go. We've spent enough time playing."

She walked to where the horses were nibbling on tender shoots at the pool's edge, took her animal's reins, and mounted up. "They'll do fine uphill. Let's ride."

She made sure to be far enough ahead of Jamie to avoid any more questions, and close enough to help him if he and Nugget got into trouble. When he crested the hill and she knew he'd be all right, she urged her painted pony on as fast as he could carry her, letting the wind dry her tears.

CHAPTER 8

*J*amie wasn't the slightest bit surprised when she raced off, purposely leaving him behind. He felt sure she regretted sharing so much about her pain, about her guilt, and about how unworthy she felt. Knowing those feelings so well, he ached for her. He could also understand the impact of losing a family member. Jamie saw the strain his parents endured during those years when he was merely estranged from them. He could only imagine the agony of losing a child altogether. He wished he had the words or gestures that could absolve Laramee of the burden she carried.

He assumed she'd be in her dorm by the time he returned to the bunkhouse. She'd bared her soul to him, and he could understand if she needed the privacy to process the effect of what she'd shared and some time to regroup before the two of them spoke again.

Jamie was fine with Nugget poking along on the return trip. It gave him time to do a little processing and regrouping himself. How does one proceed when the only person you're sharing space with is as prickly as a rose? At least he knew why now. He hoped her sharing would make her more open and willing to remain amicable during their time together.

His concerns were set aside by an unexpected development. When

Jamie reached the bunkhouse, Laramee had already loaded the wire reel and what few fenceposts Sam had delivered onto the truck bed, along with the nails and the tools they'd need to mend sections of the fence. She'd shifted gears again, and he accepted that whatever door she'd opened earlier to him was closed once more. It was time to get to work.

They fell into a good pattern, working together in tandem. The lessons learned in Jamie's desert ranch days returned quickly to him. Laramee's eyebrow rose more than once in approval of his work, but what conversation there was remained general and impersonal, as if the morning's trip to the falls, and the conversation they'd shared, had never occurred.

Sutton's cruiser showed up at the edge of the field while they were enjoying a brief water break. Jamie studied Laramee's reaction to his arrival. She didn't respond with dread, but neither did she respond with excitement or joy. His own unstable relationship with Victoria didn't give him room to judge. He wanted more for Laramee, and he confessed that he wanted more for himself too if another opportunity for love presented itself.

Laramee picked up the water jug and said, "Between the roof and the fencing repairs, we've accomplished a lot today. He ought to be able to see that, right?"

Jamie leaned back and said, "Yes, but why do you have to prove anything to Sutton? You're not engaged anymore. Right?"

She gave his comment some thought as her head bobbed in fifteen tiny nods. "Right," she said without conviction.

"But for some reason, you feel you owe him some perceived loyalty and exclusivity."

Her eyes widened in a show of defense. "I reopened an old wound."

"By simply coming home?"

"No. Because I ended things so poorly before. I hurt him deeply, Jamie. Sutton sacrificed so much to stay here and be available to me when I needed him. My mother told me he still comes by every week to check on them as if they're his family, because they were supposed to be."

"He made those choices, Laramee. Not you. I applaud your

compassion, but you shouldn't allow yourself to be guilted into a relationship with a man you don't love."

She stiffened and waved to Sutton. "You don't know if I love him. *I* don't even know that." She placed her jug in the truck and dropped a spool of wire and three more posts on the ground. "Just keep working on the fence in case he comes by to talk to you." And then she drove off to meet Sutton.

Jamie watched the greeting when she exited the truck. Sutton approached with a broad smile and a dip of his head, and Jamie tried to imagine what the deputy had likely sacrificed to bring a little hope to Laramee when she had no one else to draw upon. It was hard not to respect the guy.

He turned back to the fence and chose a rotted, splintered post as the object of his toil. He pulled it this way and that to loosen the surrounding soil. When it moved freely, he pulled up and it came out like a loose tooth. He looked back at Laramee and Sutton, hoping she noticed his accomplishment, but she was otherwise engaged, so he grabbed the posthole digger off the ground and used it to widen the hole. He pushed the two handles together and slammed them into the ground with more force than the job required to cut into the cold earth. Then he pulled the handles apart to close the cups that captured the loosened dirt and pulled the device from the ground to dump the dirt. Once that dirt was set aside, he repeated the motion, over and over, slamming the tool into the ground, feeling the strain in his back, arm, and leg muscles, and stealing glances of the two standing apart but by the cruiser.

He told himself he didn't care what they did. That their choices had no bearing on his life, and yet he couldn't tear his eyes away from them. He told himself it was like watching a replay of an equal but different train wreck called Jamie and Victoria. That watching another couple struggle through similar issues improved his perspective. Satisfied with his analysis, he took a minute to examine his work. The hole was ready for the post, and yet, when he looked back at the pair again, his jaw tightened and he slammed the digger into the ground once more, and harder still.

He'd set the three posts by the time Sutton's cruiser pulled out.

Jamie's hands ached, so he removed his work gloves, opening and closing them to work the stiffness out. Laramee headed his way in the truck, but he refused to let her see his fatigue or hear her comment that he was soft or a paper pusher or a pretty boy. Instead, he lifted the spout on his jug and chugged his water. Forgetting about his gloves, he moved on to the next post and grabbed it to work it loose, recoiling in pain as large splinters from the dried-out old wood pierced his fingers and palm.

Laramee jumped from her truck and hurried to him. "Let me see that," she said, taking his hand. Jamie flinched, expecting her touch to be indifferent and rough, but he'd greatly underestimated her. He found her workworn hands surprisingly gentle as she rubbed the skin to determine the length and depth of the wound. She looked up at Jamie and winced, and in that moment when her guard was down, the hard lines and defensive pout melted away from her face, leaving softness and compassion in their place. She smiled whimsically at him, bringing light and beauty to her cold-reddened cheeks and brown eyes. In that moment, he forgot about the splinter as he marveled at the Laramee standing before him.

"Where'd Sutton go?"

"Why? Do you miss him already?"

"Like a toothache."

"That much, huh? Don't worry. He'll probably pop in every time his cruiser has a reason to be in the area. Are your shots up to date?"

Jamie was mulling over Sutton's attentive nature, and he didn't hear the question. "What? Yes, I'm sure they are."

Her eyes widened, and she said, "Good, because about a thousand muddy, fly-infested cows and horses have rubbed their you-know-whats on that post over the years."

She laughed, and Jamie wished her parents and her brother could hear the return of her happiness, even if just for a moment.

"There's a first-aid kit in the bunkhouse kitchen. We need to clean this wound and dress it before you get gangrene or something. You're all I've got, and I need both those arms and hands."

Her humorous bullying was infused with playfulness and spunk, and her comment that he was *all she had* made his wounds completely worth the pain.

He tried to play tough guy and wave her help off, but she pulled him along to the truck, and he complied. She glanced his way more than once, and each time he saw only concern and caring in her eyes.

Back at the bunkhouse, she had him wash his hands while she searched the cupboards for the first aid kit. He sat in one chair, and she sat by his side in another, gently probing the sites with tweezers, glancing up at him sympathetically. He couldn't imagine Victoria being so patient or even willing to touch his dirty work-worn hand. He smiled knowing she'd have likely searched the Internet for a specialist who made house calls, and then she'd've overseen the physician's work, telling him how to do it better and faster.

He flinched and Laramee grimaced. "Don't mind me," he assured. "You're very good at this."

"I'm sorry if I'm hurting you, but some of these are deep."

"You're not," he said, noticing how more of her rodeo queen features were visible to him as she focused on easing his pain.

"Sutton didn't want to speak with me, I guess?"

"No. He saw you working, and that was enough. He heard from someone at the county offices that a guy was coming out to run the perk tests. He also asked if you took any soil samples, and when I told him you had, he cheered and said that you only needed to be here two more days at the most. I didn't tell him you bet me you could survive a full week. I don't suppose I can legally hold you to that. I probably ought to release you from our bet and set you free in two days."

Suddenly, he wasn't in such a hurry to leave. "I'm not a quitter. A bet is a bet."

Laramee chuckled, and then she said, "Wait! We never discussed a prize for the winner."

"That's right. Okay...if I don't make it to the end of the week, what do you want?"

"Hmmm..." she mused as she dug out another sliver. "Two dozen ginger cookies from The Alpine."

"Done!"

"And if *you* win?"

Jamie watched the way the light played off her eyes and an idea came to him. "Well...the way I see it, you win either way. If I'm still here at the end of a full week, you've enjoyed seven days of free labor, and if I die or wear out, you get cookies. So, it seems to me that if I win, I should be able to claim a very good prize."

Laramee raised one eyebrow and rested her chin in her cupped hand. "Such as...?"

Jamie lowered his voice to a whisper and said, "I have an idea of what I want but give me a few days. I'm sure I'll be certain by the end of the week."

"It sounds suspicious."

He pulled a crooked smile and offered her his own raised eyebrow stare. "Good. It's my turn to drive you a little crazy."

"No hints?"

He wondered if she noticed how often and long his glance moved to her, or how he ached over every hurt she shared. "Oh, I'm sure there'll be a few hints if you're perceptive."

Laramee shoved his hand away and stood. "Men and their games." She moved to the sink to moisten a few paper towels and carried them back to the table to wipe a smear there. It could have waited, and Jamie interpreted her actions as a need to break the mood growing between them.

"Does Sutton play games?"

"No. That man just says what he wants. He told me he still loves me."

"Just like that?"

"He said he never stopped."

"And do you love him?"

Her gaze shifted around the room, anywhere Jamie wasn't. "Yes."

"Look me in the eye and tell me that."

She stood and moved to the wall, running away and closing emotional doors again.

"Why did you leave him, and why didn't you come back?"

She threw her hands up. "I wanted a fresh start. I wanted something different than the place and things that haunted me."

"Then why are you choosing all that again?"

She sat back down and picked up her tweezers again, but when she tried to take his hand, he moved them both to her shoulders, leaving her no choice but to face him.

"Don't choose to love someone out of guilt or perceived debt. You deserve more than a best friend, or big brother kind of love for a husband. You deserve to be crazy in love with whoever you want. And to be loved in return by a man who's not only head over heels in love with you but someone who makes you the best version of yourself."

She dropped her gaze and then returned it to meet his. "Find a man you miss the second he leaves the house and who you have a thousand things to tell the minute you see him again. Is Sutton that man for you?"

Her eyes began to glisten, and Jamie knew she was either about to lash out at him or storm away. She surprised him on both counts when she drew an inch from his face and said, "Is that what you had with Victoria?"

Jamie knew he owed her an honest answer. For several quiet moments he replayed memories of his time with Victoria, and then he said, "In the beginning, but we lost it somehow."

Laramee sat back against her seatback until Jamie's hands couldn't reach her and they slipped from her shoulders. "I'm happy for you to have known that kind of love, even for just a while. I truly am. You should go back and find that with her again."

"I can't. She married someone else on Friday."

The news shocked and saddened Laramee. "I'm so sorry—" And then her eyes pinched close. "I caught you staring at that bride at The Alpine. I knew from your expression that you'd had your heart broken. Was it her? Was Victoria the bride at The Alpine?"

He nodded and smiled. "And my heart wasn't broken." He backed up and corrected that statement. "I was feeling rudderless, because for the first time in a long time, I was on my own again."

"Was she wonderful?"

Jamie sat back and stared at the planks in the floor. "In many ways. She was beautiful, smart, driven, and organized. But we were more of a merger than a romance, and I finally missed feeling loved." He looked back up at Laramee and knew she was pondering what he'd said.

"And what does that mean to you?"

"All those things I said before. Someone you miss all day and who misses you equally in return. I want someone whose biggest dream is to build a family with me, who'll be my spiritual partner as well as my lover. I want a woman who'll give me a kick in the pants when I need one, who'll be as dedicated as I am to building a beautiful, secure, exciting life. She'd be my partner in every way. That's what I want, and what I think love can be."

She focused her attention on the First Aid box for several long seconds, and then she pulled tape and bandages from their respective compartments. "As wonderful and perfect as that all sounds, few people ever know anything close to that. Most of us are just trying to find someone to get through life with."

He could see her eyes begin to well and her body relax as if the fight had gone out of her. "Oh, Laramee..." he began, but a rebuttal seemed the last thing she needed, so he pulled her close and laid her head on his shoulder.

"It's okay. It's okay," he muttered.

Her arms reached around him as her voice grew despondent in surrender. "What if a love and a life like you describe isn't in the stars for everyone? I prayed that Tyler would get better, and he didn't. Then I prayed for my parents to get past their pain, and they just moved farther and farther into their own corners. And then Sutton came along. He was good and kind and caring. I dared to believe that maybe he was my gift, the answer to my prayers. He got me back on my feet again, and eventually, I began to dream there was a better, bigger life out there for me. And how did I repay him?" She straightened and pulled back, almost challenging Jamie. "I broke his heart when I went away to find that better life, and in the end, life only got lonelier and harder as if I'd ruined the one good gift I'd been given. And now I'm back and so is he. That has to mean something, doesn't it?"

"But you don't love him."

Their eyes caught, and her voiceless lips seem to repeat Jamie's words. The weight of her worry seemed overwhelming, and she started to return her head to his shoulder, but he turned his face to hers as the distance between them narrowed. In that moment, his want equaled hers. They were two equally lonely, battered people. And for all his lofty thoughts on love, he knew what he really wanted was what Laramee also sought in that moment—closeness and connection, and perhaps a little validation that someone valued them as they were.

He could feel her sweet breath on his mouth when the alarm bells began ringing in his head. And then Laramee turned her cheek slightly away and rested it on his own.

"Thank you," she whispered.

Chills coursed through Jamie, and he drew a ragged breath. "I'm sorry."

"No. I felt you pull back ever so slightly. You knew this was a mistake."

"I-I-I—"

"What if it was wonderful? I'd be a mess when you left at the end of the week." She pressed a kiss on his cheek and whispered, "Maybe things are working out exactly as they should with Sutton. Lightning doesn't strike when we kiss, and he doesn't sing me love songs, but he does love me."

Jamie's heart sank over how little she expected for herself. "Laramee..." he groaned. But what could he say? What moral capital did he have to draw on?

She picked up the tweezers and dug the last splinter from his hand as if the conversation had never happened. She washed and dried it and applied an antiseptic salve, and bandage. When she had done all she could, she looked at him and smiled. "Good as new."

"Thank you, but—"

Her phone beeped. She stood abruptly and said, "My mom needs me. I won't be long, but in the meantime, try your gloves on and see if you're able to use that hand."

She seemed relatively unaffected by the events that had left him ashamed and empty. She was so vulnerable, and he added to her pain. He had no words to make things better, so he focused on the one helpful thing he could do. He put his gloves on, tested his bandaged hand, and headed back to the fence.

Once again, he saw Sterling Stone sitting on the porch at the very moment Laramee was in the house. A pattern of behavior appeared to emerge, of the man purposely isolating himself from his daughter, of tossing another hurt her way. Jamie couldn't bear it, so he strode toward Sterling.

Before Jamie reached him, the man called out, "You got hurt?"

"Yes." Jamie saw a chance to build Laramee up in her father's eyes. "She fixed my hand as good as new. She's really rather amazing."

"You're singing to the choir, son. Do you have any results for me yet?"

Jamie was so dumbfounded by the man's positive first response that he almost missed the second. "I-I-I uh…have the men coming to perform perk tests tomorrow, and I'll run my soil samples tonight."

"We'll talk when you get those results. No sense in speculating. I'll let you get back to work now."

Jamie felt summarily dismissed, and as ordered, he returned to his fence repairs.

⁊❧

*L*aramee was gone for over an hour when she pulled up past where Jamie was working, parked the truck, and jumped out.

He watched her carefully, assessing her mood to see if she would provide any follow-up to their strange, earlier interlude, but she offered none. He gave a huff, and nailed new wire to the end of a new post. He was determined not to speak first, but on second glance, he noticed how pallid and drawn her face seemed, and the vibe she gave off, more thoughtful than moody, told him things hadn't gone well during her conversation with her mother. The real indicator came when she moved on to the next post marked as rotted and worked it loose by slamming into it with every ounce of power in her thin body. Jamie said nothing for several moments, waiting to see if she'd open the dialogue, and when she didn't, he asked, "Is everything okay with your mom?"

"She seemed tired and distracted. My father is probably running her ragged."

"Have you had a conversation with him since you've been home?"

"I've talked *at* him and *to* him, but inasmuch as a conversation requires a two-way dialogue, the answer to your question would be a no." She slammed into the post again. "He has, however, relayed information to me through Mom. She said he thinks I look haggard and tired. No 'I love you.' No 'Tell her I'm glad she's home.' Just that."

She went for another slam when Jamie intervened and stopped her. She wrested herself free of him and reached the back of her hand across her eyes. Jamie felt his heart tighten for her. He knew how it felt to believe you've lost a parent's love, and how that loss left a child feeling like a failure, unloved and unlovable. It wasn't true, he finally discovered, but guilt builds barricades even love struggles to penetrate. *Could it be the same for Laramee?*

Jamie chose his words carefully. "I'm sorry you're feeling so hurt."

"Thanks. I'm sorry to be such a downer." She perked up and shifted gears. "Your work looks great. Have I thanked you for what you're doing here?"

"A dozen times, and you're welcome. I hope it helps your family." He questioned whether to raise his point or not and then he decided to jump in. "I had a thought about your dad. Is it possible he really was worried about you? Maybe his intent just got lost in your mom's delivery."

Hope brightened her eyes as she swung her head his way, tilting it to the side as she considered that happy notion, but the longer she pondered the thought, the dimmer that light became until it faded completely.

"What exactly is wrong with your dad?"

"Mom said she can't remember all the details, but he has heart arrythmia and some blockage in his arteries. It's not good. I want to take him to the doctors and hear the diagnosis myself, but he refuses to go until we get past this assessment."

She slammed into the post again until Jamie feared she'd bruise her own heart. He hurried to her side. "Laramee...allow me, please?"

She stepped back and waved her hand toward the post.

Jamie enjoyed the way her eyes crinkled at the corners with real pleasure when he stepped in. She'd finally learned to trust him, and he was grateful the awkward moment in the cabin hadn't ruined that. Every kind gesture he offered was met with appreciation that made him want to do more.

"How about I pull the posts out and you string the wire?"

"A brilliant and fair plan. I'm glad we're okay after…you know. We are, right?"

"In perfect synch."

She smiled again. "You're a good friend, Jamie. A little too philosophical, but still a good friend." A happy little chuckle erupted from her, and he found himself laughing, more over the pleasure of hearing her than over the moment itself.

"You have a nice laugh. It makes your eyes sparkle."

She gave him a flirty little grin, the first spark of worth he'd seen from her. "They ought to sparkle. They're worth a million bucks."

Jamie leaned back and returned her grin. "A million, eh?"

"Yes, because my dad used to tell me they were filled with specks of gold dust."

He knew his response to her show of spunk and sharing of a happy fatherly memory mattered. He closed one eye and pretended to examine her claim. "He was absolutely right. That sounds like something a loving dad would say. My guess is that he still loves you, Laramee. He might not be good at showing it anymore, but love like that doesn't just end."

She pulled her lips in and clamped down on them as she unwound the beginning of the wire. Jamie moved on to the next post and then Laramee blindsided him.

"You've got beautiful eyes too. They're not filled with gold dust, but I think you've caught me staring at them more than a few times."

He enjoyed this sassy side of her. "I've got my mom's eyes."

"They're enchanting. They remind me of a husky."

He laughed so hard he had to lean on a post. "Being compared to a husky doesn't sound too enchanting to me, but it's not the first time I've heard the comparison."

"You've got a good face. Those scars and that nose intrigue me. Tell me about those."

Her candor caught him completely off-guard. He tensed up and laughed through his nervousness. "I was just doing stupid stuff." He immediately sought a diversion, so he went back to work, and was glad she let the question drop.

He checked on her a few times to make sure she wasn't moping or angry because he hadn't been as open as she had, but she was all business again. He'd discovered a few other things about the complex Ms. Laramee Stone. She couldn't resist a good joke, and she couldn't receive kindness without responding. All in all, she wasn't as hard a nut to crack as he'd first believed, and he was about to test that theory.

"Knock knock," he said.

She looked up from stringing a length of wire and said, "What?"

"Not what. Who's there?"

She placed her hands on her hips and eyed him as if he were daft. "You've got to be kidding."

"Apparently, not very well."

She chuckled. "That joke is as lame as notoriously lame knock knock jokes get."

"Let's think this through, shall we? Consider how we met and the condition of our most personal relationships. Do either of us have any cause to be too proud for knock knock jokes?"

"When you put it that way…'Who's there?'"

They went back and forth for an hour, laughing more than working, making up more ridiculous jokes than clever ones, but it didn't matter. The sky grew gray and colder, and their hands were nearly numb, and they were still at it when Laramee got a call from her mom.

"We have food! Let's call it a day."

They packed up the tools and hopped in the truck. Laramee turned on the radio and picked up the five p.m. weather forecast.

"Freeze warning," she said. "We'll need to add extra bedding for the stock."

"Am I still on KP?"

"You bet. You tend to feeding us, and I'll tend to feeding the stock, and…wait…"

Her voice dropped off as they drew close enough to the house to see not one but two vehicles in the lane.

"That's your mother's car and that's…"

"Sutton's cruiser. I wonder how long he's been waiting. You carry the groceries in, and I'll talk to him."

From a distance, they saw Cathy Stone open her trunk. Sutton was right there, lending a hand, or two arms, that were threaded through the handles of multiple grocery bags as he carried Cathy's bags into her house. Laramee parked the truck as Sutton left the house and moved their way. His eyes shifted between Laramee and Jamie as if he were staking out the place and them. Instead of his usual warm smile, he merely nodded at Laramee and said, "I'd like a word with your ranch hand first."

Laramee started to argue but Jamie touched her arm and said, "Not a problem." He nodded toward the house, and she slowly backed away to grab the three bags of food left in the trunk.

Once Laramee had the bags, Sutton closed Cathy's trunk and sent Laramee on to the bunkhouse with a finger point, as if she were a Buick he was directing through traffic. The move thoroughly peeved Jamie, but an even less welcoming greeting awaited him as Sutton tipped his head to the side, directing Jamie to follow him back to the far side of his cruiser, presumably where they could talk out of Laramee's earshot.

Jamie leaned against the cruiser, but Sutton stood ramrod straight with his hands pressing over his equipment belt where his gun, handcuffs, flashlight, and a dozen other intimidating tools rested. "I've been here for almost an hour. I've seen you two out there, laughing and flirting."

"You mean being cordial and friendly?"

"You went way beyond that."

"We were a quarter mile in the field. How could you see us?"

Sutton pointed to the strap he was wearing bandolero style across his chest that attached to a carrier on his far side.

Jamie rubbed his fingers into his eyes. "You've got to be kidding. You didn't actually spy on us with binoculars."

Sutton didn't flinch. If anything, he puffed his chest out further for being so thorough. "I'm just watching out for Laramee's best interests."

Jamie tried to remember that this was the man who saved Laramee in those early days after Tyler's death. He took a breath and kept his voice measured and soft. "I know you love her. She's told me some of the things you did to get her through those days."

The shoulders that were hunched around the deputy's neck, lowered an inch or two. "What did she say?"

"Just what I said...that you faithfully responded to Max Stone's request for you to be there for her and her family in his stead, and that you sacrificed a lot to fulfill that request."

"She said that?"

"She did. Whatever you did or said, you pulled her through. She knows that. And she's grateful to you still."

"I never asked for her gratitude."

"She knows that too, but it's there, nevertheless. From what little I know of her past, she went through a lot before she left for Arizona, but clearly, she's been through even more since then. You see it. Worry is apparent in your eyes when you look at her. She's not the same girl who left here five years ago. Am I right?"

Sutton leaned toward Jamie and snarled, "You've only been with her a day and a half, and you think you know more about her than I do?"

"Have you seen her smile or laugh since she came back?"

Sutton didn't answer, but they both knew he'd seen the proof of her laughter in Jamie's company mere moments earlier. "You're entertainment," he growled, "but I'm her history. She came home to face hard changes in the farm and in her folks. I've been here, waiting all these years for her. Laramee respects that kind of loyalty. I still love her, and I think she loves me again."

"Then trust her."

Sutton drew his head back like a snake preparing to strike. "What's that supposed to mean?"

"You say you know her. That you love her. Then trust her. Consider what's best for *her*, not you."

"I've always put her first."

"Is that why you're here now? Making her feel guilty because she laughed and was happy? If you love her, celebrate her happiness. She needs some joy, some fun in her life."

"Don't you think I want that for her?" He slumped against the cruiser. "We had so little time for courting. Almost none. After Tyler died of that aneurysm, her father shut down. Sterling barely left his bedroom for weeks. Laramee sucked up her own pain and loss and was handling everything when I showed up, so I just pitched in by her side. The family shut the dude ranch down after Max enlisted in the spring, but they still had all their stock—fourteen or fifteen horses and ponies, a few dozen head of angus cattle, a milk cow, chickens, rabbits, and a herd of goats and sheep the kids loved to feed when the ranch was running full steam."

"And that all fell to Laramee?"

"And me. I was here at five or six each morning and we worked together until my shift started, then I was back here after work for the evening feeding."

Jamie was in awe of what this man had done. "How did you keep all that up?"

"I barely slept during that first six months. It took a terrible toll on our relationship. I saw it happening. Every conversation, every minute we were together was about this ranch or her parents. One day, I finally told her we couldn't sustain it all. I asked her to marry me, and she said yes. I thought I'd grabbed the brass ring. Then I told her father he needed to sell off most of the stock, and he delegated that to me and Laramee."

Sutton pushed away from the vehicle and paced a few steps. He took his Stetson-style hat off and pressed it against his chest. His face was slackened and sad. He turned back to Jamie as if he were confessing to a priest. "I thought we'd have more time together when the workload was lessened, but she cried every time we took animals to the auction. I've died a hundred times over that. I never should have let her go along. She said Tyler loved all those animals and that

106

losing them was like losing Tyler over and over. I think that's what finally broke her spirit."

He dug his thumb and forefinger deep into his brow. "She was lost after the stock was gone. She said the place didn't feel like home. That she had no purpose. I hoped marrying me and building our own little business would be enough. I'm a hunting guide on the side. I thought if I used my vacation time to build up my clientele, we'd have a nice side business ready when I retired, but I guess that was my dream, not hers. One day, she handed me back my ring and said she was sorry. The next day, she was gone."

Jamie wanted to give the guy a man-hug or a pat on the back. All he could do was ache for the guy and for Laramee. "You're a good man, Deputy. You have my respect. I mean that."

The deputy's eyes shifted to the bunkhouse. "I appreciate that, but I still have my eye on you. Can you still say you have no interest in her?"

"My only interest is her happiness."

Sutton stared at him for several seconds as he weighed that answer. "I'd like you to define that a little more clearly."

"I'm afraid I can't, except to say that I'll support whatever...or whomever she chooses." Jamie turned and stepped away from Sutton, but as he expected, the man challenged his comment.

"So that's how it is. I guess I should thank you for at least being honest. But just know this—I'm not going anywhere."

Jamie turned and nodded. "I'd expect nothing less. Let's agree that Laramee's happiness is the priority."

"One hundred percent."

They shook hands before the consequence of the conversation fully sank in. Jamie had all but told Sutton he was falling for Laramee.

CHAPTER 9

The longer the two men spoke, the more nervous Laramee grew. She entrusted Jamie with her most tender feelings and concerns regarding Sutton, and she prayed he hadn't used them to wound her dear friend.

She couldn't read Jamie's expression when he entered the bunkhouse. Those mesmerizing ice-blue eyes looked at her and into her as if he were seeing her for the first time. Laramee's skin prickled, and her breathing hitched. Whatever had been said between the men had changed something in Jamie. She looked for a bruise or blood and saw none, but it was clear he'd been hit by something that knocked the wind out of him.

"What happened out there?"

Jamie ran a finger along her arm and smiled. Shockwaves zipped through her at his gentle manner, and yet his touch conveyed other feelings as well, like sadness or fear.

"We just talked."

"Then why do I feel like we're standing on a cliff?"

He pressed his lips tight and lifted his shoulders in a silent gesture of "I don't know." She knew that wasn't true. He knew and didn't want to tell her.

Instead, he said, "Do you trust me when I say I only want your happiness?"

Her eyes bore into his to pull the story behind the question from him, and when he offered nothing more, she whispered, "Yes."

"Then talk to Sutton. He wants the same for you."

The look that held her captive released her when Jamie turned for his room. Her heart was racing but she didn't know why, nor did she know what awaited her in the yard. Her walk from the bunkhouse to Sutton seemed much longer than the thirty or forty steps it actually required. Perhaps it was because she had no sure plan for how to respond if he ended their chat the way he had earlier, with the same, simple, *"I love you, you know?"*

Instead, he just offered a crooked little smile she could imagine him making on elementary school picture day when the teacher pointed out that he was the only one not smiling. It made her laugh, and he laughed in concert with her.

"What's got you in such a good mood? You looked a bit cross when you were talking to Jamie."

He reached for her hands and pulled her close. "We reached an understanding."

She thought about the look in Jamie's eyes and shivered. "A-a-a about what?" Laramee backed up and cocked her head back and thought about their earlier almost-kiss.

Sutton's thumbs rubbed against her palms with an intimacy this awkward man had never shown before. It was both welcome and unsettling, and she felt off-balance, even with the very man she thought she knew so well.

"You know you don't have to mother that guy or cook his food. He's a big boy, and besides, that looked like a lot of groceries for someone planning to leave soon. Isn't he about done here?"

They were words Sutton would say. Practical words. No flowery professions. He was jealous of Jamie's presence, and he wanted him gone. She debated whether or not to tell him she had moved into the women's bunkroom, and decided not telling him was akin to a lie.

Whatever reserve of innocent, playful happiness she'd found joking around with Jamie earlier in the day was depleted by this agonizing awkwardness. Sutton had been so good to her. She decided to tell the whole truth. He deserved that.

"Those groceries weren't just for him. I moved into the other wing of the bunkhouse." When his mouth dropped open and his eyes narrowed into slits, she quickly added, "I couldn't stay in the house and endure my father's cold shoulder, so I took over the women's area. It's like two completely separate apartments."

"Are you cooking and eating together?"

"Yes. It would be silly to send him fifteen miles away to grab a pancake."

"And your downtime at night, are you sharing that as well?"

Laramee drew herself up straight, and Sutton backed down.

"I'm sorry." He quickly withdrew his implied accusation and stepped back, bringing his hands forward. "I trust you."

"Am I supposed to feel honored that you've chosen to bestow your trust on me? Well, I'm not. I'm not yours or anyone's property. I don't owe you any explanations, nor do I need to earn your trust. Jamie and I are putting in twelve-hour days, and by evening I barely have the energy to chew my food."

"You're right. I'm sorry. But I offered—"

"No. I already owe you so much, Sutton. I don't feel the same indebtedness when Jamie helps. It's business. It's just part of selling the ranch."

"Business. Sure. Maybe it's just business for you, but that guy has other ideas."

A chill zipped through Laramee as she weighed Sutton's implications against the change she felt in Jamie when he entered the bunkhouse after the men's chat. "What are you talking about? Did Jamie imply there was more between us?"

Sutton's head cocked to the side and his brow furrowed in hurt as he studied her reaction to his comment. Laramee knew her pleasure over that possibility had been too obvious.

Sutton backtracked, as if attempting to staunch the notion he'd unleashed in Laramee. "I got jealous watching you two laugh and yuk it up out there, and he said he just wanted your happiness. I guess it really wasn't anything at all, it's just that having him here, practically living in the same space with you...it makes me crazy."

She felt her heart deflate. She could imagine Jamie saying those caring, friendly words, to deescalate Sutton's jealousy and anger. *But what had Sutton said to Jamie to leave his eyes so hallowed? Or what else might Jamie have said to Sutton?* She knew there had to be more.

"Don't dwell on it, Sutton. I admit, I enjoy Jamie's company. Life has been about work and duty and carrying on for so long that it feels good to laugh. To remember that life doesn't always have to be heavy. He's been a good friend, but he'll be gone in a few days." She tried to hide the disappointment those words dredged.

"Hey. Maybe you could end a little earlier tonight and we could drive to my place. I'll grill us some venison steaks. I'd love to show you the improvements I've made on the house and the barn."

She looked longingly at the bunkhouse before finally saying, "All right. That sounds nice."

"What time?"

Once again, her gaze moved to the bunkhouse where Jamie was waiting. The happy supper she looked forward to sharing with him would have to wait. "How about seven?"

"I'll see you then."

His expectation-filled happiness made it hard for Laramee to breathe. She needed an excuse to break the moment. "There's going to be a hard freeze tonight," she said. "I should get the groceries put away and bed the stock down."

"All right."

She stepped away until he dropped her hands, ending the moment with, "See you at seven then."

⁊⹁

She headed into the bunkhouse and found it silent, with the commons area empty. She went to Jamie's door and knocked. He answered in a husky voice that was unfamiliar and foreign to her.

"Is everything all right?"

"Sure," he said with greater cheer. "He opened the door and projected a happy smile that belied the darker something in those penetrating eyes. His shirt was half off, as if he'd answered the door while dressing. She noticed another scar on his bare shoulder and one on his chest. When her eyes moved there he pulled his shirt down quickly.

"Did you and Sutton have a good chat?"

His voice was soft, and his smile was warm, but there was a tinge of bitterness in his tone.

"Yes. He asked me to go for a drive with him, and considering how I've dodged him, I figured—"

"Of course." He smiled again, and this time the tone was sweet and understanding.

"We could still cook together."

"No. You go get ready. I'll bed down the stock and rustle up something for myself. Besides, I need to run the soil samples and be up early to meet the guy running the perk tests tomorrow."

She felt as if he were handing her over to Sutton. "What did you two really say out there? Please tell me the truth."

Jamie laid his bandaged hand along her jaw. "I promise that whatever I tell you will always be the truth."

"So…"

"We agreed that your happiness is more important than two stupid men's egos."

"I still don't understand."

"Instead of making you feel you're stuck between working happily with me or pleasing Sutton, we agreed that what we really want is for you to be or do whatever you want to be happy, Laramee, and we'll both be there, cheering you on."

He walked to the peg board by the door and grabbed his coat. With a glance over his shoulder at her, he shot her a wink and slipped away into the dusk.

*L*aramee didn't know what to make of what Jamie had said, but she examined it every which way as she put the groceries away. She came to an interesting conclusion. If what he said was really true for both him and Sutton, it did open up some interesting possibilities, and she was anxious to explore them in the morning.

She stood back from the fridge after placing the last item inside. The shelves still looked empty, but then again, she was used to seeing a bulging fridge when the dude ranch was running. Mom always did the ordering, which varied little week to week, and she and Tyler put it all away. Everything about the dude ranch was so exciting back in those days. In truth, she could say the same about everything in her life back then. She and Tyler and Brenda were the darlings of the rodeo, and they felt they owned the world.

More thoughts of Brenda poured over her. The two had been as tight as sisters. How had they drifted so far apart? For the same reason she'd drifted from everyone...Tyler's death.

The phone felt prickly in her hand. She wanted to call Brenda and she dreaded the thought, knowing that for all the happy news of her baby and chit chat about old times, the conversation would inevitably circle back to Tyler.

Sam had surely told Brenda that Laramee was back, and delaying the call would just make the conversation harder. She had to pause and think about the number she had once known as well as her own. She dialed it, and the phone rang six times. She was just about to give up, relieved that she could say she tried to call, but anxious about what kind of message she should leave, when Brenda said, "Hello."

"Hey. Hi, Brenda...It's Laramee."

"Hey! Sam said he was making a delivery to your ranch today. When did you get in? How long are you staying?"

Laramee answered the first part and avoided the second. She heard a cry in the background and used it to divert the topic. "And I heard you had a baby. Congratulations! Tell me about your little guy."

"His name is Knox. He's almost two. Have we not spoken since he was born?"

Guilt stabbed Laramee at all the calls from Brenda that had gone unanswered. "That's my fault."

"You kind of went dark on me. In fact, when Sam said you might call, I didn't actually expect that you would. I just figured you'd moved on to that more exciting life you always wanted."

It was said so matter-of-factly, without intent to cause hurt, but it did. Laramee felt her throat tighten, and she needed to sit. Brenda was the one person she could tell everything to, and what she wanted to tell her now was that life hadn't gotten better. It had gotten smaller and harder and lonelier, but all she could eke out was, "I'm sorry."

The baby cried again. "Things change. I, of all people, know that. Even if you'd stayed here, our fun would have come to a screeching halt after Knox's first seizure. But I sure missed our talks."

"Seizures?"

"Yeah...from his cerebral palsy."

"I'm sorry. I didn't...I didn't know."

"I wondered. When your mom and Sutton both said they didn't hear from you often, I wondered if you knew. Yeah, we had our own adventures back here. Not all of them were ones we wanted, but we're managing, and Knox gives us smiles that make our hearts burst, so we're doing okay."

Laramee was still processing everything and had no ready reply.

"Maybe we can get together before you go or sell the ranch or whatever is happening over there."

"I'd like that," Laramee said. "I'd really like that."

"Well...gotta go. My little man needs me."

"Sure. Sure. I'll call you in a few days."

"K. Bye."

Laramee ended the call and headed to her room to dress for her date, but Brenda's situation stole her peace. Her best friend had a baby with CP, and she hadn't even known about it. She thought about all the ignored calls she purposely avoided because she had been wallowing in her own guilt and self-pity, and there was Brenda, needing her friend, her sister.

So many people she loved had needed her, and she'd left all of them, hoping to run away from her own guilt and pain, but she soon realized that all she'd done was carry those burdens with her, to a place where she was completely alone and without support.

She thought of her mom. She needed her, and like a miracle, a knock came at the door. When she answered it, she found her mother standing there in a thin jacket, with a basket of fragrant muffins in her hands.

"What are you doing out there, Mom? You'll catch a cold or worse. Come inside."

"No, thanks. I won't be but a minute. I know you have plans, and you need to get ready. Sutton stopped by the house before he left and told me you two talked. He said you were going to have a dinner date tonight, and I thought these might come in handy. That man can hunt a deer, skin it in field, process the meat, and grill like a chef, but I don't think he bakes, and—"

"I know. I know. And neither can I."

"I wasn't going to say that. I really don't know what you've learned in these past four years." Her mother's face pinched, and then she beamed a smile that was too bright and too cheery. "You might be an award-winning chef now for all I know."

Laramee tried to ignore the hidden hurt in her mother's comment and shifted the conversation. She sat on one of the porch's two benches and patted the space beside her. "At least sit for a minute, Mom."

"All right. Just for a minute."

A pregnant silence set in until Cathy said, "Young Mr. Cannon seems like a pleasant man. He always smiles and waves when he sees me."

"He's a good person. I thought he was going to be a nuisance, but he's actually kinda wonderful." Laramee quickly backed her praise down for her Sutton-loving mother. "He's been a huge help."

"How long will he stay?"

"Just a few more days, I imagine. He made me a bet that he could survive a week as a ranch hand"—she chuckled through the sadness the words caused her—"but I think he's feeling restless. The men come tomorrow to do the perk tests, and once he runs his soil samples, his work here will be done."

"And we'll have our answers so we can make a plan. I'm ready for whatever comes next. I've missed you, Lar. We both have."

Laramee didn't pursue the point about how much her father missed her, but that point raised another. "Are you really ready to give up the ranch?"

Her mother leaned her head back against the wall and set her gaze on the house. "I always imagined myself growing old here and dying in my own bed, with my family close by, but your father's health is declining, and you and Max live elsewhere now…"

*And Tyler is gone…*Laramee added in her own mind. "But what if I decide to stay and revive the dude ranch?"

"Are you seriously considering that?"

Her mother's doubt punctured Laramee's thin dream. "I haven't ruled it out." She stood firmly for a short time, as if to emphasize her point, and then her posture, like her resolve, weakened and she leaned against a beam.

"The ranch blessed our family for generations, Laramee, but each generation made sure to leave a better life behind for their children than the one they enjoyed, and that's what your father and I want to do for you kids, whatever that means to you. The real question is, what life do you want?"

Laramee looked out over the barren land. "I wish I knew."

"So, these past four years haven't clarified things for you?"

She knew the sad expression she'd find on her mother's face before she turned her head and saw her mom's pinched lips and hollowed cheeks.

"I guess I didn't consider what my leaving would do to you. I tried staying, but I couldn't after—"

Her mother's hand flew forward. "Don't, Laramee. Let it go."

"Are you asking me to forget Tyler?"

"Never. I'm asking the same thing of you I've asked from your father, to not stop living your life because Tyler's ended."

"I don't know how anymore."

"Do you love Sutton?"

"Why does everyone keep asking me that?"

"Because it's not fair to him if you don't."

Laramee slid down the wooden beam to the floor and sat there in a lump.

Her mother made the uh-uh-uh sound she made when she was mulling something over. "I love that women have so many new opportunities and such independence now, but I'm glad I was born when and where I was."

"What? Why?"

"I think I had it easier than you. Partly because we were more sheltered back here in this county. Oh, some of the local kids headed off to universities and cities for work, but that never interested me. There were only fifteen boys in my graduating class. That seemed like the extent of my world, and I was fine with that. I fell in love with your father when I was fourteen and loved him every day after. We knew we'd either live on his family's ranch or on mine, and when my brother Jack died in the war, it was just assumed that we'd live here, and your father's brother would take over the Stone family's place. Simple, neat, perfect."

"But didn't you have dreams, Mom? Didn't you ever want to see something beyond the shadow of the Rockies or swim in an ocean or fly on a plane or work in an office?"

"Maybe in random moments here and there, but my dreams were small and easily satisfied by the life ahead of me. All I ever wanted was to simply be a mother and a rancher's wife, like my own mother. It suited me. Now, I did fill out a contest form on the back of the TV guide once. I drew the little reindeer on the back cover and sent it in, and I won! They sent me a nice letter with an offer to take an online art course. They even said they'd place my sketch in an art journal I could buy, but that letter was enough approbation for me. It gave me the confidence to keep doodling for my own pleasure, and here with the guests. And I passed everything I knew on to you. But early on, I saw that you were someone with bigger and broader dreams. That's why seeing you come home after all these years, still lost and sad, breaks my heart. I'm delighted you're here, but I really did want you to find all that happiness you were chasing."

"Thanks, Mom." Laramee felt like an even bigger disappointment. "I talked to Brenda."

"Good. She's had a rough go of it, poor thing."

"Her little boy has cerebral palsy?"

Her mother nodded. "Such a beautiful child. I've babysat for them a few times so she and Sam could attend a family funeral or wedding. Little Knox is so loving, but those seizures are scary."

"I could have been a help to her."

"Be one to her now. Keep close, no matter what you decide to do." Cathy Stone pulled her jacket more tightly around her. "I'm starting to feel the cold in my bones. Florida sun would feel real good right now. I ought to go into the house and check on your father."

She stood and blew out a rush of air that left steam trails in front. "He should be in the prime of his life. He's only fifty-three. Dr. Mathers says he's on a slippery slope. He still has time to make changes and get healthy, but if he doesn't start soon, the effects on his heart will be irreversible."

"Why doesn't he listen?"

"It's like telling a person to be happy, Laramee. In some cases, feeling happiness is a choice. In some, feeling happiness requires help. Your dad needs both. I can offer him help, but I can't make him accept it or choose happiness. But I think you two could do that for each other."

So, there it was. Her mom's counsel about happiness was also meant for her. After delivering her message, her mom turned to leave, but Laramee couldn't resist asking the question that haunted her.

"Does he ever ask about me? I don't mean when you tag his name onto your thoughts. Does *he* ever ask about me?"

"Yes, Laramee. Every time you and I talk on the phone, he always asks about you." She leaned in closer and added. "And he always asks me the same question, whether you ask about him."

Her mom left without apologizing for the uncharacteristic but noticeable bite in her final comment, as if it was intended to pierce Laramee a bit, which it did and continued to do as she dressed for her date. The aroma of sautéing onions hit her like a welcome when she opened the door and stepped into the kitchen where Jamie was cooking.

His smile was like a lifeline, soothing her burdened heart. "I saw you talking with your mom. Good chat?"

Not wanting to get into it, she brushed the comment aside, saying, "Sure."

Jamie raised a sauce-covered spoon. "I'm whipping something up in case Sutton's a terrible cook and you need a midnight snack when you get home."

She laughed, but what she really wanted was to fall into Jamie's arms and lay her head on his shoulder, where she felt protected and at ease. "It smells great, but the truth is, Sutton is a wonderful cook."

"I had a feeling..." Silence followed as Jamie turned back to the stove. "I was torn between two of my favorite recipes—spaghetti or corn bread pizza. Both are Cannon family favorites, but I chose the pizza. Mom had to make two giant pans of either because we scarfed them right up."

"My only two recipes are heat and reheat," she said as she walked close to see what else was sizzling in his pan. "What's corn bread pizza?"

"Just picture moist, sweet cornbread as your pizza crust, then top it with meaty sauce and lots of cheese."

"I'm amazed you can still fit into your britches eating like that."

"It's like you said. Ranch work is much harder than going to a gym. I figure I've earned this and a horse cake."

She laughed at the mention of anything called a horse cake. "What the heck is a horse cake?"

"Picture it."

She huffed and said, "I'm picturing a pile of dung."

"That's it," he teased, "except it's a small dung-looking pile of deliciousness made from chocolate and oats and coconut."

She laughed and leaned against a pole. "Do you always travel with a copy of the Cannon Family Recipe Book?"

"You may have noticed that I've been ignoring a ton of calls and texts. They were from my helicopter parents." He circled a finger in the air. "But I started craving cornbread pizza, and a call home for the recipe seemed a good excuse to reach out to them and have a chat."

"You're a good son."

"Not always, I'm sad to say." He turned and faced her straight on to make his point. "They make me crazy sometimes, but they've given me some great advice when I needed it."

"Did you need some tonight?"

He studied her face for several long moments before answering. "More like a priority check."

She wondered what he was trying to tell her. His eyes remained on hers, inviting her to inquire further, but she broke the mood with a quip of her own.

"It must be nice to have ready advice *and* unlimited Cannon family recipes from your happy childhood."

He flinched, and she knew her sarcasm had wounded him. She wanted to apologize, but she felt as if she was already drowning in guilt after talking with her mom, facing her failure as a friend to Brenda, and preparing for an evening with ex-fiancé Sutton. Another word about the perfectly loving Cannon family would be the anchor that would sink her.

Sutton's headlights appeared through the window. "He's here. Time to go."

Jamie nodded. "I hope you have a wonderful time. Really."

Her throat grew thick as she opened the door. She felt as if Jamie was handing her off like a two-dollar purse at a flea market.

CHAPTER 10

*L*aramee was surprised when Sutton offered her his arm. He escorted her around to his truck's passenger side, stumbling over the choreography of where to place her while opening the door. This new attempt at courtliness left him as awkward as a fourteen-year-old boy at his first church dance.

The twenty-minute ride to his small spread felt like fifty. Neither of them appeared interested in opening topics about the past or the future, leaving only the rather dismal present for discussion. Sutton sprinkled the silence with reports on the county's crime rate, neighbor news, and the high price of feed.

His ranch was comprised of seventeen fertile acres with a creek running through it. Sutton had laid it out beautifully with the house in the southwest corner so his view from the front porch was one of animals in the pasture and fields of corn and wheat.

"You painted the house yellow. It's lovely, Sutton."

"A butter-colored house. That's what you said you wanted someday."

His expectations weighed on her and she found it hard to draw a good breath.

"Come see what I've done with the barn." He took her hand and walked her up a slope to where the red barn sat, except it now had an addition off to the side. He slid a large barn door on its rollers, revealing a concrete floor with drains and broad channels running along the sides. Large pulley and chain systems hung from tracks mounted to the ceiling, and at the end was a block wall with a large metal fridge-style door.

"This is my game-processing shed. I processed over forty deer and elk here last season. My reputation has spread so wide that hunters reserve space with me months before the season opens. It's a lucrative side income, Laramee. I get a straight per pound fee or they pay me in meat, which you're going to sample tonight."

Laramee liked venison just fine, but she preferred not visiting all the details of how her steak made it to her plate.

Sutton noticed her lack of enthusiasm and asked, "Don't you remember how we dreamed about building the place up so we could be self-sufficient? You were going to raise organic fruits and vegetables, and I was going to build up my hunting and fishing guide businesses so I could retire after twenty years on the force, and we could work the farm together?"

"I remember." And she did, but that dream hadn't crossed her mind in years.

"I have other good news. A cable show on the Explorer Channel did a piece on Colorado fly fishing, and they asked me to guide them on a segment. My guide business tripled overnight. I kept thinking how the only thing I needed to make that moment perfect was you. Imagine vacations spent camping by the most beautiful rivers in the country and cooking supper over an open fire—fresh trout pulled from those clear, sparkling waters."

Sutton repeated tales of an adventurous future he'd dreamed of during the tedious hours spent trying to save The Stone's Throw Ranch. They were dreams woven once upon a time, before she ran away. Did that old slipper still fit her anymore? Was it ever the life she wanted, or was it the life she believed she owed to the man who'd saved her and her family?

She walked around the property. The little wishing well, the glider swing, the garden bordered with river rocks—they were still here in exactly the same places as if time had stood still. Not a rake or a bucket out of place. Even the doormat was the same. In the months after Tyler died, when everything in her world was changing, nothing in Sutton's did. When her parents were lost and stumbling, Sutton's steadiness was comforting. She'd found security in his love of sameness and history and tradition.

A few things had changed. He added on to the barn since she left, and he'd given the house a facelift with the butter yellow paint she favored when she was nineteen. Both projects felt like tethers intended to pull her back to who she once was. Not who she had become. She had changed. Sutton had not. She felt sure if she looked in the hall closet she'd find his waders and his short boots in the same spots, his mail in the same caddy, and his butter would be sitting on the table in the same hen-shaped butter bell his mother once used, the one with the red bow on top. In short, she felt she was looking at both her past and her future.

The same dreams.

The same plans.

The same life.

She couldn't breathe.

Sutton jumped into the silence, detailing plans for their future as if his ring were back on her finger. She was half afraid he'd drop to one knee and pull it from his pocket, so before that happened she said, "Whoa, Officer Bryndall. You're racing down the track, and I'm still at the gate."

"I'm sorry." He blushed and folded inward. "Brenda warned me not to do that."

"Brenda?"

"Yeah. I got an emergency call to the market a few days ago. Little Knox was having a bad seizure. I got there twenty minutes before the paramedics made it from Pine Creek. The seizure ended, and Knox was tired but otherwise fine. Brenda and I sat for a few minutes, and I told her you were coming home for a while. She warned me to play it cool. To be patient and not overwhelm you. I guess I failed."

"Tell me about her. About her son."

His face tightened and his jaw tensed. "I don't know how they do it." He proceeded to lay out the obstacles of life with a small family-run business, a mortgage, and a seriously ill child whose needs upended every day's plans. She asked questions through dinner and on the ride home, seeing places where she could have filled in and offered support if she'd been there. By the time they reached the bunkhouse, Laramee was drained. She laid a hand on Sutton's, thanked him for supper, and dragged herself through the bunkhouse door.

*

*J*amie breathed in the aroma of the cornbread pizza. It smelled like heaven but the thought of eating it alone diminished its appeal. He decided to let it cool and attend to the soil tests. The routine of lining up vials in holders, adding some of the liquid created when he mixed the soil samples with water, and administering drops of reagents to each was a good diversion. This miniscule contact with the earth, with land, took him back to Sipapu and the stories told through its painted walls and dig piles.

He literally thought he had been sentenced to Hell when he arrived at the flat barren land of sand and stone that extended as far as he could see. Sipapu had no streams, no trees, no homes. Nowhere to run. Just the same cactus-dotted nothingness in every direction surrounded by mountains a million miles away.

He grumbled like a tough guy when the bus dropped his group off and drove away, and then fear set in at his complete inadequacy to survive there. He and his seven troubled companions sat down and hugged their backpacks, which they had packed that morning with only a bowl, a fork and spoon, a bottle of water, one change of clothes, and a food bar. Jamie figured he was one scant meal away from death.

A weathered man appeared from behind a giant cactus carrying only a pottery bowl. Without addressing the group, he began walking toward a rock formation. The group stared and laughed, and then one of the kids stood and started following him. One by one, they all accepted their complete vulnerability and need for help. Placing their blind trust in this man, they too followed along to the large rocks.

The sun was setting behind the formation, leaving a patch of shade. The man pointed to the shade where the sand was cool, before moving on to a large prickly pear cactus. He pulled a knife from a sheath, cut a pod off, trimmed it and ate it, all without uttering a word.

Over the next two days, the group did whatever he did as he taught them to follow, to trust, to work hard, and to help one another. Rewards appeared along the way. A tent. A shovel. A map to a spring. A basket of fruit. A few loaves of bread. Simple things that felt like treasures. Their hearts began to change.

They loved and revered this quiet man who respected the ancient Indians of the region—the Anasazi. When the group was ready, he took them to the ruins of Anasazi's city—an ancient metropolis of hardened mud-and-stone dwellings, many of whose walls were covered in paintings. The guide told them how old the paintings were and explained the peoples' history, as written in their drawings. This ancient art was a record of wars and harvests, of changing seasons, some of hunger and some of plenty. Through it all was family. He told the youth that like these people, they were writing their own stories. Stories of successes and failures, of love and loss, of hopes and dreams. He promised us that someone would find it all beautiful, just as we found beauty in these stories.

The dig piles held other lessons. They were shallow landfills where generations discarded items no longer useful. The piles were small for how ancient they were, a testament to how little was wasted over the years. The Indian guide advised the youth to be careful before they cast anything or anyone aside, for value can be found in almost everything and everyone.

As the desert unveiled her secrets to the group, the youth came to love the dirt, the rocks, and even the barrenness. It was quiet, simple, reliable, and beautiful, a stark contrast to the lives of chaos the group had been pulled from. They spent a week creating sand art from the soil beneath their feet. They scoffed at first over the ridiculousness of making art from beige sand, and then they began to see the subtle differences and beauty in grains of sand and stone, until the bland desert became a gorgeous palette to be admired. They likewise came to see the subtle beauty, obscured to others, but becoming increasingly apparent, in each other and in themselves.

All from sand and dirt.

The reagents turned the liquid from Jamie's samples into a variety of colors indicating acidity, alkalinity, and levels of nitrogen, phosphorous, and potassium in the soil. Jamie wrote the numbers down on a chart. A text came in telling him that tomorrow's perk tests were being postponed because of the impending rain. He wasn't terribly disappointed. The tests were essential to reveal the rest of the data he needed to assess the best use of the Stones' land, but the delay validated his hope to stay around a few days longer.

He checked the clock for the seventh time, wondering when Laramee would be home and whether she and Sutton were picking up where they left off years ago. The thoughts rattled him, so he grabbed his coat and headed outside to sit on a bale of hay. He'd ignored his phone most of the day, and when he checked his emails there were two from his dad. Neither was urgent. One actually contained questions he'd answered before he left Denver. It was another check in, and as annoyed as he felt, he politely answered the questions again and turned the phone off.

The moon was obscured by the rolling storm clouds. He was glad he'd more than doubled the animals' bedding. A dusk-to-dawn lamp cast an eerie yellow light over the paddock, and Jamie sat there, looking over the land, trying to find some good news that might save the ranch or fund the family's increasing needs. His mind kept going back to the turquoise that Laramee refused to touch.

A squeak off to the right drew his attention to the porch on the main house. Sterling Stone appeared, wrapped in a thick quilt. His legs were unsteady as he made his way to the rail for support. He too stared out over the land, and more than once, he wiped his eyes.

Jamie rose quietly from the bale, intending to withdraw and give the man the privacy he sought, but Sterling's craggy voice called out, "Stay. I see you."

Jamie froze, not knowing whether the words were an indictment or an invitation. He walked over to the porch and said, "Good evening, sir."

"You've got a load on your shoulders. Is it the land or Laramee?"

The man was blunt. Laramee didn't seem to appreciate his style, but Jamie found it refreshing. He avoided the topic of the land and gravitated to the subject of Laramee.

"She's out with Sutton. I'm sure that pleases you. I know he's very close to everyone in your family."

"Yes. We're indebted to him. He's kept us going and kept this place afloat. We love him like a son."

There it was. Sutton had the Stones' vote.

Sterling pointed to the empty paddock and smiled as if he were seeing something wondrous. "You should have seen my girl dressed in her spangles and spurs. She was audacious."

Jamie had seen that Laramee in photos, and glimpses of her when they laughed and worked. She was still in there, more tested and strong. In his mind, she was more audacious than ever.

Sterling drew the quilt more tightly around him and turned for the house. He stopped before passing through the doorway and threw a final odd comment Jamie's way.

"Do you suppose Laramee would want to spend the rest of her life dancing with her brother?"

And then he closed the door leaving Jamie in the dark in every way.

He was cleaning up his testing supplies when Laramee came home. He rose, excited to see her at first, and then his face clouded. "Are you all right?"

"Just tired. I'm going to bed."

Before she reached the door, he asked, "I was just about to dish up some cornbread pizza. Do you want to eat and talk about what's bothering you?"

She turned away from him to hide the tears he'd already seen and said, "No thank you. I'm sorry but I'm just not feeling very well tonight." She turned and headed for the women's dorm door, hiding her eyes from Jamie until the door was closed.

His fists curled at the thought that she came home crying from a date with Sutton. He'd grown up in a house full of boys where crying was rare, and when it occurred, it was quickly dispatched with an arm across the shoulder and an invitation for a game of catch. Victoria was rarely emotional. She saw it as a weakness that gave opponents an advantage. The few occasions that broke her resolve left her more angry at herself than sad. In those moments, Jamie gave her some personal space followed by a sumptuous meal. By the time the last course arrived, dinner conversation had generally restored her calm.

He had no idea how to respond to Laramee's tears. He counted the twelve-inch tiles on the floor between the men's dorm door and the women's—twenty-two. Twenty-two feet of shared living space that felt as barren as Sipapu's desert. Ignoring her pain was impossible and allowing her hurt to linger unabated felt cruel. He didn't think a game of catch would cut it in this situation, but he had vowed to bring happiness into her world.

He moved to Laramee's door and called her name softly, but there was no reply. Hungry, he dished himself a big square of the cornbread pizza and opened his laptop to check his email. He was looking for one email in particular, and there it was. Once Laramee told him her ancestors once mined the turquoise, he contacted his brother, the company's lead real estate attorney, asking him for two favors. He took a forkful of the pizza knowing he'd be digging into two things tonight—the pan of cornbread pizza, and this email's information to see whether there might be new threats to the Stones' future.

CHAPTER 11

Sunday, March 26, 2023

Laramee didn't want to talk to Jamie, but neither could she sleep, so when she tired of tormenting herself with her failures, she turned over in her bed and finally nodded off, imagining being back in Arizona. When she awoke before dawn, her dreams were still of red-rock vistas.

When things didn't work out as she'd hoped at Arizona State University, she'd fallen back on what she knew best—ranching and horses. The Indian Council on one of the reservations built a casino and racetrack called the Wild Pony Resort. A big brand hotel chain built a beautiful hotel and spa there for the high rollers and weekend dreamers who came by. For those that wanted a cowboy experience, the Wild Pony Resort offered long trail rides and riding lessons. Just a mention of the fact that her family ran a dude ranch in Colorado and Laramee was hired.

She looked at her watch to check the time and noticed that it was Sunday. Sundays on the Wild Pony Resort were just another workday for her, filled with as much stall mucking and horseshoeing as horse riding, leading novices on trail rides out into the desert. If truth be told, she preferred mucking stalls to dealing with people most days, and after hearing the wind and the icy rain pounding on the windows and roof, she found herself almost missing the desert's warmth.

Her conversation with Brenda and the things Sutton explained about her friend's life still nagged at her. There was some comfort in knowing she'd crossed the "first call" barrier, but something still pained her. In truth, she knew it was several things. She'd run away when life got messy and hard, but Brenda had stayed and not only faced her problems head on, she found happiness despite the pain. There was more. Brenda had been with Laramee every day those first few weeks after Tyler's passing, until Sutton slowly edged her out and filled her space. In stark contrast, Laramee had neither celebrated Knox's birth nor helped Brenda through his hard diagnosis. She had selfishly failed her friend in every possible way.

Laramee put all her regrets in a text and sent them to Brenda with a reiteration of the promise to get together. Her phone rang immediately.

"Can't sleep either?" Brenda said with a yawn.

"No. Are you up with the baby?"

"Bad night. His monitor went off three times."

"Is that how it usually goes?"

"Not always. Sam and I trade off checking on him and rocking him back to sleep, but the bigger seizures leave me so nervous I'm afraid to close my eyes."

Laramee heard the exhaustion in Brenda's voice. "I could run over there and take a turn."

"Thanks. Friends and family offer all the time, but Sam and I won't let them. I guess it's the guilt we carry around."

"Guilt?"

"We blame ourselves for Knox's condition. We missed our final ultrasound. It was snowing and the community hospital is an hour and a half away. I felt great, and the baby was active and kicking like an MMF fighter. We justified missing the appointment by saying we were safer at home than on the roads, but Knox came three weeks early and before we could reschedule."

"What caused his CP?"

"All that flipping around those last weeks caused the cord to get wrapped around his neck. Every time I pushed, his heart rate went down. By the time we reached the hospital, he was in distress."

Laramee barely heard her friend's voice crack over the pounding of her own heart.

"When Knox was released from the hospital, Sam and I called the paper and went straight to the County Office. We begged them to get a qualified doctor and a clinic with imaging equipment out here so this doesn't have to happen to another family on the plains."

"Did they agree to do it?"

"They said they'd take it under *advisement*. The commissioner said he was sorry but his call to the hospital verified that I missed my appointment, so the real fault was ours."

Laramee felt blood in her mouth and realized she'd bitten her lip. "It was just like Tyler. There was no place nearby to take him."

"I've thought about that more times than you can imagine."

"I'm so sorry, Brenda."

"I just keep telling myself that it could have been worse. At least we still have Knox. I can't wait for you to meet him."

"I-I-I will. Tell me when it a good time to come."

"Probably not tomorrow. He and I will both be wiped out. But soon, okay? I'm so glad we talked, and I'm glad you're back. Gotta go. Bye."

Laramee's hands were shaking so badly she could barely hit the "end call" button. She heard a knock at her door, followed by Jamie's voice calling out to her. She tried to ignore it, but he knocked again, harder, and called out in a teasing voice, "Good morning, Mary Sunshine. Breakfast is ready."

"I'm not...I'm not hungry."

"You didn't feel well last night either. Are you okay?"

"I'm all right. My stomach is just upset."

Concern colored his normally cheery voice. "Are you getting sick?"

"No." She just wanted to be left alone with her grief and her pain.

He jiggled the doorknob. "Just poke your head out and show me, please."

She wiped her eyes and tried to pull herself together so he'd be satisfied and leave her alone, but as soon as she cracked the door open and saw the worry in his face, the tears began.

"What's wrong," he asked, taking her by the shoulders.

"It's too hard to explain," she said between shudders.

"Just try. Please," he said as he led her to a kitchen chair.

She resisted his efforts to herd her. "Just let me go back to my room. Please."

But Jamie took one of her shoulders and laid his other hand across her forehead. "You're not hot, but you're shaking. You might need a doctor." He pulled out his phone.

"Don't! And who would you call, anyway?"

"Then tell me what's going on."

Laramee didn't even know where to begin or how to explain how a conversation about little Knox dredged up her worst memories. "I called my friend, Brenda. Her husband delivered the supplies yesterday. She had a baby, a perfect little baby growing inside her, but there were complications and now he has Cerebral Palsy because we don't have a hospital or clinic with imaging services nearby."

Jamie stood in the center of the floor, his arms limp by his side as if he had no idea what to do or say. "That's terrible. I'm so sorry. I take it you didn't know until just now."

"No, I didn't because I wasn't here. I didn't even know she'd had a baby because I was in Arizona."

"Is she angry with you? Is that why you're taking this so personally?"

"I'm taking this so personally because it hits so close to home."

His head turned as if he were tuning into her words but missing their meaning. Her frustration mingled with her fear of exposure, pushing her words out as more of a growl than a conversation. "You don't get it. You don't understand."

His hands came forward. "I want to. Explain it to me. Help me understand."

"I can't. I can't because I can't bear for you to know. No one knows but my parents, and it destroyed us."

He pulled her from the chair and into his arms. "Shhh…You don't have to tell me anything." He brushed her hair back and laid his hands on her face as he looked into her eyes and into her heart. "All I need to know is that you're safe."

All I need to know is that you're safe. They were the most beautifully comforting words she'd ever heard. No expectations. No recriminations. No guilt. Just caring. She wanted to stand right there, like that, forever, with Jamie's body supporting hers and his hands caressing her face. She moved her own hands over his and clasped them, holding them there. Holding Jamie right there. The thought and wish that had run through her mind a thousand times was before her, and without a thought about anyone else's need but her own, she pulled Jamie close and kissed him.

He didn't pull back or hesitate. His hands held her to him as his lips pressed harder to hers. She felt vibrant and alive for the first time in her adult memory. She had almost forgotten how sweet it felt to simply be happy, but Jamie had shown her, day by day, with his offers of help and his kindness and smiles. He'd made her laugh over his knock knock jokes and reminded her how easily forgiveness could be given each time they argued. Sleet pounded the rooftop, but the heaviness that had weighed down her heart lifted, and the very air seemed bright and filled with light and love.

A distant tone sounded in her room. She ignored it, wanting none of her senses to focus on anything but the touch and feel of Jamie. It ended and started again. The annoying ringing. The intrusion of the world into this serenely tender moment.

Sutton.

She knew it was Sutton. Checking on her as he did each morning since she came home. No matter how deeply she wanted to run away from it, her past kept pressing back in.

She pulled back slightly, but Jamie smiled and pulled her back in to that warm happiness. And then the phone rang again. She couldn't ignore it. Sutton was reminding her that these fairytale days would end shortly, when Jamie's work was completed, and he moved on.

Sutton would still be here. Always. Along with the life and problems and pain she ran away from.

The bitterness of the future soured Jamie's kiss. Laramee pushed away from him crying. "I can't. I just can't." She grabbed her jacket off the hook by the door and ran out into the freezing rain, tugging it on as she ran. Jamie grabbed his own coat and ran after her, but she had picked up a fencepost and was swinging it wildly at the fence as if trying to knock it down, all the while yelling, "I hate this place. I hate it. I hate it!"

He held her there for several long moments as her crying eased and her body stilled. He asked her to put the post down, but she spun into a second rage that left her past reason. She swung the post again and again at the fence, and even though her efforts were futile against the newly set post, they were enough to keep Jamie at bay, and to delay the moment when he'd discover the truth.

She felt the sting of icy rain on the half of her not covered by the partially dangling coat. Her T-shirt and sleeping pants did nothing to protect her, but she swung again, even though her frozen hands could barely maintain a grip. The force of her final concussion with the post sent shockwaves of pain up her arms and into her shoulders as it spun her back and down into the wet, muddy ground.

Jamie scooped her into his arms. She gave him one final fight, pushing back against him as she cried out, "Don't! Don't! Don't you see? I killed him. I killed him."

Her energy was spent, and she slumped against Jamie, but she felt a change in the steadiness of his arms as they held her, and she knew he was shocked by what she'd said.

"What are you talking about?"

"Tyler. I'm the reason he's dead."

She died inside during the silent seconds Jamie needed to process her words. He lifted her against him and carried her into the kitchen, setting her on a chair while he added another log to the fire. She was too ashamed to face him and too wrung out to make her way to the bedroom, so she crossed her arms on the tabletop and buried her face in them as she cried.

Jamie didn't ask any more questions. He grabbed towels and

blankets to pull most of the water from her clothes and hair. "We need to get these wet things off you. Can I trust you to change and come back out here?"

When it was apparent to him that she was unwilling to cooperate, he simply wrapped her in another layer of dry blankets. She felt warm again for a few moments, and then the deeper cold set her body shaking again.

Jamie moved to another chair where he'd laid the stack of hastily gathered blankets and pulled two of the softest from the stack. He laid one on the floor by the fireplace and then turned to face her. In that minute, she was two versions of herself. An exhausted woman yearning to be held and protected like a child, and a wary woman fearful of her confession's impact. She could see hesitancy in Jamie, and she worried her blunt admission had caused irreparable damage between them.

He spent a moment surveying her before he moved toward her. He stopped and held his place nervously as if she were a cougar cub, vulnerable and defenseless one minute and ready to claw him in the next. She prayed that he would take another chance on her, and her prayer was answered when he moved to her and wrapped the other blanket around her. He sat on the first blanket and leaned against the ottoman. Then he took Laramee's hand and pulled her down without resistance, until she was leaning against him, her back being warmed by his chest, and her front being warmed by the fire.

They sat that way for a time. Laramee didn't know how long. Exhausted in body and soul, she enjoyed a feeling of peace she hadn't known in a very long time, and surrendering to that comfort, she fell asleep. When she opened her eyes, Jamie's attention was fixed on the smoldering fire. Laramee watched him for several seconds before he realized she was awake. Unprepared to speak yet, she knew she'd have to tell him everything. She stirred, and he placed a hand on her forehead, as if checking for a fever. After a moment, he leaned his head back against the ottoman, saying nothing, and perhaps worse, asking nothing, placing the burden to begin squarely on her.

"I told you we got Tyler home safely and into bed, but what I didn't tell you...what I've never told anyone but my parents, is that after we all went to bed, Tyler came to my room and asked me to ride with him out to the falls. I refused, but he kept pressing me, saying it was our tradition to ride out and sit there under the full moon." She felt her heart rate increase and felt her chest tighten until her breaths came in shallow gasps.

"I didn't want to do it, but he begged me, and instead of saying no or telling my parents, I gave in."

She felt Jamie's hand on her head, rubbing over her wet hair, supporting her. His kindness tore at her. She hadn't known such a gentle, strong touch since her father held her when she was a little girl. Sutton was still a schoolboy in many ways. His touch was strong, nervous, unskilled in the tender needs and wants of women. He didn't understand that a woman needed a gentler hand than a man used to comfort a horse or even a foal. Jamie understood and demonstrated that understanding in small ways—how his warm fingers occasionally moved from her temple to her crown, pausing from time to time to massage her head in small circles, releasing the tension that built up like knots. His touch provided her with the assurance she needed to stop her story and relax her trembling, while also offering a promise to stay with her and hear it through to its conclusion.

She breathed in a long draw of air that released in tiny shudders. She was approaching the worst part. The horrible, life-altering end. "We made it to the ledge okay, but Tyler seemed disoriented, so we turned right around." She took another thready breath. "He slumped in his saddle before we reached our gate." Her heart began to race as the mental conflict of those moments returned. "Precious, maybe life-saving moments passed while I debated what to do, whether to leave him and get my parents, or stay with him so he wouldn't be alone. I didn't want to leave him, but I finally decided to run in and get my father."

She groaned at the memory and pushed on. "My mother seemed confused by everything I was saying, but my father looked at me with his face drawn and pale and his mouth agape, as if he knew what I was going to tell him before I said a word. He looked at me...I can't get his expression out of my mind. No matter what we're doing or saying, or how his face really looks, all I see and hear now is the groan of his voice and the horror on his face when we ran outside and found Tyler on the ground."

A moan broke from deep within her, and Jamie tucked her head under his chin and tightened his arms around her.

With her face buried in his chest, she pushed on to the end. "We raced to the nearest clinic, but they didn't have the equipment or specialists he needed, and Tyler just slipped away and died there." She pressed her face back into Jamie's chest and cried. It felt liberating, even healing to finally tell someone whose happiness wasn't tied to Tyler.

His hand rubbed a diagonal pattern across her spine as he held her. Understanding and empathy flowed into her under his touch, giving her the courage to face the impact of that night.

"Everything good about my life died with Tyler. My father and I didn't speak other than the duty conversations required to keep the minimum done here. I couldn't blame him really. What would a man say to the daughter who murdered his son?"

Jamie turned her to face him. "You didn't murder your brother, Laramee."

"The official cause of death was a cerebral aneurysm. He survived the shove into the gate, but the bouncing of the horseback ride must have caused it to tear. That ride killed him, and I allowed it."

"Did a doctor tell you that?"

"I just know it."

"Or that weak vessel in his brain was a ticking time bomb destined to kill him unless he received intervention, which no one was prepared to offer him. Maybe you gave him a final sweet moment with you in his favorite place before the inevitable happened."

It was the one bit of relief she'd held on to all these years. "Thank you for not judging me." She scooted away from him and stood.

He reached for her, saying, "You've got to let go of that guilt you carry around."

"Easier said than done." She tucked the blanket more tightly around herself and stepped back again. "I know you mean well, Jamie, but you don't understand. Maybe I didn't actually murder Tyler, but I had several opportunities to intervene and save him, and I missed them. Every one. That's on me. Only me. At the end of the day, the outcome's the same either way."

She turned for her bedroom and closed the door.

ॐ

*H*e gave her an hour, and when she still hadn't come out, he thought about knocking on the Stone's door and asking her parents for help, but initiating a conversation between Laramee and her emotionally estranged father seemed a risky option right now, and despite Laramee's anemic assurance that the last conversation had been good, Jamie felt sure it had been one step on the downward spiral that led to the day's outcome.

Jamie considered the burdens he knew she was carrying—the ranch, her parents, Sutton, Tyler's death, and her friend Brenda's son. Those heavy worries were enough to crush anyone, and he knew he'd probably added a few others to that list—the confusion caused by him and their kiss. He didn't want her to feel rejected again, but the truth was less noble than that. He'd wanted to kiss her since the moment she bandaged his hand. But he had his own issues—concerns that made it difficult to commit to another woman. It was less about Victoria and more about their painful history. He didn't want to repeat old mistakes, and yet he'd given Laramee a hollow kiss without any promise or expression of affection. Without those elements, a kiss was little more than an impulse, and that's not what he wanted for her. Hadn't he said as much the other day in his lofty speech about love? And what had she said?

*What if that kind of love isn't in the stars for everyone?...Most of us are just trying to find someone to get through life with...*That tepid pronouncement on her relationship with Sutton ripped at Jamie. This one was no better. *Lightning doesn't strike when we kiss, and he doesn't sing me love songs, but he loves me...*

Jamie wondered if lightning struck when *they* kissed.

His head and heart hurt, and his nerves were on edge. He was smothering in this small space, but he was afraid to leave Laramee.

What should I do?

142

The simple answer came to him. *Just keep caring.*

He could do that.

But how? What did she need?

He thought about the sweet silly hour spent telling knock-knock jokes, and he headed for the cupboards, not certain what he was looking for. The available entertainment was grossly limited—a few dusty boardgames in dubious condition, some puzzles in tattered boxed that portended they were likely missing pieces, a ruffled stack of paper, and some random, partially dried up art supplies. One other option presented itself—a guitar hanging on the wall. It inspired a memory from days gone by, of campfire singing by the lake when he was young. He pulled the battered instrument down and attempted to tune it. The third, or G-string was missing, and the five remaining metal strings had lost much of their spring, producing a dull sound at best. The tone was perfect for his use.

The old guitar proved Laramee right about his soft, paper-pushing hands. The strings cut into his tender fingertips, making it hard to produce solid notes. All the better, he decided with a smile, as he set his fingers in the right places and began to strum a little cowboy ditty his grandfather used to sing called, "The Old Grey Mule."

The first strums produced sounds that were somewhat familiar. The missing G-string left something to be desired in the tone, but terrible music would serve his purposes as well as beautiful music would, and perhaps even better.

He strummed the guitar again and slurred, "M-m-m...M-m-m... Mmmyyyyyyy..." as he slid between two or three notes, searching for one that matched the current ghastly chord he was producing. Settling on one note, he wailed out a rubbery half-speed version of the first line.

My uncle had an old grey mule...

He stopped and played with the tuning keys, producing an even more offensive sound, and continued on with—

My uncle had an old grey mule,
His name was Simon Slick;
He'd roll his eyes and switch his tail,
My, how that mule would kick.

He heard the bed squeak in Laramee's room, but he couldn't tell if she was rolling over to hide from the music or sitting up to hear it better. Pleased for any response, he turned up the volume and let 'er rip on the second verse—

He took him down
To the bottom of the hill
To try him out one day,
He kicked and fought and pawed the ground
And here is what he'd say,
He'd sayyyyyyyy—

He held the word "say" out, adding a little yodel to the end as his eyes remained peeled for any sign of Laramee. When the door remained closed, he moved into the refrain, the "*pièce de résistance*" he felt she most assuredly would not be able to ignore.

He set the guitar across his lap, lifted his chin to the ceiling, and brayed like a mule. As hoped, the door opened a crack, revealing Laramee, bent forward to hide her face. He hit the "*He'd sayyyyyy,*" line three or four more times, using a different mangled chord for each repeat as he headed into the bray. After the fourth repeat, he saw her shoulders shudder, and knew she was doing everything in her power to hide her laughter. Once she was more composed, she straightened and gave him a sober look through the cracked door.

"You're mangling my favorite song."

"*The Old Grey Mule* is your favorite song?"

She opened the door a bit wider, placed a hand over her heart and fluttered her watery, reddened eyes. "It's a tender love song…"

Jamie resisted the urge to run to her and comfort her again. A mood change seemed to be the best gift he could offer her. "About a man and his mule?"

"Maybe…maybe he was allergic to dogs."

Her serious expression exploded into laughter and Jamie followed suit.

"But you really are butchering this masterpiece."

Jamie set the guitar down and issued a sweet challenge. "Then come here and help me get it right."

She moseyed from her room and picked up the guitar. "First of all, this is no longer an instrument. It's an item of décor. Notice the missing string?"

"I did, but I was determined."

She sashayed over to the mantel where her mother had set a box of tissues. Laramee pulled one out to blow her nose and tossed it into the fire. Then she moved to a different cupboard from which she pulled a black guitar case. After setting it in Jamie's lap, she said, "*This* is an instrument."

She opened the case and pulled out a shining guitar, complete with a strap, picks, and a tuning harp. She slid the strap over her head and commenced to tune the instrument from ear. After a few strums and twists of the keys, a rich and mellow sound poured out when she strummed.

"You play?"

She shrugged. "I used to. I haven't touched this thing in years."

Jamie leaned back and interlocked his fingers behind his head. "Play me something."

"I'm the teacher. You're the performer. Now, let's try to save that song. Grab your lower jaw about an inch up from your lips."

His eyes crinkled in embarrassment. He knew where she was going with this, and he humbly complied.

"Now pull it all forward so you look the part."

"Of a fool?"

"Of an authentic western folk singer. Do it. And when you sing the chorus, I want you to really engage your nose."

"My nose?"

"Yeah. Some really deep nasally snorts. That was definitely missing. I'll play and you bray."

She played a little intro, and Jamie repeated the first verse. When he came to the refrain, Laramee's eyes were wide with playful expectation. It was more than he dared hope for, and he chuckled his way through the braying.

Laramee scolded him. "Get back in the saddle and give it another go."

The second attempt was just as laughter filled, so Laramee slipped the guitar off and set it aside as she moved to him with a devilish look in her eye. "You're not holding your lip tight enough," she said, grabbing it herself and pulling it forward. Jamie's appearance cracked her up, and she snorted a little laugh.

"You can't stay focused on your art either," teased Jamie.

"Who are you kidding? I just demonstrated the snort of a perfectly engaged nose."

Jamie leaned back and hooted, and when he came forward, he grabbed Laramee and began tickling her until she fell into his lap. He soaked up the sound of her happy laughter, the innocent happiness she exuded, the appearance of her face when alighted with joy. He didn't realize how his tickling had slowed to an embrace until her laughter faded, leaving the joy and happiness in place. Her rosy cheeks held a constellation of freckles that crossed over her perky nose, and he thought, if he had a pen handy, he could draw the Big Dipper and Orion on a face whose eyes already seemed to hold a universe of understanding.

A look, tied to a hundred questions, passed between them. Jamie wanted to close the distance between them with another kiss. His thoughts must have registered on his face because Laramee tilted her head and smiled with a look that invited him in. He remembered their earlier kiss, the brush of Laramee's mouth over his and how he melted as she pulled him close. The lightness of her lips didn't deliver lightning strikes of passion that stole his control. Instead, it brought warmth. Closeness. She had piloted the kiss, leaving him merely a willing passenger, free to feel and experience that kiss on a different level than any he'd ever shared before. An entire new degree of intimacy with a woman.

And then he pressed his lips into hers—deep, firm, full. The feelings she stirred in him nearly freed his heart to share how happy she made him, and then she pulled away, looking ashamed or filled with regret, and leaving rejection as Jamie's last memory of the kiss.

And here they were again.

Her eyes stayed fixed on his and she leaned in, as if checking his willingness to share one more tender moment, but Jamie pressed a finger to her lips, stopping the kiss. Then he set her in the chair and stood.

"I need to tell you something." He rubbed a finger over his lips that still felt hers upon them. He shook his head because he really didn't know where to begin. "I'm a bit gun-shy right now where romance is concerned."

Laramee leaned back into her chair and struck a sympathetic look. "I'm sorry. I should have realized you're still aching over losing Victoria."

"It's not so much about losing Victoria. It's about *how* I lost her."

"There was another man."

Jamie knelt beside the chair to be sure Laramee understood. "*I* was the other man."

"You stole Victoria?"

Her response stung, and he jumped in to explain. "More accurately, she dumped her fiancé to pursue me, but in either case, the result was the same. I interrupted someone's love story because I ended up with his girl." He stood again and sat on the hearth. "I swear I didn't know she was engaged at the time. She wasn't wearing her ring. My father was the keynote speaker at a regional investment conference. I was starting out in the company, but he took me along. We had these nametags on from the conference that identified us and our corporation. I think she was initially drawn to my family name and my father's connections in the business world, but when this beautiful woman approached me, the woman every other man in the room was trying to meet, I thought I was the luckiest man on earth."

"I saw her. She was beautiful."

Jamie heard the intimidation in Laramee's voice, but there was no way to soften the story. "She was also brilliant and driven, and she completely captivated everyone in any room she entered. I had just come out of a dark time in my life and I was still a little lost. Victoria reinvented me, from my clothes to my hair to what music I listened to and what restaurants I frequented. She taught me how to work a boardroom until I became successful in my own right. I had the connections to open doors, and she had the skill to close the deals. We were a power couple, but the longer we were together the more I depended on her advice and approval, and then, one day, I realized I had lost myself and become someone I didn't recognize. We broke up and got back together three times because I wanted to pull back from the work and the money and the hectic lifestyle we'd adopted, but she didn't. I ended things a few months ago, and she went right back to her former fiancé without a glance in the rear-view mirror."

"I'm so sorry." The room filled with the weight of Laramee's unvoiced questions, and then she pieced her thoughts together and asked, "Are you saying she married the first guy?"

"Exactly."

"I'm sorry, Jamie. Your heart must be broken. You're still reeling from losing her, and I've made this—" she swirled her hands around as if identifying the bunkhouse and their time in it, "—all about me and my problems. I'm so sorry."

He took her hand. "You've been the best medicine for a wounded ego, and you've opened a heart I didn't believe I could open again. But I can't be that guy again, Laramee. The guy who gets swapped in for a man the girl isn't sure about, just to be swapped back out when she changes her mind. I'd love to spend time together and see if we could be more than top-notch fence fixers and crooners—" his eyes began to shine, "—but I can't risk that pain again, and I won't take a chance on hijacking something good you and Sutton might already have."

"You're right. I don't know my own mind or what future I want." She raked her hands through her hair, bringing her head to rest in her palms. "Coming back here has made me even more confused, and sadly, you and Sutton are the ones getting caught up in Hurricane Laramee." When she lifted her head and met Jamie's gaze she was calm and serene. "I'm a different person around you." She smiled and shook her head. "Let me clarify. I like who I am when I'm with you, but I heard the warning bells, telling me not to kiss one man when another man's still carrying my ring. Especially when the first one is probably leaving in a few days."

Jamie wondered if she paused there so he could promise to stay, but he didn't. Not that he wouldn't have liked to, at that moment, but because the timing felt wrong to make promises.

Her eyes glistened, and she blinked rapidly. "I hoped a sweet kiss from you would magically make things clearer about Sutton, but it only blurred the lines more. That was selfish of me, and I'm sorry, because you're right. I need to back up, slow down, and figure a few things out for myself." She stood and tipped her head to the side. "Still friends?"

It was more of a plea than a question, and Jamie's heart broke a little too. "Of course…with possibilities for more?"

"Once I know my own mind."

He smiled through eyes that were pinched in sadness. "Bring it in for a hug."

There was a stiffness to her posture when Laramee moved into his arms. Their talk had changed things between them, and Jamie wondered if they'd ever return to the playful closeness they'd achieved.

Laramee's phone rang in her room. She glanced in that direction, but she didn't rush to answer it. "I'm on KP tonight. How's chili sound?"

"I thought you only heated and reheated."

"I also dress up precooked food *before* I heat it. I'm adding onions to canned chili to make it appear less processed."

"I see. You surprise me again."

"That's me, all right."

Her attempt at overt perkiness didn't fool him. She was sad. Heartbroken even. Not just because of the talk about the kiss, but because of all of it—Tyler's death, her guilt, Sutton's goodness, her parents' distance, the ranch's decline, and wants she might never get to explore. He wanted her to know his feelings towards her hadn't changed because of today. And then the phone rang again.

She ignored it and said, "We need to eat early. Sutton and I are—"

"—Got it." He cut her off, not wanting to hear the details. "Don't worry about making dinner. There are plenty of leftovers." The phone rang again. "You should get that. It's probably Sutton."

She pressed her lips tightly and nodded. "I'll just go get dressed."

She slipped from the great room, leaving Jamie to mull over the day's events. He thought of a dozen things he wished he'd said to her, and now he wondered if there'd be another chance. An hour passed while Laramee showered and dressed. A knock sounded on the door. When Jamie opened it, Sutton stood there, beaming as he held a bouquet in his hands. He pushed the flowers forward with pride and gave Jamie a wry victory smirk as he stepped inside, scanned the interior, and mouthed, "Where's Laramee?"

Jamie pointed to her door and waited as Sutton knocked. He wondered which version of Laramee would appear when she opened it. The playful woman who kissed him earlier? The sad woman who saw her future set in stone? The guilty woman who couldn't forgive herself?

The woman who appeared was none of those. This Laramee was more like her rodeo photos, and the sight of her made Jamie's breath hitch. Her soft-brown hair was pulled back, but not tightly as it was for ranch work. This time it was pulled back softly, leaving curly tendrils around a face that looked more like an artist's portrait of her. Her brown eyes popped this evening, with eyeliner, mascara, and some smoky brown shadow that set them off and pulled him in. Her cheeks had a tint of pink color, but Jamie was most awed by her lips. They were lined and moist and shiny, as if sending out invitations for a kiss. Her jeans were fashion-fitted, with every piece hugging her body perfectly. She wore a pink button-front shirt with lace inserted from the shoulder to the pocket. She looked stunning. In short, her missing sass was back on full display. He didn't realize that his jaw had literally dropped until she smiled his way and tapped under her own chin to point that out.

If her purpose had been to make Jamie jealous, she exceeded all expectations. And if her second purpose was to provide Jamie with a comparison to his earlier description of Victoria, she succeeded there as well.

She looked past Jamie to Sutton and his flowers. "Are those for me?"

She received her bouquet, but when she kissed Sutton on the cheek, Jamie turned and began retreating toward his room's doorway, all the while looking back over his shoulder as Laramee moved to the kitchen to place the flowers in a half-gallon Mason jar.

He noticed how her eyes likewise held on to him no matter where she or he moved, as if he were her scaffolding and anchor. No matter how audacious she appeared to be, there was a timidness behind the sass, a discomfort behind the confidence. She was shaking inside, and in that moment, he saw himself in the way she sought his approval, the same way he had leaned on Victoria's. He didn't want to be either her Svengali or her plaything. If her objective had been to take his breath away, she'd succeeded, but he worried that she'd achieved something else she hadn't foreseen. Sutton was clearly, unabashedly lovestruck, and Jamie wondered if Laramee was prepared to handle what he might read into all of this.

Sutton slid his arm around her and pulled her close, whispering what Jamie assumed was a string of compliments in her ear as he claimed her for his own.

"Don't wait up," Sutton tossed back. "We're having dinner and a long chat at my place."

Jamie caught the hint. Sutton wanted him to know their chat was going to be an important one.

Laramee grabbed her coat and a Stetson from the hook, then turned back to look at Jamie before leaving. She must have sensed worry in his face because her parting words to him were, "Remember everything I said."

He nodded, remembering everything she'd told him, and every word and smile and laugh they'd shared. As he watched the pair head to the car, he saw the way Sutton kept one eye on her and one on the window where Jamie was holding a watchful vigil. Moments later, their headlights disappear.

"Be strong, Laramee."

He said it for her, but he meant it for himself.

CHAPTER 12

*H*ours later, Laramee waved goodbye to Sutton and headed for the bunkhouse. Her heart raced when she didn't find Jamie inside. She checked outside to see if his SUV was still there. Finding it in its place, she took a deep breath and headed back inside.

He came in mere moments after she arrived. She glanced at him and smiled as she began pulling ingredients from the cupboards.

"How was your *talk* with Sutton?" asked Jamie.

"Good." She opened the fridge nonchalantly. "Where were you?"

"I took Nugget for a ride."

"Good." She pulled onions from the fridge and started trimming them. "So, you had a good evening."

"Yep…Good. Very good. We're both good. Just dandy," Jamie said with evident sarcasm. "It's nearly midnight. Why are you cooking?"

"I'm not tired, and I figured I might as well get a head start on dinner tomorrow."

He picked up the can opener and started opening the cans of beans she'd set out. "Did you and Sutton come to any conclusions tonight?"

Laramee heard the attempted indifference in his voice and wasn't quite sure what to make of it.

"I told him I wasn't the same person who left here four years ago, and that we'd have to take things slowly to see if we're still a good fit."

Jamie nodded over each word. "That's good."

Despite everything awful happening around her, from Jamie's perspective, everything appeared to be *good*. Just splendid.

She directed her frustration to the poor onions, chopping them into oblivion when she saw Jamie set the can opener down and lean into the table near her.

"We need to talk about what happened today," he said.

Laramee set her knife down and stared at the table. "Could we please not do that, at least not tonight?" She laid her hands over his and peered into his eyes. "You've been incredibly kind and caring to me. I'm probably stretching the limits of your kindness." She cast her eyes around the bunkhouse and smiled. "But can't we just be the most wonderful friends tonight? Let's cook together and laugh and push responsibility and reality back for at least a few hours? Then we can talk. I promise. All right?"

When he picked the cans off the counter and carried them to the sink, Laramee still wasn't sure if he'd go along with her wish.

"Put me to work."

"How about browning the ground beef?"

He got to the task without saying anything more, and Laramee knew he wasn't all-in on her plan.

"Tell me about your family. We hardly know anything about one another. Not anything personal, anyway."

"What's the point if we're just going to be *friends* for a few more days?"

She picked up her pulverized onions and placed them in a skillet, moving beside Jamie at the stove. He glanced at her and his entire countenance changed from frustration to sympathy. She assumed he noticed her moist eyes, and she feared he might try to comfort her. Rather than share a resolve-crushing hug right then, she blamed her drippy eyes on the onions rather than admit that this entire experience was killing her.

Jamie stabbed at the lump of beef he was browning as if it were the cause of her tears. "I'll share if you promise to unlock the doors you've been hiding behind."

She expected such a trade. "All right."

"All right then. What do you want to know?"

"Just anything. Tell me about your family. Start with your parents."

"Okay," he said with reluctant surrender. "Dad was from southern Utah. My mom was from Idaho. They met in college. Mom was a music major, and my father was a senior in the business school. He was taking a shortcut through the music building and heard Mom singing in a rehearsal room. He looked in, saw her, and dropped an elective to sign up for choir. They were married a few months later."

Laramee stopped frying her onions and turned to see if Jamie was pulling her leg with that story. When she was sure it wasn't a joke, her throat tightened at the beauty of their family's beginning. "That sounds so romantic."

"They still are that way."

Laramee wiped the counter, and asked, "Where do you fit into your family?"

"Well...that depends on your definition of family. There are just four of us living. Mom and Dad wanted a big family but after three miscarriages, they finally had two living children—my older brother Mike and me. So, I'm either number five if you believe families are united with every life they're blessed to create, or number two if you only count the ones who were born alive."

Laramee's hand stilled as the concept grabbed her heart. "Which do you believe?"

"That the siblings I never met are still part of our family, and that I'll meet them all and know them some day."

Tyler suddenly felt very near. She wiped her eyes again and resumed cleaning the splatters coming from both frying pans.

"Mom and Dad are as much in love as ever, and they love us just as passionately. Too much, sometimes. They're hoverers."

"So basically, you have the perfect family."

"No family is perfect, but mine is actually pretty great. It sounds like the Stone kids are also a loyal team."

Laramee weighed that supposition as she stirred the wilted onions.

"Tell me some funny stories about your family that prove you're normal."

"Well…we all felt Mike would either win a Nobel Prize in literature or end up in prison."

Laramee laughed so hard she nearly dropped her spatula. "Connect those dots for me."

"Skiing is his first love, and as soon as the first flake dropped, he began forging the most creative notes to get out of school early. He didn't go for the standard, 'Mike has a doctor's appointment' kind of excuse. Oh, no! He'd concoct some ruse about comforting a dying aunt or that he needed to shovel snow to spare his father's back. My favorite was when he forged Mom's name on a note excusing him to go home to help care for a litter of rabbits because they were his project for the fair."

"Were there any rabbits?"

"Oh, sure. And he did send a card to our ninety-three-year-old great aunt before he hit the slopes, and he did shovel the sidewalk."

"So, his lies were actually based on truths."

"Truths he stretched until they cried 'uncle!'"

"I think I'd like your brother."

"Everyone does. He's the best. It did take having his hide tanned a few dozen times to help him get more intimately acquainted with the truth, but he's very honest and focused these days."

"How'd you stay such a straight shooter?"

Laramee noticed how Jamie tensed before diverting to a joke. "How do you know I'm not an international jewel thief or a terrorist?"

"I'd know."

Her voice was tender rather than playful. He looked at her with wonder in his eyes, as if her assurance of his goodness was an incalculable gift. "I love how you see me, but if truth be told, I wasn't always a standup guy. I was a too-big-for-my-britches jock in high school," he said, cracking open a door to his past. "All-State running back my junior year, county wrestling champ, and a fairly reliable shooter from my sweet spot at the three-point line."

"Did you have a million colleges looking at you?"

"Only a half-million," he scoffed. He twisted the toe of his shoe into the floor and started again. "I had five partials and two-full rides by my sixteenth birthday."

It didn't surprise her. He was strong and muscled, and she could easily see how his work ethic could have been honed by coaches, on practice fields, and in the crucible of competition.

She touched the scar on his chin. "You said you got these scars doing stupid stuff. Like playing football?"

His lips parted as if he were about to answer her, and then he turned back to his cooking and merely answered, "Something like that."

The cost to become a champion athlete was physically and emotionally high. She understood that. She'd had her own share of sporting accomplishments and tumbles, which Jamie knew very little of, and she was still paying interest on some of those prizes.

"I don't know much about the rodeo, but from what I've seen, you have to be tough and have guts, and I imagine it also comes with plenty of adoring fans."

Her world had plenty of groupies and prestige, but she didn't want to discuss her past. She wanted to explore this rare glimpse into Jamie's world, so she smiled and waited for him to continue.

"The attention, the people wanting to be your best friend...not just girls and other players. Their parents too. It all kind of went to my head..." He drew in a long, slow breath, and let it out with equal deliberateness. "I blew it. I let it all slip away."

She knew the details had to be agonizing, but she wanted to know more about Jamie, so she pressed him. "How?" She asked the question so softly she wasn't sure he could even hear, but he had, and his answer cut her to the core.

"I just got lost. So very lost."

His twisted features testified to the pain the memories still conjured. "I broke my parents' hearts, and my brother's too. I've spent the last nine years trying to win their trust back. I never want to disappoint them"—he drilled his eyes into hers—"or *anyone* again."

She understood the hold demons had on people, and she didn't want to make Jamie face more than he was able to at this time. She set her sponge down, intending to comfort him, but Jamie stepped away until his back was pressed into the fridge. She assumed he wanted to avoid another emotion-driven moment that would again bring them too close and then pull them apart, and he completed his withdrawal by dropping his gaze to the floor.

"I know what you're feeling," she said.

"That's why you're the one person I could say those things to." She reached a hand to him, and he took it, giving it little squeezes until he was able to meet her eyes again.

"I've told you my worst secret," she said. "You know you can tell me anything."

"You're braver than I am. Or you're more whole."

"Only because you made me feel safe enough to face it. I'll be here for you when you're ready."

He gave her hand a final squeeze and let it go, offering her a crooked smile as he shifted the mood once more. "You're a much better friend than Mr. Tears."

"What a terrible name. Is that really someone's name?"

"He's not a person. He's a thing, but he's very real."

Laramee didn't know what to make of the story, but the gotcha-smile pulling at Jamie's mouth egged her on. "Oh...I need to hear that story for sure."

"You know those paddles that have a long rubber band attached to a ball? Mom bought us each one of those for some holiday. She noticed how they were shaped like a teardrop, and that gave her an idea. When the rubber band broke, as they all did, she drew a face on that paddle and named it—"

"Mr. Tears!"

Jamie raised one eyebrow. "He was someone you didn't want to meet. Most of the time, all Mom had to do was say his name and we'd straightened right up."

"*Most of the time*? I take it you had occasion to meet Mr. Tears more intimately?"

"Very intimately." He wriggled his eyebrows again.

"Sounds like she's a fun mom."

"She is. My parents both are, actually." His voice grew husky. "I owe them everything."

"And now, you work with your father. Do you like being a businessman?"

He walked to the stove and turned it off, giving the browned beef a final stir before answering her. "I'm still not sure."

She wondered if he was leaving room for her to fit into his fancy world of Range Rovers and business conferences and getaways to The Alpine. Even if asked, and that was a huge *if,* could she possibly make the giant leap into his world? Or could he ever be content with a simple life like hers?

"Do you have a colander?"

"What?" she asked, returning to the present conversation.

"To strain the grease off."

"Uh...sure. Over there." She pointed to a cupboard, unable to completely push her musings away. "Did Victoria work for your family's company?"

"No. She invests in small startups and buys struggling businesses she can build and sell for a profit."

Victoria sounded like a woman of wealth and privilege. Someone already on Jamie's social level. "She sounds very successful."

"She is, because of hard work. Her parents were schoolteachers. They told her the greatest thing they could do for her was to inspire her to learn and become an achiever so she could get into the best schools. She took their advice and got a scholarship to Columbia. That got her an internship with one of the big banks and she kept investing and building her business from there."

Hearing that Victoria wasn't born to that high-energy, big-money life gave Laramee hope. Victoria grew into it. Maybe Laramee could as well...But Victoria had an Ivy League education and had built and sold businesses. Laramee wondered what she had accomplished. Her life was tiny by comparison. She had nothing valuable to offer a man like Jamie or a family like the Cannons. Reality crashed back in. And what about sweet, loyal Sutton, and her parents?

What about *them?*

With shaky hands, she haphazardly added the onions, beef, and cans of chili into a pot, slopping sauce and bits of onions and beans all over the cooktop. "It all needs to simmer together for a while," she explained as she wiped up her mess.

The lull in the conversation worried her. Jamie might ask her to keep her end of the bargain and talk about the walls she retreats behind. It was a topic she didn't want to revisit right now. She set her dreaming aside and thought about her parents. No matter what course her life took, she needed to know they'd be okay. That they could enjoy their later years. It all came down to the ranch.

"Jamie, have you had time to give your best estimate for the ranch?"

He cocked his head to the side, as if the change in topics had given him mental whiplash.

"I don't have all the data yet."

"I understand that, but surely you have a feeling about its potential and value."

He pulled out a chair, inviting her to do the same. "When you told me your ancestors mined and sold off some turquoise, I sent an email to my brother who's our firm's lead real estate attorney, to have him see if the turquoise is a matter of public record. He wrote back and told me that it is."

"What's that mean?"

"It means that buyers will know about the turquoise, and I seriously doubt anyone will buy the land without getting that ridge and the turquoise too."

"You're saying we can't protect it."

"How long has it been since your father did anything to improve the acreage, like fertilizing it or overseeding it?"

"I don't know. I don't remember him ever doing that."

"The soil is poor, Laramee, and without an entire irrigation system, which you can't afford, it'll never be good for farming or even good for grazing more than a few head per acre. I assume your father knew that and that's why you had so few animals."

"What about development? Houses or a school or a hospital? You said that was an option."

"I don't have any home developers who would invest in acreage with so little access to water. A school? Maybe. Or a small community clinic, but those types of projects take years to happen, and I don't think you want to wait that long."

"And if someone else buys our turquoise you think they'll mine it?"

"I do. I'm sorry, but I think that's exactly what they'll do."

Laramee laid her head on the table to think. "So, selling the stone is our best option."

He placed his hand on her neck and gently massaged it. "My father went to school with a guy who owns a mining company. I'd like to see if he could give you an estimate of the stone's worth. Please don't do anything until I can get a team up here to test the potential yield of the turquoise. At least make your decision based on accurate information."

"How long will that take? My mother is pressing me for a decision on whether I want to keep the land."

"I don't know. I'll try to get someone here as quickly as possible."

"Can we do this quietly? I don't want to build my parents' hope up until I have the answers to the questions they're surely going to ask."

As much as he hated to admit it, Jamie knew the best solution was to speak with his dad. Forgetting what time it was, he pushed his pride down and picked up his phone to call his father. "Hey, Dad. Hi. I'm good…I'm good. Oh, man. I'm so sorry. No…no. Everything's fine. Really. I promise. I completely lost track of time and forgot that it's well after midnight. I have a question for you, but it can wait until tomorrow. No, really…it can wait. Are you sure? Okay, thanks, because we're running out of time to save the Stones' ranch. I don't think there's much hope of it ever being profitable as a ranch again, but it has a beautiful vein of turquoise running through a grotto, and I'd like to get the stone evaluated. Who's that friend of yours who owns that mining company in Utah? Yes, that's right. Richard Brockbank and The Silver Buckle Mine. Do you still keep in touch with him? Oh, great. Do you know if they work claims besides the Silver Buckle Mine?" Jamie looked at Laramee and nodded that they did. That's great. Could you see if he would send someone up here soon to take a look at this turquoise soon? Thanks, Dad. Love you too."

Laramee listened to the call. She was even able to hear some of

Jamie's father's responses at this late hour. They weren't snippy or aggravated. Just caring and concerned. She marveled that Jamie could pick up the phone or send an email to his powerful father and brother and ask for instant favors with the ease of a simple hello. It picked at the scab of her family issues, but she accepted that his positive relationship with his family, strengthened through forgiveness, might help her save her own.

CHAPTER 13

They washed the pots together, keeping the conversation on general topics like favorite music and movies and foods. Jamie didn't force the conversation into places that were painful or awkward, but when the last dish was wiped and put away, he asked, "Anything else you want to know about the Cannon family before we call it a night?"

Laramee rubbed her hand across her brow and winced. "It's probably time for me to open a few of my locked doors."

"It's after midnight. Do you want to do this tonight?"

She pulled out two kitchen chairs and sat in one. "I'm too keyed up to sleep. I might as well honor my promise. Where should I start?"

"With whatever you want me to know about you."

She returned a lopsided grin Jamie was powerless to ignore.

"This is going to be good, isn't it?"

"We'll see." She pulled supplies from the messy art cupboard, closed the cupboard doors, and sat. The bunkhouse had no TV or stereo, so she picked up her phone and opened her music folder, choosing a soothing shuffled mix by a ballad-singer. As the music played, she closed her eyes and moved her head and fingers. It seemed to Jamie that she was internalizing the tune, absorbing its emotion, and channeling it into her hands. Jamie barely heard the music because its impact on Laramee held him spellbound. The transformation in her was subtle and yet profound, softening the muscles of her face, erasing the worry lines around her eyes, while bringing confidence and peace to the whole of her.

When filled by the music, she reached up and smiled at Jamie as she brought her hand forward to cradle his chin in her hand. She studied every part of his face while avoiding eye contact, as if admiring him as an object rather than as a man. She turned his head this way and that, and when she was pleased with the angle and light, she said, "Hold steady right there." Then she put pencil to paper and began to sketch.

"Ah, ah, ah!" she scolded, each time she looked up to capture another glimpse of him, only to catch him trying to look down and steal a glance at her work. The two spent the next forty minutes in outward silence that belied the internal storm brewing inside him whenever they were alone.

He stopped caring about the drawing because posing for his portrait provided the opportunity to study her face without discomfort or explanation. He loved catching her unawares, when she was simply gazing off at the land or watching a hawk fly overhead. She was most comfortable in stillness, a skill she likely honed during hours in a saddle, guiding tourists through the Arizona desert. She was beautiful, he concluded, but not with the cheeky attractiveness of her rodeo days. If wisdom and empathy described beauty, these were her attributes. He loved her perceptive eyes that felt everything deeply and spoke volumes with a simple roll or the rise of her brows. He was fascinated by how busy her mouth became, pursing, pouting, and smiling as she worked. It fascinated him, particularly since she said little when she had something to say, and she was generally comfortable remaining silent the rest of the time.

She looked up and caught him studying her and blushed. Her eyebrow arched in that way he adored, in a silent command for him to stop. He couldn't prevent the grin that followed, or the double-eyebrow arch that followed that. He wanted to kiss her. Just thinking about it made prickles rise on his neck. He wanted to hold her in his arms and kiss her while sitting together listening to ballads and eating cornbread and chili. To soak up the wonder she effused into the simplest pleasures, like the way she soaked up the music. He silently prayed she'd choose him and offer him her heart, but he kept his promise to care more for her happiness than for his own and focused on what she was creating.

She held her sketch up for him and he fell back in awe. But how could it be? The detail and shading made the image look more like a photo than a pencil sketch. More than illustrating him there, as he sat at the table, Laramee placed him under the falls, by the pool, with water falling all around him. But it was the tiny details in his face—expressions of worry and want and determination—that sent shivers through him, as if she had read his heart and brought his most inner self to life in graphite and paper.

"Laramee..." he muttered. "I don't know what to say. It's amazing. *You* are amazing."

Worry clouded her face. "Then you like it?"

"I love it. I'm awed. It's the most beautiful gift anyone has ever given me."

Her face squished into a smile of relief. "I'm so glad."

"How did you sit here and draw the falls so perfectly?"

"That place is seared into my mind."

"And my expression..."

"I needed to see your angles and how the light plays off them, but that complex expression is also seared into my mind. That's how you look when you think no one is watching. It's how I see you. Worried about everything and everyone, always looking for solutions, all while searching for your own answers."

"So, this is who you are. An artist."

"Who I was. Who I wanted to be."

He reached across the table and took her hand. "No. It's who you are. You have a magnificent talent."

"ASU evidently didn't think so." She pulled her hand back and stood to put her supplies away.

"I can't believe that. What happened?"

"My mom taught me everything she could about sketching and wood burning. I did the burning on the posts in here."

"I figured that."

"But I wanted to do more than just sketching and western art. I wanted to learn about sculpting and real painting techniques. I wanted to make beautiful art"—her voice took on a dreamlike quality filled with the power of those dreams—"so I saved all my rodeo money for art school. And then I had to set that dream aside."

"When Tyler died."

"Of course. I was needed here. And then Sutton entered my life." She leaned toward Jamie, and he knew she needed him to understand what she was about to say. "He saved my life, Jamie. He literally kept me going, day to day. His calls pulled me from my bed each morning, and he took my hand and walked me, dragged me, from the house to the barn each day for months."

Jamie hated himself for wishing there was no angel named Sutton, but there was, and he was a fine man. What Laramee felt for him—gratitude, friendship, love, or all of it—was honest and true.

He swallowed his own hurt and asked, "Did you tell him you dreamed of going to art school?"

"He knew. And he didn't try to stop me. He did ask me to try to satisfy those dreams here, without going away to school." She laughed an anemic little laugh. "He spent hundreds of dollars on videos, art sets...He even hired a local artist to come and give me lessons. They helped, but every compromise felt like another loss. I'd lost Tyler, I'd lost the family I knew, and now I'd lost my dream of college and all the adventures and new doors that would open to me, like attending the School of Art and studying other artistic mediums." She slumped back in her chair as if the oxygen left her body. "I can't put it all on him. My family needed me here, and as pathetic as it sounds, my self-sacrifice was modest—only one year. I set my dreams aside for one year, as a small penance I felt I owed."

"To whom? To Tyler? Do you really think that's what he would have wanted you to do?"

"No. Not Tyler."

"Then who? God?"

She didn't correct him, and he assumed he'd hit the answer. "Torturing ourselves is not what He wants either. He loves us. He loves you, Laramee. That penance you're exacting from yourself has already been paid...by Jesus Christ."

"I know the doctrine of forgiveness, Jamie, but I can't find the peace or comfort that's supposed to come if His love extends to me in spite of the mistakes I've made. Aren't those the fruits of forgiveness?

"You've got to trust what He said, Laramee. That His love and sacrifice extends to all. Forgiveness and Grace are as available to you as anyone else."

"There's nothing you can say that I haven't already read or prayed to feel. I know the words. I've read all the promises. That's the problem. I've read it all and I don't *feel* forgiven or good or absolved. I just feel burdened all the time."

She broke down and leaned against the wall. Jamie empathized with her agony and yet he felt powerless to help her.

"I left everything—Colorado, the ranch, Sutton, my family—hoping that if I couldn't be forgiven, maybe I could at least find some peace somewhere else, like at ASU by throwing myself into art school. I had enough savings for one semester, so I paid the tuition and invested everything in my classes because I desperately needed to get a scholarship for the next semester. But I didn't get it. I wasn't good enough, and again, I felt like a failure."

"Laramee..."

"So, I dropped out of school and got a job doing the only other thing I was good at. I worked at a resort on an Indian reservation, caring for horses and giving riding lessons and leading trail rides. The work was hard, and the days were long and hot and brutal at times, but the work suited me because I didn't want to feel anything except tired. What I didn't want or expect happened anyway. I became as hard as the work."

Jamie reached a hand to her but she declined his touch. "And then Mom wrote to me about selling the ranch, and I decided to come home to see if the ghosts and the pain were gone now. But they're not,

Jamie. They're still here. They're everywhere, and I don't think or expect I'll ever be happy, so I'm just setting my sights on being useful to my parents and kind to Sutton who has been so good to me. And maybe I can be helpful to Brenda and her baby. Hopefully, if I serve others instead of myself, I'll find that peace and absolution I want so badly."

She sat at the table and folded over, laying her head on her crossed arms. Jamie reached out and touched her elbow.

"I've been in that same dark place, Laramee, thinking the things I did made me undeserving of ever being loved or forgiven. That's a terrible place to be, but I found my way out, and so can you."

Her voice turned bitter. "Good grief, Jamie. I didn't share my story so you could try to save me."

"Then let me just tell *you* a story."

"No." She lifted her head and put her hands forward like a shield. "No pitying, no saving, no stories. We're done. I'm getting a drink of water and going to bed."

Jamie watched her head for the sink. He closed his eyes, and asked, "*Please help me.*" No obvious revelations poured into him, but when he opened his eyes, the first thing he saw was the sketch, and the answer was there. He picked it up and held it out to her so she could see it.

"I don't know what happened at ASU. You were still suffering. Maybe it hampered your gift. You were lonely and sad and afraid." He stood and moved toward her, holding the drawing her way. "But look at it, Laramee. How can you doubt that you have a gift? It's not just *what* you draw, it's *how* you draw. More than just features, you capture a person's beauty and *spirit*. The essence of a person. Their souls. You have talent, Laramee, but more than that, you have a gift...a gift from God. This gift He's given you is one evidence that He loves you and that His influence is in you."

She halted her retreat, as if the ideas captured her interest, and Jamie moved closer without her recoiling. "You think you have failures? Let's count mine. Do you know where I learned to love rocks and soil and to ride horses and mend fences? I was so messed up on drugs and alcohol that my parents had to send me away to a rehab center in the middle of the desert, to a place where I had nowhere to run. Where I had two choices—follow and listen or literally die. That's the risk it took to pull me back."

She hovered between shock and wonder, hanging on his words.

"I'm ashamed of my choices, but I saw how my parents refused to give up on me, and neither did God. He never stopped loving me or wanting me to find my way back. He loves me now, and He loves you too, Laramee, despite our failures. I've felt your spirit. It's kind and gentle and loving. You're not hard. You protect yourself because your heart is broken. I get that, but you let everyone else's pain seep into you through the cracks of that broken heart."

"But it was selfish of me to run away."

"I can't speak to your mindset or your decisions back then, but you're a horsewoman. You understand an animal's need for a safe space and time to lick its wounds and heal. Maybe that's what you needed too."

"My choices sound better when you say it like that."

Jamie's heart lifted at the hope seeping into her. "You are good and kind, and if you don't feel His comfort, it's not because God is withholding it. It may be because you need to forgive yourself and give yourself permission to feel it."

Moments passed without movement. Jamie prayed and held his breath, waiting for Laramee, a woman of few words, to respond. She walked to the chair she had been sitting in, straightened it, and said, "It's late. I think I'll turn in."

Jamie didn't want her to hide behind that door again. He stood quickly and reached for her hand across the table. "I'm not tired. We could do a puzzle, or I could play you another tune on the guitar."

She dipped her head and shook it with a laugh. "As tempting as that is, I'm afraid I'll have to pass." Her smile faded into soberness. "I need some time alone, to think."

Any further debate would be futile, he surmised, and could possibly overwhelm her. He watched Laramee enter her room and close the door without looking back.

He stayed up for another hour in case she needed to talk some more, but she didn't come out again. Instead of heading to his room when he grew tired, Jamie made his bed on one of the sofas so he'd catch Laramee when she awakened. His sleep was a ragged series of short naps between worried futile hours spent standing outside her door, wishing she'd come out. He wondered whether he'd eased her burdens or added to them. It crushed him to watch her extend grace and forgiveness to everyone except herself.

CHAPTER 14

Monday, March 27, 2023

*J*amie was awakened by a knock on the front door. He was shocked when he saw the hour—after ten a.m. He ran a hand through his mussed hair before opening the door and did a double take when he saw his father's worried face. Mike was standing beside him on the stoop dressed in jeans and heavy work coats. Two other men were with them. Their faces were unfamiliar, but each had dark hair and eyes and their features were similar. The taller of the two looked several years older, and his cheeks and chin were rugged and scarred. His build was more muscled while the younger of the two men was slim with broad shoulders and a smooth face.

Jamie's emotions were mixed over the group's appearance. His father and brother were two of the people he loved most in the world, but their hurried arrival here, at this moment, with two other men, was like the collision of two worlds—the innocent bubble Laramee had asked them to enjoy together for a few days and the reality they were trying to push back.

"What are you two doing here?" Jamie asked.

His father, William Cannon, moved his hands to his hips before answering. "Your call last night. You said you needed a favor, and we came to deliver. This is Reese and Harrison Brockbank."

The Brockbanks…Jamie had asked for their help, but he hadn't expected this. "Of The Silver Buckle Mine?"

"Yes, but they're now the Silver Buckle *Mining Corporation* because they now own five mines. That's why they're here. They're interested in looking at the turquoise on the Stone's Ranch. Harrison is the lead geologist for the corporation," his father continued, "and Reese is both a principal at the company and he also knows a lot about ranching on desert plains. Harrison is going to pull some samples of the turquoise, and Reese is offering to give you an assessment of the ranching potential of the land. Wasn't that incredibly generous of them?"

This was not the favor Jamie wanted or expected, but he knew how ungrateful he sounded. His father had underscored that very point during his introductions. He pulled himself together.

"Yes, yes. Of course, it is. Thank you all for coming." He rubbed his fingers into his eyes which were adjusting to the morning light. "Sorry. It's just that I didn't expect the ranking principals of one company, let alone two, to come take a simple rock sample."

His father answered again. "We all chatted early this morning and decided it was a good excuse to take a play day."

More likely they'd come to check on him. The thought rankled Jamie. "I just assumed you'd send someone up with the equipment. That alone would have been favor enough."

Mike leaned in and whispered, "There was something about that urgent request to help Laramee Stone that made us think there was more to this favor than just mining potential, so we decided to check it out personally."

Jamie watched his brother's teasing grin spread. Yes, the family clearly had questions about Jamie's extended "business" trip here to The Stones Throw Ranch. Lots of questions. He felt a sheen of sweat rise over his skin. "How'd you get here so soon, anyway?"

"As luck would have it, Reese and Harrison were already in Denver, recruiting at the Colorado School of Mines. Mike and I flew the Cessna up to the private airfield of a friend who has a place an hour from here," said his father. "I called Mr. Stone early this morning to see if he knew of a closer landing spot, and he offered to pick us up from there."

His father pointed to a truck behind him where a weathered old cowboy leaned. Sterling Stone looked like a page from another era. He was dressed for the part, from his boots to his oiled duster and up to his weathered hat. His face was covered in scraggly whiskers and what parts of his face could be seen seemed ashen and gray. Jamie remembered Laramee's request that her father not know about the plan to evaluate the turquoise, and now he not only knew, but he had been rousted from his sick bed to facilitate the study.

"I wish you hadn't called him, Dad. He's not well, and Laramee specifically asked—"

Jamie stopped as he heard the thunder of hoofbeats coming from the right. He looked up and saw Laramee racing Patches across the pasture toward the driveway. When she drew near, she pulled a rodeo-worthy stunt, jumping down beside the slowed but still moving horse and landing on her feet.

Her features were twisted in worry as she called out, "Dad? I couldn't believe it when I saw your truck coming down the driveway. What are you doing standing out here in the cold? And who are these men?"

Before Jamie could head him off, his father, ever the gentleman, was removing his hardhat and bowing slightly for Laramee. "William and Mike Cannon, Miss Stone. Jamie asked us to take a sample of the turquoise. We brought some experts with us. This is Reese and Harrison Brockbank of The Silver Buckle Mining Corporation in Utah."

Her eyes darted from her father to Jamie, and before she said a word, Jamie braced for the betrayal and fury flying from her eyes.

"Why didn't you tell me what you were doing, Laramee?" her father asked.

She drew in a deep breath. "Jamie said we probably can't protect the turquoise from buyers because it's part of the property's public record now. I wanted to see how strong the vein was before we decided what to do with the land."

"You could have explained that to me."

"I-I-I was planning to, once we knew how rich the vein actually was. I didn't want to give you unfulfilled hope or additional stress in case it turned out not to be valuable after all."

Sterling Stone dismissed the explanation with a wave of his hand, but Jamie noticed how badly that hand was shaking.

"Didn't trust your old man, did you? You don't think I'm capable of making a wise decision?"

"It's not that, Dad." She couldn't even look her father in the eye, and Jamie felt heartsick for her.

The shaking spread to Sterling Stone's limbs and left him unstable where he stood. "I know what it was. Sure, I know. You don't trust me. I know why. I live with it every day."

By the time he finished delivering his comment, he was slipping down the side of the truck. Laramee gasped and the Cannon men rushed to hold Sterling up and get him into the house. Once he was safely in bed, Laramee snarled at Jamie.

"Get them out of this house. All of you, get out. Now."

Jamie knew no explanation or apology would matter at that point. Her disappointment was personally aimed at him. He was the man who vowed to make her happiness a priority, and instead, he'd violated her trust and thrown a wrecking ball into her relationship with her father. The anger he'd spent nearly a decade learning to control flared up like a geyser in his gut. He rushed his father and brother from the house to the yard, excusing themselves as he directed them past the stunned Brockbanks, and to some privacy on the side of the bunkhouse. His teeth clamped and his fists curled as he faced his father, who turned as ashen as Sterling had been.

"I'm sorry, Jamie. I shouldn't have surprised you this way. And I should never have called Mr. Stone last night without consulting you. Tell Laramee I'm terribly, horribly sorry."

Jamie shoved a finger toward his father. "No, *you* tell her, *Dad!*" He spit out the once sacred name. "You have no idea how much harm you've done here, to Laramee, to her relationship with her father, to her...her trust in me. She's my...my *client*. Mine!" He hated minimizing what she had become to him, but he wasn't going to share any more with his family. "I was handling things in a way to protect her until we had solid data, and you blew it all up."

Mike tried to lay his hand on Jamie's shoulder, but he shoved it off. "No! You came here to check on me. Admit it." He paced three feet away, turned, and fired another round of angry accusations. "All those calls and texts and emails. You both thought Victoria's marriage threw me and that I might go rogue again. Admit it. That's what you thought. Right?"

Mike made another move to cool the moment, but William begged him off. His face twisted as he absorbed Jamie's anger and disappointment. "We just love you, son."

Jamie strode twenty feet away and waited for a time until his thoughts calmed. When his shaking body quieted, and his breathing stilled, he turned back toward his family. His anger was still there, but it was in check by the time he returned to speak to his father.

"I don't doubt that you love me, but the way you love me?" He dropped his gaze to the ground and shook his head before squaring back up and facing his father again. "It's not healthy. Not for me or for us. I know what my choices cost you all, but haven't I atoned enough? Made amends? Proven myself to be a solid man? Your fretting makes me feel weak and useless and childlike. It dismisses the solid life I've struggled and sacrificed for through almost ten years of sobriety. You still don't respect or trust me as a businessman or...or as a son. So here it is. If you want to be in my life, this hovering has to stop. Either you trust me, or you don't."

*L*aramee's very presence agitated her father, and out of concern for him, her mother asked her to leave his bedside. She'd never felt as alone and lost as she did at that moment, banished to the hallway, while listening to his grumblings and struggles from beyond the door.

She'd started the day holding on to the thin hope Jamie's words about forgiveness had provided the previous night, weighing them as she lay in bed. She'd risen early and found Jamie keeping a vigil outside her door. His concern for her strengthened her determination to ride Patches out to the ridge where she felt closest to Tyler, hoping to repeat Jamie's words of comfort there, hopefully to find that peace Jamie had spoken of.

Comfort did come to her, and her heart clung to it, until she rode home and faced her angry, unyielding father. If *he* couldn't forgive her she would never have peace from any source.

She looked back at her parents' bedroom door that was still closed to her. The only thing to do, she decided, was to honor their request and leave. She'd come home to help, but all she'd accomplished was to deepen the rift between them.

A few hours had changed so much in her, for the better, but the damage the morning's events had caused to her family relationships spread broader than before. The entire world seemed to be swirling into chaos as she opened the front door and found the Cannon men arguing. The dysfunction in her own broken family was spreading to theirs. Jamie saw her come through the door and he stepped away from his father and brother. He froze at the bottom of the steps, mouth agape, his empty hands spread wide, looking emotionally bereft and begging for her forgiveness. "I'm sorry," he mouthed again.

Wrung out and spent, Laramee dropped to the step and leaned into the rail.

"Please," he pled. "Please talk to me."

She had been ready to pound her angry fists against his chest, but his penance was brutally apparent in his beaten and pained countenance.

She nodded and he approached her tentatively. "He doesn't even want me near him."

"I'm so sorry, Laramee," Jamie said as he climbed the first step and waited. "I never imagined my father would come in person or bring the Brockbanks, or that he would call your father for a ride. I'm so terribly sorry."

She dropped her head into her hand, feeling naked and exposed to every awful thing life kept throwing at her. "It's not your fault. My father's right. I should have asked him before ordering the test on the turquoise. It's his property."

Jamie rose another step. "You were trying to protect him."

"He doesn't see it that way." She laughed, but her brief laughter broke into a sob. "Why should that surprise me?"

"I know your intent was loving. He'll see it that way, in time."

Jamie climbed the last two steps, and when he sat beside her, she willingly fell against him and welcomed his arm as he slid it around her and pulled her protectively to him. Safe again, she cried into his shoulder, falling apart and allowing the broken pieces to fall where they might. She trusted Jamie would stay with her as long as she needed, that he wouldn't leave her on her own when she was ready to put herself back together again.

Jamie brushed the stray hairs from her wet cheek. "How is he?"

"He sounds terrible. Mom says it's how he gets sometimes. But how would I know that because I ran off and left them?" She braced for another of Jamie's protective rebuttals. Instead of hollow reassurances, he rubbed his hand up and down along her arm.

"What's his medical diagnosis?"

"A-fib and a leaky heart valve." Laramee straightened and wrapped her arms around her knees as she gazed up the lane. "His doctor wants him to see a specialist in Denver. He's being stubborn. He says he just needs more rest, but I really think it's because Denver is nearly a ninety-minute ride each way, when you factor in how long it takes on rough local roads before you hit the highway."

"I'd be happy to drive him."

"I don't think the drive is his worry. I think it's being sick so far from home in case..."

"Oh...I understand. I understand."

Laramee followed Jamie's gaze shift toward his Range Rover where his own father and brother stood with the Brockbanks, all of them looking lost and without a place to be.

"Maybe this is one time when having a pretty-boy paper pusher around can be a good thing."

"What do you mean?"

"Hold on a minute, okay?"

He stood and headed down the steps, stuffing his hands into his pockets as he apologized to the Brockbanks before approaching his family members. Laramee read contrition in his father's face and a mixture of annoyance and sadness in his brother's, as if Mike were equally worried about Jamie and his anger's impact on their father. Jamie spoke first. He said little, but whatever it was caused his father to nod and smile with relief. William Cannon laid a hand on Jamie's shoulder and patted it. Eventually, Jamie's pride or hurt eased enough for him to move into his father's offered embrace. Mike joined the circle. Laramee marveled that with a few minutes to cool down and a few words of forgiveness or apology, fences mended, relationships healed, and love was given space to return.

It appeared so simple. She wondered why she and her father could not get past step one and even cool down.

Jamie returned, nearly skipping up the steps. "I spoke with my dad and Mike. We'd like to help you help your father."

"How?"

"We have the means to comfortably and quickly move your father by air wherever he needs to go."

"What? Do you have your own plane or something?"

"I don't personally, but yes, the company has a Cessna. That's how they got here this morning. And we have a small helicopter we use to survey properties from the air."

She knew the generous offer was made in kindness, but the news behind the offer felt disturbing somehow.

"And if you need a specialist or a second opinion, we have other resources at our disposal, like access to great doctors and hospitals."

"How do you have all that?"

"Over the years, we've gathered investors for big medical projects—clinics, hospitals, trauma centers. Along the way, my father has built personal connections with doctors and chiefs of staff in some of the best facilities in the country. All we need is a word from your family, and we'll get your father the best care possible."

Laramee leaned away from him without realizing it.

Jamie apparently noticed the shift. Worry erased the previous happiness from his face. "What's wrong?" he asked.

"You tell me your family has powerful friends and airplanes and helicopters to whisk people off to the best hospitals in the nation, and you wonder why I'm a little stunned?"

"Are you judging me because we have money? Money doesn't mean anything."

"Says the guy with a Cessna and powerful connections." Laramee stood and walked to the far end of the porch. "I knew you were successful, but I thought you were the normal kind of successful."

"What?"

"Like successful enough to own a nice big house and to buy fancy cars and take awesome vacations. Owning planes and having not one but multiple chiefs of staff of cutting-edge medical centers on speed dial...? That's an altogether different kind of wealthy."

Jamie stepped closer and said, "Because it doesn't matter."

"You can say that because you *have* it. Access like that means life and death to regular people. Like Brenda and her baby. And it would have meant everything to me the night Tyler died."

❦

*J*amie saw the wall coming up again, brick by brick. "Of course, I understand that, but I didn't know you then. I couldn't help what happened to Tyler, and I'm so very sorry for that." He placed his hands on Laramee's shoulders. "My family's wealth doesn't make anything between us different, except it does is make it possible for you to get your father the care he needs right now."

She smiled a too-winsome smile and nodded as she wriggled her shoulders free, stepping completely away. "Let me talk to my mother and check on my dad. I'll tell her about your offer. If she's willing, I'll gladly accept your family's help to save my dad."

And there it was. *Your family's help*...Why did it sound like a giant step back in whatever was beginning between the two of them. Jamie didn't offer a rebuttal. He knew it would be pointless in that moment when everything Laramee cared about seemed to be swirling in a blender.

Laramee went inside, and Jamie headed off to see where his father and brother had gone. He found them near the barn speaking to a man in a red pickup with a county insignia on the side. *The perk test!* Jamie had completely forgotten. The man was scheduled to come at first light, and he appeared to be finished. By the time Jamie reached the little huddle, the man was getting back in the truck. He rapped on the window, and the man wound it down.

"I heard you were having a family emergency, so I gave the report to your worker. My report should be available online in a few days."

The man drove off before Jamie realized his father was the presumed ranch hand. It touched him that his modest father hadn't corrected the man's assumption. He moved to his father and placed a hand on his back.

"Thanks for having my back with the county agent."

"I didn't have it this morning, and I certainly wasn't going to fail you twice."

Mike leaned in. "I take it Laramee is more than a client."

Laramee headed their way, and Jamie hurried his family members along. "Why don't you invite the Brockbanks into the bunkhouse. There's oatmeal, eggs, and bread. Make whatever you want. Just clean up after yourself so my *client* doesn't get upset with me for wrecking the place." Once the men entered and the bunkhouse door closed, Jamie's focus was solely on Laramee.

"What's the news?"

"Mom really appreciated your offer of help, but she took Dad's blood pressure and oxygen readings and called the information to the doctor. He says Dad's stable, but he wants Mom to check him again in half an hour and then call. He'll decide then if he wants her to bring him into the clinic."

"That's good news. How far away is it?"

"Forty-three miles. Over seventy to a hospital with a critical care unit."

"That's terrible. I could—"

"I know." She nodded. "I know what you can and are willing do, but Mom thinks all that fuss will be too upsetting for Dad. She'd prefer to take him to the clinic first, and accept your offer if things get urgent. Now you see what we're up against out here. The state says they can't justify the expense of an emergency facility for the few families spread out over these big areas." She rubbed her fingers deep into the corners of her eyes. "Can you imagine how different everything would have been if we'd've had a way to magically whisk Tyler or Brenda off to the care they needed?"

She shook her head in frustration, and Jamie realized how ironic and painful his offer of a helicopter ride to any facility her father needed must have sounded to Laramee. She would have paid any price for such access for her dying brother or her friend's baby.

"I wish I had known you then. I would have—"

"What would you have done? Would you have given me a hotline to call you whenever someone I loved had an emergency?" She dropped her face into her hands. "I'm sorry. I believe you would have. And it's not that I'm ungrateful for today's offer of help. It's the fear about tomorrow's emergencies. It's the powerlessness I feel over the inaccessibility to something as essential as critical medical care."

"It's your call. I'll support you in any way I can."

"Thank you. I know you're trying to help. You're a good friend, Jamie."

You're a good friend, Jamie. He wondered if she noticed how badly that reference stung him. Laramee kept her attention focused on the front door of the house, and Jamie fixed his gaze there too as they talked. "When did you leave this morning? I didn't hear you pass through the living area."

"You forget that I spent my childhood sneaking out of my house at night."

"Where'd you go? I was going to make you breakfast."

"Patches and I rode out to watch the sunrise over the plains. I might not have many of those opportunities left. But mostly, I wanted to speak to Tyler. I feel close to him there."

"Did you get any answers?"

Her head bobbled left and right. "I see all the ways this can possibly play out, and I'm preparing for each scenario."

"Stop being cryptic, Laramee. What 'this' are you referring to? Your future? The ranch? Sutton's proposal? Us?"

They heard the squeak of the home's storm door and looked up to find Cathy Stone supporting Sterling. Laramee called out, "Let me help you!" as she and Jamie took off in a dead run, followed closely behind by William and Mike Cannon. Together, the men got Sterling into his truck.

"I'll drive," Laramee said as she opened the driver's door. Cathy Stone pulled her back a few feet to talk to her. In the end, Cathy drove away with Sterling alone. Laramee kept her eyes fixed on the truck's bumper until it rolled out of sight.

Jamie slipped an arm behind her and tried to come up with a comforting explanation of why her offer to drive was rejected. "Your mom probably felt more people would make it appear that this episode was something really serious. That would upset your father even more."

"Thanks. I'll try to tell myself that."

"We could drive separately and follow them."

"No. This is how they want it. The loving thing would be to respect their wishes, right?"

Tears pooled in her eyes, spilling over as she watched the truck disappear over the first rise.

William and Mike came to where the two were standing. The Brockbanks stood a few steps away. "I'm so sorry, Laramee," William began. "I didn't know Sterling hadn't approved the plan to test the vein."

"It's not your fault, Mr. Cannon."

"Please, call me William."

She smiled at him and walked to where the Brockbanks stood. "Thank you for coming today. I'm sorry about all this. I thought I was protecting my father by requesting a study without telling him. As you can see, I made a huge mistake, and I'm sorry you got caught up in it."

"No, Laramee," William Cannon hung his head and shook it. "I'm responsible for all this. Not you. And not Jamie. I'm especially sorry about upsetting your father. All things considered, maybe we should forget about gathering a sample today."

Reese Brockbank removed his hat and laid a hand on Laramee's shoulder. "And you don't owe us an apology either. I, of all people, understand how complicated family and family businesses can be. Don't be too upset. Family things have a way of working out." He winked. "And we'd love to see your turquoise vein sometime."

Laramee sniffed and pulled herself together. "No. Please. Gather the sample. The damage is already done. Now that Dad knows, he'll be expecting a report. Besides, we need accurate information so we know what this place is actually worth. Especially now, for my folks' sake."

William looked off in the general direction of the falls. "Are you able to lead us down to the site now?"

"Of course. Just give me a minute?"

"Take all the time you need."

Laramee slipped into the bunkhouse, leaving the men alone. Jamie watched her go with worried eyes. His father seemed to notice his concern.

"I'm sorry, son. Our little surprise visit has caused trouble and stress for everyone, especially for you and for Laramee."

Jamie glanced back at the bunkhouse. "It's complicated."

"That's an understatement," said Mike. "I feel for you, brother."

Jamie winced at Mike and turned to the Brockbanks. "I'm the one who asked Dad to contact your company about the stone. Despite all this, I appreciate you coming so much. I'm in your debt."

"Believe me, if the turquoise vein is a good one, it will all be more than worth it," said Harrison.

"Great. Then let's saddle up. The ranch only has five horses. Laramee and I will ride double."

Reese again stepped up. "Harrison is the geologist. He'll ride to examine the stone. I'll take my truck and check out the land to see if it can ever be profitable as a ranch."

Jamie nodded. "I'd appreciate that, Reese. More than you can possibly know."

Reese pulled Jamie aside. "I have a pretty good idea. You see, I've just recently made my way back into my own family and our business. I made some big mistakes that hurt them. They never stopped loving me, but I thought I felt a shift in their love. I've only recently come to understand that the shift was in me more than in them. So, I'm still proving myself, and I'd love to help Laramee have a win." He inched closer to Jamie. "I get the complicated relationship stuff too." He rolled his eyes. "I almost blew it a million times with my wife."

Jamie wondered if Reese knew his story was also Jamie's story. "Thanks, Reese." He pointed in the direction of the grotto. "We'll be out there pulling the samples."

"I hear you also ran soil samples."

"The results are on the kitchen table in the bunkhouse."

"Sounds good. I'll look them over, check out the land, and meet you back here."

Jamie shook Reese's hand and led his father, brother, and Harrison toward the barn. "Let's be ready to ride when Laramee comes out."

Nothing more was said about the morning dilemma as they saddled the horses. Laramee returned and they rode to the falls with William Cannon asking questions about the ranch to break the silence. Laramee and Jamie headed down to the bottom first and backed away to give Harrison, William, and Mike space to examine the turquoise. Their initial reaction was similar to Jamie's—wonder and awe.

Harrison rubbed his hands over the blue/green protrusions and laughed with childlike pleasure. "It's incredible, Laramee."

"It's very personal to her. She's not sure she wants to sell the place or whether she'll agree to mine the stone. She just wants to know what it's worth."

Harrison placed his flat palm on a patch of blue and left it there as he turned toward Laramee. "I understand that feeling. The practical side of you wants the life the stone can provide, but the romantic side of you recognizes the privilege and responsibility you feel to protect it."

"You do understand," Laramee said, "but it's more. Precious memories are attached to this place."

William winced as if he were feeling her pain. "I'm afraid that's an issue only you can resolve, Laramee."

"But you'll still take the samples?"

"If you want us to." He touched a crack in the stone. "Right, Harrison?"

"You bet. We'll pull samples from crevices, so the marks are hardly noticeable. Jamie, I hear you've got experience pulling stone samples. Do you want to do the honors?"

Jamie planned to stay back by the far side of the pooling water with Laramee, and though he was tempted, he deferred back to the expert. "No, thanks. This is too important. You do it."

"Okay. If you're sure." Harrison grabbed a drill-like device fitted with a diamond-point barrel. "I'll start with a half-inch boring tool."

Jamie noticed how Laramee shuddered as the drill approached the stone. "Come closer, Laramee. Let him show you what he's going to do."

She moved to Harrison's side and touched the turquoise reverently. "I hope I'm doing the right thing here."

"Gathering the sample doesn't obligate you to any particular decision. I'm just going to bore some holes into the stone to pull samples out. The marks won't be very noticeable, but you'll know how deep the vein runs and the quality of the stone. After that, your family can decide what to do with that information."

She nodded, but Jamie could see she was still unsure.

"It's going to be okay. Most turquoise is deeply embedded and must be blasted loose or pulled from beneath tons of overburden rock with heavy equipment. But nature and your ancestors left this beautiful vein right here in plain sight. Now all we need is to see how deep it runs."

"I can't watch. Besides, it's lunchtime. You're all probably hungry. I'll go make sandwiches."

Jamie knew Laramee's past, present, and future were tied to this ridge and vein, from her last hour with Tyler to the family's destiny. He knew where he was most needed. "I'll go help Laramee."

She rode to the bunkhouse without waiting for him, as if he was a nonissue. By the time he arrived, she was in full sandwich-making mode.

"Do you want to talk about it?" Jamie asked.

"Talk about what?" she asked as she smashed a slice of bread on top of some ham and cheese."

"You're upset with me, and I deserve it. I caused all this."

"I'm not angry with you," she said as she shoved five sandwiches into plastic sleeves and then into a paper bag, showing them no mercy.

"Don't we need six sandwiches?"

She shot him an undiscernible look that shut the questioning down.

"I'm not hungry," she said.

"What's really going on here, Laramee?"

She pulled five sodas from the fridge and slammed the door shut as if it were the enemy. "Not now, Jamie. Not now."

They rode back to the site and Mike raised his eyebrows Jamie's way as if he'd picked up on the tense vibe between Laramee and him.

"How much longer will it take?" Jamie said with a tone that implied how happy he'd be to see them go.

His father looked up and gave his younger son a look that made it clear he got the message. "We'll be done here in another hour or two."

It took almost two hours, but when four deeply bored samples were slowly pulled from the wall, William stepped back and called Laramee over to see the twelve-inch samples that slipped out of the bore tools. Each showed variegated blue, green, and brown color, end to end.

"How does it look?" she asked Jamie, but Harrison answered.

"Really promising."

Jamie concurred. "When I heard your mother's people mined the stone over the years, I wondered how much of the vein had been harvested, but this sample proves that the remaining vein is at least a foot deep."

"At least," Harrison agreed. "Reese and I will take the samples back to the mine office to score them for color and color transitions. It won't tell us exactly how much turquoise is left here, but we'll know what each carat weight is worth."

"How long will that take?" Laramee asked.

"A day or two."

William and Mike labeled each sample and placed them in the plastic cases Harrison brought while the geologist packed up his tool. Jamie pulled Laramee to the side. "I just realized that my father and brother don't have a ride back."

"You need to drive them."

"Come with me. I don't want you to be alone right now."

Reese had arrived and was standing on the ridge above. "We'll drive them back to the airfield."

"Are you sure?" Jamie asked.

"It's on the way."

William smiled as he snapped the last case shut. "Thank you, Reese. I've muddled enough things up for Jamie and Laramee for one day." He pulled Jamie aside. "Laramee needs you. You've got your priorities straight."

"Thank you all for coming, and thanks for responding so fast. It means a lot."

Harrison shook Jamie's hand and packed the samples and tools into his horse's pack. Jamie needed some private time with his father and brother, so he suggested that Laramee ride back to the bunkhouse with Harrison while they had a word. Fortunately, she agreed, and when she was gone, he moved close enough to the men to be heard over the sound of the falling water.

"Promise me that you won't tell Mom about Laramee."

"Is there something to tell?" William asked with a smile and wink.

Jamie laughed. "Exactly. Her former fiancé is back in the picture, and she's not sure how she feels about either of us, so this could all end before it really begins."

Jamie knew his father was on board, but what about Mike? As his father mounted his horse, Mike took Jamie by the arm. "Be careful, little brother. Are you sure you aren't rebounding from losing Victoria?"

Jamie braced for an argument and then backed down. "I don't know what's happening here. I've only known Laramee for three days, but I already care deeply about her. But I hear you. Trust me, I want to be sure of what I'm feeling, whether it's worry or sympathy, or if I'm really falling in love with her. That's why I need time and privacy to sort it all out."

Mike rubbed a hand over his mouth and glanced at the ground. "This is your business, Jamie, not mine. Laramee's great, and I have to admit you seem happier than I've seen you in a long time, but you don't have a lot of time to figure things out, so don't let your feelings overrule your head."

"What are you implying?"

"Just that there's a lot at stake here—for you, for the family, for the company—so be wise."

Jamie homed in on *for the family, for the company*, and his ire flared. "Just exactly what does my decision about who I care for matter to the family or the company?"

"Because you're an important part of each one. Let's start with the corporate interests. You've brought us a business prospect with great potential. I suspect the tests will prove this vein to be quite valuable. If it does, we'll make the Stone family an offer that's good for them and good for us. But you're the key to their decision, so use your head."

"Stop. Just stop, Mike. I'm asking for your help as my brother, not for business advice from the senior attorney of the firm, and I'm certainly not going to advise Laramee or her parents to make a decision based on how it will affect our bottom line!"

Mike shook his head at Jamie. "There's more at stake here, Jamie. Do you really think Laramee or her parents want her to break her back on this rocky land for the rest of her life? She wants an honorable out, and she's asking you to give her that. You said it yourself. You hardly know her, and you don't know what you feel for her. Unusual circumstances bring people together. Her life is like a sad novel. She's losing the family ranch, her father is sick, and she's looking to you to save her. It's only natural that you two would be drawn to each other under this very emotional situation. But what happens in a week? A month. A year? I know you too well. The only way you could advise her to stay and work this land would be if you planned on staying here with her. Am I right?"

Jamie glared back as Mike untangled the very threads of his confusion with painful clarity.

"What will you do if you sort your feelings out and realize you don't love each other, after you've convinced her to stay here? Could you ever leave her high and dry? She'll have her heart broken and still be forced to sell to survive, or guilt and obligation will force you to stay in a relationship you don't want. This is where the family responsibility comes in. As noble and romantic as it might sound to stay with Laramee out of guilt and loyalty, remember what your last exit did to Mom and Dad. So, all I'm saying is use your heart, *and* your head." He turned for his horse and mounted, leaving Jamie speechless and angry.

Jamie's heart was pounding in his chest, and he didn't have a rebuttal for the case his astute brother had laid out. It frustrated him, even angered him that the company's master negotiator, who could read a clients' wants and needs from a single meeting, had read Jamie's worries and Laramee's heart and mind so accurately. Was he in the same position Laramee was in with Sutton? He could hear Laramee making these same arguments in her own head, and he knew they factored into her reasoning about whether to sell the ranch or marry Sutton. Guilt and obligation or love? He felt sick because in just a few days, he had become the factor affecting the other two decisions that would determine the rest of Laramee's life.

He rode back to the bunkhouse and saw Mike hand his mount's lead off to Laramee. Mike got inside Reese's truck without a final goodbye. In a moment, his father and brother would be gone, and yet, Jamie knew Mike's words would continue to haunt him.

Jamie walked to the truck and asked Reese, "What do you think about the land?"

Reese bit the side of his mouth and said, "Your father told me what your initial assessment was. You were right. I don't see a future for ranching here. Did your dad tell you that the initial perk test results were disappointing?"

The critical information had gotten lost in the chaos of the day. Jamie shook his head.

Reese continued, "You'd need access to a steady water source *and* a sizeable investment for irrigation equipment, and the Stone's don't have the resources for either. I'm sorry, but the land won't support ranching or much development."

The news wasn't unexpected, but the finality of it still pained Jamie. "Then the turquoise means everything."

"It appears so, but that news is good. Harrison thinks the vein is rich."

Harrison jumped in. "Don't say that to Laramee until I send the final report. The last thing she needs is another disappointment, but I really do think they've got something great here."

"Thanks. I won't inflate her expectations. Again...I owe you both so much. Let's stay in touch. Let me return the favor."

He turned away from the truck in time to see William Cannon taking Laramee's hand. "So lovely to meet you, Laramee. Please let me know if there's anything we can do for your father."

"Thank you, Mr. Cannon. I will."

William turned toward Jamie. "Please let me know how Sterling is, will you?"

"Of course, I will."

His dad looked directly into Jamie's eyes. "You're doing a fine job here, but you might not be able to save the place, no matter how much you care about Laramee."

Jamie heard that worry in his father's voice again. "I know that."

"Okay then. Take care of yourself, son. I'm proud of you."

"Thank you, Dad."

William set one foot on the running board and looked back at his son. "I'll email you the test results as soon as they're in. Love you, Jamie. Come home soon."

The longing in his father's final words haunted Jamie. He'd been away from the office for only a few days, so his absence wasn't the cause of his father's distress. It was as if his father was grieving the future loss of him. Mike had likely gone two for two today, accurately defining Jamie's dilemma, and nailing the source of their father's worry. Jamie glanced at Mike, who shot him an expression that seemed to declare, "See? I told you so."

CHAPTER 15

The two spent a few hours brushing the horses and settling them in. Neither spoke much, and Jamie figured Laramee was as lost in her thoughts as he was in his. Reality returned with the ring of Laramee's phone. "It's Sutton. I need to take this and tell him about my father."

"Go. I'll feed the horses and bed them down for the night."

She headed into the bunkhouse leaving Jamie alone. He took his time. His thinking was clearer when she wasn't around, and he knew the last thing he wanted was to listen in as Laramee and Sutton chatted. He walked to the paddock and stared out over the ranch as he tried to sort through Mike's argument, but everything turned his thoughts to Laramee. He headed back into the bunkhouse. When he entered, Laramee had her back to him while she stood at the stove using one of her two recipes—heating. The main ingredient seemed to be two cans of stew. And stretching her culinary skills to the max, she was about to boil some rice.

"Stew for dinner?"

"Yep. A cowboy staple."

"But we still have a pot of chili."

"Now we'll have a choice."

Jamie heard the quiver in her happy-sounding voice. He hung his jacket and hat on a peg and ventured a little closer. "Any word on your father?"

She nodded her head but never turned to face Jamie. "Yeah, as a matter of fact, they're getting ready to release my dad, but Mom is still worried about bringing him all the way home in case he has a relapse, so she wants to spend the night in a motel near the hospital to make herself feel more comfortable. Sutton is there now. He said since I'm not with my folks, he thought it might give me comfort for him to be there, listening to the doctors' reports and supporting my mom." She broke down and brought her left wrist to her mouth and sobbed into it. "He's a good man."

Jamie leaned into the long table and hung his head. He had to admit, the guy was practically a saint.

"Anyway," Laramee began again, "they should be home again tomorrow. Isn't that great?"

She broke down again and this time Jamie stepped closer to her. "That's great news."

"Uh-huh."

"I'm sure you're relieved to know he's doing well."

"Uh-huh." Jamie stepped to her and, with one hand, turned her to face him. "Is there anything I can do to help?"

She handed him her wooden spoon. "Can you take over here while I pull myself together?"

It wasn't the help he intended to offer, but he took the spoon and said, "Sure."

Laramee grabbed her coat and headed outside. He didn't know where she went, but he knew she'd want to be alone. The food was ready in ten minutes, but it sat in bowls for another hour before she returned with the mail that had accumulated over the past two days.

They ate, saying little. Laramee absently turned the pages in a farming catalog, and needing a diversion of his own, Jamie picked up the local paper with the grocery ads, pretending to be interested in the cost of jelly and chips. Finally setting the catalog aside, Laramee looked at a piece of mail addressed to her father. Her head fell into her hands and the tears started again.

Jamie stood and moved to her chair. "Come here," he said as he took her hand and pulled her to him. She stepped into his embrace, placing her head on his shoulder as he rubbed little circles in her back.

"I can't lose him without setting things right between us, you know?"

"I know. I'm sure he loves you very much," he whispered into her ear. He wanted to add, *Who could not love you*, but he didn't.

"I just need to get this right."

"You will. You will."

He held her in silence, and she relaxed into him, allowing him to bear a portion of her slight weight. It was easy to love her, especially in moments like this, when he was her white knight and protector. She made him feel needed in ways Victoria never had, and strong in ways Victoria never needed, but he still couldn't shake Mike's words about how their situation was not reality.

Tomorrow would be different, he told himself. Her father would be home, and Laramee'd be calmer, feel safer, and be less in need of his comfort. By then, they'd be clearer about the attraction building between them.

Yes, reality could wait until tomorrow, and tonight I'll simply be there for Laramee and support her...

But ten minutes in each other's arms took its toll on his resolve. Laramee smelled like the valley air, scented with pine and a cleanness that had no name he could attach to it other than fresh. He felt her breathing even out the longer he held her, as did the little sniffs and sighs she made as her anxiety settled. The arms that had simply lain on his shoulders to support her weight now enfolded him and she moved her head ever so slightly to fit it more tightly into the crook of his neck. All the well-thought-out plans and resolve he'd conjured evaporated, and he knew another minute holding Laramee this way would completely do him in.

His breathing became ragged as he pulled his head back to check in with her. She set her eyes on his parted mouth and sat up, placing her forearms on his shoulders. "What are you thinking about?" she asked.

Jamie took her arms and peeled away from her. "My mind is filled with confusion."

"We're a mess."

He couldn't agree more. He slid his hands down to hers and gave them a squeeze before letting go. "Let me help you clean up."

A look of disappointed finality came over her. "No need. I've got this."

When he persisted, she touched her fingers to his lips and shook her head. "Let me…please. My mind is swirling, and I need to stay busy."

He took her hand and held it, holding her in place, wanting to pull her to him again, facing the same dilemma they'd faced moments before.

"Stay and keep me company?" she asked.

He knew if he stood anywhere near her, he'd gravitate back to her, like magnets, and they'd be knotted up with want and guilt all over again. And he could think of no topic of conversation that wouldn't eventually loop them to the primary hurdle between them—what did they each want? Only one solution seemed reasonable.

"I think it's best if I take a book and head to bed to read."

CHAPTER 16

*T*uesday, March 28, 2023

*J*amie felt as if he had wrestled an elephant all night. Mike's warnings left him crushed by the weight of responsibility he felt. Another flop and turn left him at the bitter edge of the lumpy bunk and almost on the floor. He took his blanket to move out to the sofa and found rest equally elusive there.

His thoughts were coming in at warp speed, leaving him unable to sort them out.

What did he love about Laramee?

What were the hurdles between them?

What did they have in common?

What about her made him better?

What about him made him worthy of her?

He strode to the cupboard and pulled out a drawing tablet and a pencil. In a few minutes he'd made five lists, and as he studied them, he began to feel a sense of clarity, not only about Laramee, but about his own insecurities. He moved from making lists to writing down thoughts and phrases that made him hungry to speak with Laramee when she awoke. Was he ready? He folded that page back, revealing a clean page. This time he'd write out what he wished he could say. An hour passed, and three pages had been crumpled into balls. By the fourth page, he thought he'd finally found the words he sought. He read it through, deciding it still needed work. Fatigue hit him, compounded by the hour spent dredging his soul, so he threw the crumpled pages away and tucked the pad and pencil into the cupboard with plans to return to it later.

The moon gleamed through one of the front windows. He wrapped a blanket around himself and allowed the moon to pull him outside where the air was refreshing and clean and crisp. It reminded him of Laramee, and he couldn't imagine her anywhere else but here. Before that thought carried him away, he heard a slight scuff off to his left near the bunkhouse and followed it. Laramee was already up and dressed and in the barn with the door wide open, mucking a stall. He leaned against the wall, studying her, wondering which of her many worries had ruined her sleep. He also wondered whether she'd made her decision to keep the land and was simply doing what a rancher does, arising at first light to tend the animals, even though she had so few anymore.

She was whistling a familiar tune. He soon recognized it as "The Old Grey Mule." He smiled as memories of their playful moment flooded over him with warmth and joy. He loved the feel of her in his arms, her laughter, her childlike simplicity about what mattered and what didn't. But it was more. He liked how he felt about himself in that moment. He had recognized it immediately, and then lost it when the kiss ended and Laramee was so upset. He tried to pull that feeling back from his memory—relief, as if he'd returned to a place or sense of himself he'd been missing.

Simply said, he felt happy.

He marveled over that seemingly simple word. Had he felt happy with Victoria? He could see himself laughing and enjoying himself with Victoria and his family, but there was always some distraction limiting his joy, things like overscheduled calendars and the need to maintain a lifestyle as irritating as too-tight shoes. Something Victoria once said pulled at him.

Successful people sacrifice the luxury to be footloose and fancy free.

Maybe that was all it was. Maybe that was what Mike meant, that being here with Laramee, being footloose and fancy free with nothing to do but be together wasn't real. However delightful this attraction for her might be, would it suffer when the pressures of real life closed in?

But oh…how he loved how he felt…

With her mucking concluded, she turned to brushing Patches and talking to her old equine friend as if she were chatting with a child. Her voice was higher in pitch, and every few words were punctuated with a kiss or a hug. The horse responded to it all, bobbing his head as if agreeing with her assessment of how good and handsome he was. The more he bobbed, the more she laughed, and on and on the game went as if Patches were reminding her how much she'd been missed.

She led him out to the paddock, but she didn't like the swing of the gate. A minute later she was out there hitting the main post with a sledgehammer until the swing corrected. She was a git 'er done kind of woman.

Lines from a song came to mind about a man who lost everything and had to start all over, but he knew he'd be okay because of the woman he'd married. It could have been written about Laramee, he concluded. If her house burned down or got swept away by a tornado, she'd grab an axe and start felling trees for a new one.

It occurred to Jamie that Sutton was her perfect match, a determined helper, a man who could likewise survive a disaster and rebuild his world with his two hands. Could the same be said of himself? Jamie considered his earlier personal assessment. Within the bounds of his own world of commerce and business, he was smart and capable, the detail-oriented son who dotted all the I's and crossed all the T's. The personable Cannon brother who followed through on assignments and schmoozed clients, but had he ever built anything?

Laramee's nicknames for him returned—Pretty Boy…Paper-Pusher…Maybe that's how she actually saw him, as an adornment, a resource with business acumen. He suddenly wondered who needed whom between the two of them.

She set the sledgehammer down and gave Patches another hug. Jamie wished he had his phone or a camera to save the moment. She rested there in utter stillness while Patches soaked up her love. Jamie couldn't take his eyes off Laramee, enjoying the brightness the cold brought to her cheeks, lips, and nose. Standing there, yards apart, he could map the freckles on her face that gave her more character and natural beauty than any tube or color stick could ever add. Her hair was long and loose. Some meshed with the horse's mane while the rest fell in tangled waves down her back, as if she'd just climbed out of bed. It was then that Jamie noticed she was dressed in the clothes she'd worn the previous day, and he wondered if she'd slept in them, and if so, why?

He moved and made the slightest of sounds, but Patches picked up on it, and so did Laramee. He savored her first response upon seeing him. Her mouth dropped open in wonder, settling into a smile that brightened her entire face. Her eyes widened at first, then relaxed into crinkled slits, and then, in a flash, everything shifted from pure happiness to sorrow, and back into that pasted happiness she sent out to others who wanted her to hurry up and feel happy again.

Jamie suspected the reason for the mood shift. He cocked his head to the side and walked toward her with the blanket draped over his shoulders like a robe. Neither of them spoke, and when he drew close, she stepped toward him. His blanketed arms opened wide as they slipped back into loving friend mode. It was as if they both knew what was coming before a word of news was shared, so they avoided *the* topic, making small talk instead.

"Couldn't sleep either?" Laramee asked.

"Nope."

"The lumpy mattress or other worries?"

"A bit of both." He laid his head against hers. Did you sleep at all?"

"Some. On the sofa." Laramee took Jamie's hand, pulling him along. "Watch the rest of the sunrise with me?"

The ladder was still leaning against the bunkhouse roof. He

thought about the day he became stranded there and had to be rescued by Laramee. "What if we both get stranded up there?"

"Today I'm tempted to kick the ladder down myself."

Feeling more certain about his suspicions regarding her mood, he avoided taking the bait and climbed the roof instead.

The blanket was big enough for two, and they sat on the edge of it. Jamie wrapped the rest of it around them and tucked it tightly, until they looked like a two-headed burrito. They sat in silence during the march of brilliant morning light across the eastern plains until it illuminated the mountains. He tried to enjoy the moment, and savor the memory, perhaps one of the last they'd share together, but his mind was racing. Then Laramee's melancholy whisper entered the silence.

"Some people look for pictures in the clouds. When Tyler and I were kids, we'd look for images in the mountain peaks. Some mornings, when I was working in Arizona, I'd go to a place on the ranch where the sun broke over the mountains and try to find pictures in those peaks the way Tyler and I did here, when we were young." She managed to work her arm loose enough to point out a spot in the mountain peaks. "See that series of pointed rocks?"

Jamie didn't know if she was waiting for a reply, and when she hurried on, he had his answer.

"Tyler and I named that series of peaks 'The Statue of Liberty' because it reminded us of her crown." She pointed further left. "And that stretch there with the rounded peaks? We called that Buffalo Ridge. We dreamed of riding our horses to the top one day."

Jamie understood why, but he also sensed that this exercise was more about Laramee's need to talk about Tyler than about pointing out geological formations. "Tyler's on your mind a lot today, isn't he?"

"Yes, but the memories are happy now." Laramee looked into his face. "I have you to thank for that."

Jamie slid his arm around her, and she continued.

"I stayed up long after you went to bed..." She nudged him as if calling him out for that error.

He raised one eyebrow and gazed down on her. "We both know perfectly well why I pulled myself away and headed to bed."

"Nothing happened between us but a hug."

"It might have if I'd stayed," he said, his voice conveying all the seriousness the moment deserved. He moved his eyes away from Laramee before those feelings returned again. "Is that why you couldn't sleep?"

"Partly." She laid her head on his shoulder. "I thought how grateful I am that you came into my life for this little moment." She looked up at him again. "What you said to me about God working in me? It healed something broken inside. You were right about me pushing Him away. I didn't feel worthy of His love, so I pushed it away, but I can finally feel God's love again. I even welcome it. Now I want to feel my father's love equally. While I stayed up, I worked up the courage to finally talk to him honestly about Tyler's death, so we could both heal those last hurts."

"Did you call him? It must have been very late."

"Like a little miracle, Mom actually called me. She said the nurses had to put Dad on oxygen last night. He's probably coming home today with a tank."

It was a tough mix of blessings and more heartache. "I'm glad he's coming home so soon."

"Me too. I need to talk to him to finally have peace."

A thought struck Jamie, and he pulled out of the blanket. "What do you hope that will look like?"

"I'm going to tell Mom and Dad to sell the ranch. They deserve to spend their last years in comfort, not staying here to help me and not worrying about me every day."

"I think there's a high probability the Brockbanks will make you an offer on the ranch. Our real estate company will handle everything."

"We'll gladly entertain all offers, Mr. Cannon," she teased.

"You're sure you're ready to give the place up?"

"I don't feel a need to run from my memories of this place anymore, but I don't see my future here anymore."

Those last few words sent a zip of hope through Jamie. "So, you're not marrying Sutton?"

She shook her head and looked at him. "I didn't say that."

"But you said you didn't see your future here. I'm confused."

"I don't see my future on this ranch. What good would it do to rid myself of the guilt over Tyler's death and my parents' grief, just to take on a new load because I destroyed Sutton again?"

"Because you deserve to love yourself at least as much as you love everyone else."

She tilted her head sideways. "Thank you, but do you tell yourself that? I saw you with your father and brother. You're different around them than you are with me. As if you feel a need to prove yourself."

The chill set in through his sweatshirt, and Jamie pulled the blanket back around him. "Since being here, around you, I've felt the most at ease and like myself that I have in years."

"You're one of the finest men I've ever met, Jamie. I hope you hold on to what you've found here when you leave. The last test results will be in by tomorrow, and your work here will be over. We'll each pick up our real lives again."

It was the news Jamie suspected earlier when Laramee's expression shifted after seeing him, but hearing the words out loud made his stomach flip like a dip on a roller coaster. "Is thinking about that what kept you up last night?"

Slumping in resignation, she sighed and played with the edge of the blanket grasped in her hand. "My mother and father met in grade school. From the time I was little, Mom told me she knew she loved him from the first day they met. I remember asking her how a person knows when they've fallen in love. She said, 'You just do.'" Laramee paused to brush at a piece of litter on the blanket and went on. "I held on to that promise until after I kissed Sutton for the first time."

"No bells or fireworks?"

"Love changes over time. It ebbs and grows. I saw it in my parents' marriage. It's just that...well...my mother's promise that I'd just *know* scared me after that kiss, because I didn't actually *know* whether I loved Sutton. At least I wasn't sure enough to table my dreams and be content with the sweet quiet life I'd have with him, so I ran away."

"And you didn't return for him, Laramee."

"No, I didn't."

"Listen to yourself. Tell me you didn't feel something wonderful when we kissed, because I know I did. I felt alive and whole and hopeful for the first time in a very long while. Did you feel the same? Because I think this Sutton and Laramee thing is based on guilt. You think you owe him for being kind to you when Tyler died."

"Maybe at first, but I'm not sure anymore. I think my time away from here changed me. Mellowed me."

"You're not sixty, Laramee. You're in the most exciting season of your life."

"Excitement is relative." She pointed off to the left. "There are two hot springs within an hour's drive of here. One is so hot that steam hovers above it like an eerie cloud, and the ground around it is so warm that nothing can grow, so it's barren and feels like Halloween all year-round. It's dramatic and spectacular, a huge make-out spot, but it's unsafe to be in it for very long. The water in the other hot springs is more temperate. Greenery and flowers bloom there in season. It's safer and relaxing but less exciting, so you find older couples and families with children. That's the hot springs my family visited."

"Meaning???"

"Sutton makes me feel like a dip in that second hot spring—warm, safe, welcome. That's not a bad start for a marriage, but I haven't felt that spark, that special storybook thrill with him yet, and I wanted to know what it feels like, so I'll be ready with a better answer when my own children ask me that question."

"Wait, wait, wait. So…He drew the words out, encouraging her to explain. "Are you admitting you felt that spark between us?" Jamie tilted his head to the side and eyed her, trying to determine if the conclusion he was drawing was written in her eyes. "Are you admitting you love—"

"I'm not admitting anything." Her head started shaking before any words came out. "I'm just tucking these fairytale days we've shared away in my heart. But I believe I'll have a better answer for my children than the one my mother gave me."

She turned away again. Jamie sat staring out over the sunrise's glorious impact on the prairie, while feeling as if something were setting in his own life. He couldn't reconcile the wrongness of the situation, that she was going to marry a wonderful man she loved more as a friend than a husband while kisses shared with Jamie from their fairytale days still lingered in both their senses. He reached across her and tipped her chin around to meet his gaze.

"What if this is more than just a few fairytale days? What if this *is* our new real life?"

"What?"

"Mike saw something brewing between us and said we couldn't know if what we felt was real because we were all alone and cut off from reality."

She turned away from him and then back again to challenge him. Instead, she ended up burying her face into his shoulder.

"Don't you owe it to yourself and to Sutton to be sure he's the person you're meant to be with?"

A sparkle lit her eyes, and Jamie plunged ahead.

"We've got a day, maybe two to get those answers. I propose we find out."

"How?"

Jamie threw the blanket off his shoulders and turned to face Laramee. "Laramee Stone, will you do me the honor of going on a date with me?"

She shot a hand to her mouth and started laughing. "Where? Here? What exactly did you have in mind?"

"I have no idea!" He laughed, feeling sixteen and awkward again, like the time he worked up the nerve to ask Melanie Dickson to their homecoming dance. After racking his brain for clever invitation ideas, he went to her house and left a candle and a pack of matches on her porch with a note that said, *Will you go to prom with me? If the answer is yes, light the candle and leave it in your window.* When he drove by to get his answer, the candle was not in the window, and the house was pitch black. It appeared she'd even removed the bulb from the dusk-to-dawn light so there'd be no mistake about her answer.

He brushed that nightmare away and focused on Laramee. "What do you say?"

She threw her head back, laughing and clapping. "How can I turn down an invitation like that?"

"Let me take you into the city and show you the town. We'll share

211

a delicious meal, and maybe grab tickets for whatever's playing at the theater."

The excitement in Laramee's eyes quickly dimmed. "I can't. My father…"

Jamie wanted to kick himself for forgetting that her mother was bringing her father home today. "Okay…we'll do something special here." He quickly racked his brain to assess what tools he had available to create a magical date for Laramee. He'd found a few items in a bunkhouse cupboard the day he cleaned, and something interesting in the shed. They gave him an idea. "Head back into the barn for ten minutes while I dress and grab a few things in the bunkhouse, then it's yours. Get dressed for the day and maybe pack a few sandwiches and a thermos. I'll pick you up in an hour."

"Pick me up?"

He bobbled his head. "In a manner of speaking. Just be ready, okay."

The very thought of planning this random, homespun date for Laramee filled him with a nervous excitement he hadn't experienced before. He quickly pulled a few ideas together and saw roadblocks ahead. *No matter*, he thought. The remote location of the ranch complicated things but it didn't prevent him from enlisting help. He began making notes on his phone and searching for what and who he needed.

A text came in from Mike. "*Call me when you get this.*"

Jamie knew this had to be about the turquoise samples. His time to prepare for the date was limited but this news was too important to put off. He dialed Mike's number. "I take it the report is in."

"It's good news. The Silver Buckle Mining Corporation is going to make them a very lucrative offer that'll be good for everyone. The Brockbanks get the turquoise, the Stones get a hefty price, and Cannon Capital will get a hefty commission fee."

"That's great. Laramee is ready to sell."

"Good work, little brother."

"I didn't *work* on her, Mike. She's agreeing to let it go to assure her parents a comfortable retirement."

"Okay…we're being a little defensive, aren't we?"

"This is more than a business deal to me, Mike. It's personal, and I'm taking the lead on this project. There's more at stake here than just profit."

"I know. You like this girl. I'm happy for you. Tell Laramee I'll make sure a contract gets there by tomorrow."

Jamie ended the call without responding. The deal would be good for the Stone family, but the last thing he wanted was to talk business with Laramee today of all days.

CHAPTER 17

*L*aramee dug through the things she brought back from Arizona, searching for something to wear. After years working at The Wild Pony Resort, she owned very few shirts that weren't well-worn or that didn't have the logo of her former employer emblazoned across the back. She hadn't refreshed her wardrobe in years, and she didn't want to wear the outfit she'd worn on her date with Sutton. The remaining selection was disappointing, comprising two skirts, a few tops, jeans, and T-shirts in varying stages of wear. Jeans it was, she decided, and she chose the white button-front top she had not worn on her last date with Sutton.

She combed her hair and pulled it into an elastic band. Wanting something a little more special, she pulled it loose and French braided her hair, leaving the long ends in a sweet braid that she rolled into a bun at the base of her neck. Pleased with the look, she added some mascara and a sweep of lip gloss and felt a slight return to the person she once was. At the last minute, she tied a red bandana around her neck.

She made three sandwiches and stuffed them into zipper bags. Next, she grabbed grapes, two pudding cups, and two napkins and packed them all into an insulated bag. Then she filled a thermos with lemonade. With the requested lunch made, she tidied up around the bunkhouse, watching the clock. When the hour had nearly passed, she received a text from Jamie asking for another fifteen minutes. When that grace period was nearly past, he texted again begging for a little more time. She didn't mind. In fact, the delays only raised her curiosity over what he was doing with that time.

A few minutes after nine, she heard a knock on the door and found Jamie standing on the porch dressed in his own clothes again—a black Henley, designer jeans, and a denim jacket that likely cost as much as her entire wardrobe. A white bag and two cups containing a steaming beverage were in his hands.

"How on earth…"

Jamie stepped back and smiled as he scanned her from head to toe. "Wow. You look amazing."

Heat flushed her cheeks as she dropped her gaze away from Jamie, whose compliment and eyes, which were still on her, made her self-conscious.

He blinked and shook his head comically as if shaking himself back into his senses. "Were you asking how I worked this culinary magic?"

"Something like that."

"Venmo…and I'm a great tipper for home delivery."

"I see."

"I was going for fresh scones but the best I could do were Betty Jean's fried donuts from the Sav-A-Lot next to Sam's hardware store."

"Was Sam your driver?"

"Yes. It was a win/win. You said he and Brenda needed money and I needed his help."

Laramee laughed and then shrank behind the door when she compared herself to his appearance.

Jamie stepped inside, set the food on the table, and peeled off his outerwear. "What's wrong?" he asked.

"You look like you stepped out of Nordstrom's catalog. She studied her ensemble from her faded pant's legs to her scuffed boots. "I look like my outfit was designed by Yard Sales are Us."

Jamie rushed to her and took her arms. "That's not true. You're beautiful. I just wanted to be myself today, but I can change back into Tyler's clothes if—"

"No." She caught his arm as he turned for his room. "It's a nice change. Shall we eat?"

Jamie pulled two plates from the cupboard, plated a glazed donut, and handed it to her. "The cocoa came in a thermos to stay piping hot."

"I bet that required a hefty tip."

He winked and set his hand on hers. "Totally worth it."

Laramee felt little shivers race up her arms as a teasing smile tugged at Jamie's mouth, crinkling his eyes. They had spent hours together, working side-by-side and sharing looks and touches and kisses, but today seemed very different. There was a nervous innocence between them as they navigated this first real date.

"So, what have you been working on out there?" she asked, drawing the attention away from herself.

Jamie wagged a finger at her. "No, no, no. No telling and no peeking."

She broke a piece off her donut and stuffed it in her mouth to give her something else to focus on besides Jamie's teasing blue eyes. They finished the donuts and cocoa, and Jamie became quiet. "Is everything all right?" she asked.

"I'd rather not talk business today, but Mike called. The turquoise samples were very impressive, Laramee, and The Brockbanks are going to make you a very lucrative offer on the ranch and its mining rights."

She sat back. "How lucrative?"

"The contract will be here tomorrow. You'll see then."

Laramee stood and clapped her hands as she paced around the kitchen. "I can't wait for Dad to hear!" She rushed over to Jamie. "I want you to present the offer to him."

"I'll be happy to speak to him as soon as he gets home and settled in. For now, get ready. We're going riding, so grab whatever you need to stay warm."

Laramee nearly skipped to the pegs where her coat, hat, and scarf hung. Her gloves were in her coat pockets. When they were both dressed for the cold, Jamie grabbed the packed lunch sack and thermos and extended his free hand to Laramee. "Ready?"

Even through their gloves, warmth and security spread into her when her hand slipped into his. "I go where you go."

As soon as they stepped onto the porch, Laramee heard the crunch of tires coming down the lane. She recognized the truck immediately. Two contrasting emotions filled her—excitement and tension. She was thrilled to have her father home, but the old emotional distance between them slid over her like a shroud, and despite having found a measure of *divine* forgiveness and love, she worried her father's love would never be hers again.

The truck pulled to a stop, and she was surprised but not shocked to see her father behind the wheel.

"Your father drove home," Jamie muttered. "He's one tough old cowboy."

"You have no idea," said Laramee.

She waved to her parents and saw her mother gathering up the oxygen tubing and pump. Before the woman made it around to the door to help her husband exit the vehicle, Sterling Stone was halfway out, waving her off with an assurance that he could manage on his own. She placed the walker near her husband, backed up a step, and watched nervously as he climbed to the ground and rested breathlessly against the truck body,

"Water, please, Laramee," said her mother as she checked on Sterling. "I think he needs a drink."

"I'll get it," Jamie said as he ran into the bunkhouse.

Her mother called a thank you to Jamie and then looked at Laramee with urgency in her eyes. "Sutton had a full day in court today. He asked us to hold off getting your father discharged until he could come and help us get him settled in, but your father wouldn't wait."

Her father's stubbornness didn't surprise Laramee at all, but she had a new concern. Sutton would head here right after court to check on her father, and that could spell the end of the date Jamie had planned for her.

When Jamie returned, she and he stepped behind her father. Each of them grabbed one side of her father's belt to support his efforts to walk while her mother followed behind, carrying the pump.

When they reached the front door, Sterling glanced at Jamie. "Thank you. I can manage from here."

Laramee noticed no word was said to her. She released her own hold and stepped away. When Jamie looked back at her, she waved her hands forward, reminding him of his promise to speak to her father about the proposed offer on the ranch. Jamie shot her a "not now," glance, but she persisted, as if they could all use some good news at that moment.

He turned to her father as he entered the house and said, "Sir, I have good news for you. My company is expecting an offer on your ranch tomorrow from The Silver Buckle Mining Corporation."

Laramee barely breathed as she watched and listened for her father's reaction. He turned around and glanced back at her, but there was no acknowledgement of her. Nothing. She took his glance as a summary dismissal, and in that instant, whatever progress she'd made in forgiving herself diluted into nothingness. Her eyes caught Jamie's empathetic gaze as she turned to go, but her last view of her father wasn't of him looking at her, to invite her back, but of him pointing to two chairs on the front porch as he addressed Jamie saying, "Sit. Let's hear it."

❧

*L*aramee's slow trudge back to the bunkhouse tore at Jamie. He wanted to shake Sterling Stone for being so cold to a daughter who loved him so much. He refused to sit on the porch as if the two were respected business associates or old friends. He was doing this for Laramee and Laramee alone. He'd be her advocate, say his piece for her, and then he'd leave Sterling Stone the way Sterling had left his daughter.

Cathy Stone dismissed herself to make her husband a plate of food, but only after shooting a worried look and a plea to Jamie, asking him to watch over Sterling. It tore at Jamie. He didn't wish the man further ill, but neither did he care for the man who purposely wounded Laramee. He would do what he came to do and leave.

Jamie's jaw was tight, causing his words to come out clipped and cold as he delivered the news. "I don't have the final details, but the contract will be here tomorrow with exact numbers for your consideration."

"And they plan to mine the turquoise?"

"In a responsible way that doesn't leave the land barren and ruined."

Sterling nodded. "That's good."

"Then we're done here?"

The older man eyed Jamie. "You don't much like me, do you?"

The man's abruptness took Jamie by surprise, but the thought of the pain on Laramee's face as she turned back for the bunkhouse steeled him. "I don't much like the way you treat your daughter."

"How should a man treat a daughter who despises him?"

Jamie cocked his head back and drilled down on the man. "You're wrong. You're so wrong. She loves you. All she wants is your forgiveness."

Sterling's eyes squinted in disbelief. "Me? Forgive her?"

"How can you deny her that? What kind of man would take pleasure in watching his own daughter suffer?"

The man seemed to honestly not understand, and Jamie came back again. "She's so loving and giving, but she's in so much pain, and you're the only one who can relieve her of the guilt she carries around. Why can't you forgive her?"

"*Her* guilt? There's nothing to forgive her for." He hung his head until his chin rested on his chest. "I'm the one with the guilt. I desperately need *her* forgiveness."

Jamie wasn't sure he was hearing the man correctly, so he slipped into the chair and faced Sterling. "She thinks you still blame her for Tyler's death because she took him riding that night."

Tears filled the man's eyes. "That ride to the falls didn't kill Tyler. Maybe it hurried the inevitable along, but he was already a dead man walking that day. I didn't know it at the time, but I should have...if I had listened."

"I don't understand."

"I had a surprise planned, and I didn't want anything like a headache to mess it up. I just didn't listen."

"To what? To whom?"

"To Tyler." Sterling ran his hand across his whisker-scraggled face. "He'd begged me all rodeo season for permission to ride a bronc, and Laramee begged me to give him his chance, so I set it up for that last night. I was so excited to give him his wish, but Tyler complained of a headache that afternoon. That boy loved to ride, and I should have known something was up when he talked about pulling out of the evening's competition. But no...I was going to be a hero. I had everything arranged for his big debut, and I convinced him to ride that night. I might even have teased him about using a headache to run away from the bronc."

Sterling's hands came up to cradle his heavy head as he began to cry. Jamie could see the rest of the story clearly. Tyler's brain was already at risk before he even arrived at the rodeo. His evening's events alone would have likely been enough to cause the rupture of the vessel, but the time on the bronc and the crash into the gate sealed Tyler's fate. The lack of a readily accessible neuro center hindered him from getting an accurate, possibly life-saving diagnosis, and they went home where Tyler most likely would have died in his bed before first light whether he and Laramee had taken that ride or not.

He felt sick...for Laramee, for Sterling, and especially for Tyler, whose death was a senseless, unnecessary tragedy that should never have happened. The agonizing part that tortured Laramee to this day was that such a thing probably would never happen where most people live. But it was as Laramee had said, a clear danger to those who lived in sparsely populated areas where the local governments couldn't justify the cost per capita of a cutting-edge facility. Like here, in the eastern Colorado ranchlands.

"How does Laramee not know this?"

Sterling drew in a deep, shudder-filled breath and straightened. "I thought she knew and blamed me. She avoided me for days, so I withdrew and hid from her, and then Sutton came along, filling her time. I figured he was helping her manage her grief, and I hoped the tension would ease between us as time passed, then one day, she just packed up and left."

"Did your wife know the truth?"

"Some. Cathy knew I allowed Tyler to get on that bronc. She thought he and Laramee wore me down until I gave in and let him ride. I could never bring myself to tell her I wanted it as much as they did, and that I had dismissed those warning signs in Tyler's head earlier in the day." He cried again. "I couldn't do it. I just couldn't do it."

"So, she thought Laramee was partially to blame."

"She thought we both were, and she asked us to forgive each other and ourselves."

"But what she didn't know was that Laramee laid all the blame on herself."

Sterling wiped his eyes again. "Neither did I until just now. Don't blame Cathy for any of this. Fixing things looked simple to her. She thought it would all get better if we just started talking, but my girl and I just couldn't find our way back to each other. Poor Cathy walked on eggshells around us, watching guilt break me and then watching Laramee leave. We let Laramee go without a fight because we thought she needed to deal with her grief on her own terms. Cathy had already lost Tyler, and Max was deployed and in harm's way. I think my poor wife worried she was holding on to Laramee by a thread, and she didn't want to push her away. But she was grateful for every little phone call from Laramee, and she avoided the topic of Tyler as much as she could."

He dropped his head back into his gnarled hands. "I'm not proud of how I've handled things. We didn't know she'd laid Tyler's death on her own shoulders."

Jamie rose to his feet to make his last point. "You do now, and you can't let things go unsaid any longer."

"You mean like you?"

Jamie sucked in his next breath. "Excuse me?"

"I might be sick but I'm not dead. I've watched you two through the window and seen how you flirt and tease one another. Have you told her you love her?"

Jamie's tongue felt thick, and he garbled his response. "I...She still has feelings for Sutton."

Sterling Stone cursed and made a face that looked as if he'd bitten into a lemon. "I made excuses too, and I passed her off on Sutton just like you're doing. As terrible as that decision was, I only hurt Laramee. What you're doing will damage her and others far worse. Have you considered what marrying a woman who loves another man will do to Sutton? Or to their kids? And how will you live with your regrets? Think about that."

Jamie had lost the moral high ground with Sterling Stone. Sterling was implicating him in the spirit-sucking muck destroying Laramee.

"I thought you loved Sutton like a son."

"I do, but I wouldn't want her marrying her brother."

Jamie now understood some of Sterling's previous and obscure comments, shared while he sat on his deck in the dark. "Of course, I feel something for her," he began. "I care very deeply for her, and she knows that, but I can't say whether it's love just yet. All I know for sure is that I want to protect her from any further hurt."

"Like the hurt you're going to cause her when you leave?"

Sterling's accusation was a gut punch that left him reeling.

"We're going to spend the day together to figure some things out, but I want your word that you'll speak to Laramee and tell her the truth. Regardless of what happens between us, she needs her father."

Sterling nodded slowly. "I don't know how to begin. I need some time to sort things out...to figure out how to mend things. Maybe you could tell her for me."

"No! No way!"

"Think about it."

"This is not my business."

"It is if you care about her. She trusts you. You could relieve her of all that weight and help make a way for us to meet in the middle. Take her out for a few hours and get your answers. Figure out how you feel about her. And maybe keep an open mind about talking to her for me. Either way, send her to me when you return so I can celebrate with her...or bind up the newest break you're going to cause to her heart."

The man had summed it all up precisely. Be part of her joy or the cause of her sorrow. On the surface, it seemed an easy enough choice. Jamie did think he was falling in love with Laramee, but Sterling didn't have all the facts. Jamie wasn't certain he was the best man for Laramee, and he had only a few hours left to find out.

*L*aramee had watched the exchange between the men from the window. She expected the conversation to be a happy one, at least for her father, but as the two men parted ways, neither of them seemed happy or satisfied.

She stepped outside as Jamie approached the bunkhouse. "Well, that didn't appear to have gone very well."

"Your father is a complicated man, but I think he was happy with the offer."

Laramee blew out a rush of air in relief. "Thanks for handling that."

"I won't say it was my pleasure, but I can say I'm happy to have done it…for you." He tapped her on her nose. Are you ready to head out?"

"Can't wait. Let's go."

"I just need another minute."

The glint in his eye sent shivers up her neck at the wonder of what he had planned. No sooner had she returned to the bunkhouse and closed the door than she heard a knock. When she opened it, she curiously found Jamie standing there ramrod straight with his hat in his hand.

"Morning, ma'am. You sure look lovely."

"Well, thank you, kind sir," she returned in an equally playful tone.

"Please forgive my manners. I'm Jamie Cannon, your date."

Laramee got the message. Jamie wanted a redo and a restart to their relationship, beginning this moment.

"Pleased to make your acquaintance, sir."

"I'd be delighted if you'd call me Jamie, ma'am."

"Shall we go, Jamie?"

He swept his hand forward, and she followed his directions. One of Jamie's surprises appeared as soon as they turned the corner. A white sheet was stretched across the barn wall like a movie screen, and the old projector was set up on a table, aimed at the sheet. Two chairs and a table were in position for a show, reminiscent of the way the Stones showed movies to their guests during the height of the ranch's popularity.

Laramee's hands flew to her mouth in surprise. "You're taking me to the movies."

"Do you like it?"

"I love it!" She thought she might cry at the sweetness of the gesture. "How did you find the projector? I haven't seen it in years."

"It was in a crate in the barn. I found it when I was looking for tools to fix the roof. But I could only find three movie reels, all westerns I'm sure you've seen a *few* times." He wriggled his eyebrows playfully.

She turned against him. "I've never watched them with you, and that makes it perfect. Thank you."

"There's more." He took her hand and drew her to the corner where the table was set with a tablecloth and dishes. "I ordered dinner from a restaurant in Denver and paid a ridiculous fee to have a driver deliver it around six." He closed his eyes and chuckled. "But it will likely arrive cold so we might have to max out your cooking skills and reheat everything."

Something her mother said came back to Laramee, draining the fun from the moment. She wondered if they had until six. "Sutton is coming later. I don't know what time, but he's been checking on my dad and supporting my mom, and now that they're home, he wants to see if they need anything."

"And to see you." Jamie's tone carried a hint of jealousy, which he quickly masked as he painted on a cheerful smile and said, "Then we'd better get going."

He pointed the way to the paddock where Laramee saw Patches and a bay gelding named Caruso saddled with packs. She found it interesting that Jamie had traded Nugget in for a more difficult, stronger, and faster horse.

"Are you sure you're ready for Caruso? You could barely handle Nugget when you got here."

He shrugged his shoulders and smiled. "Maybe I'm not that same man."

She shivered again. It was true. He was different in so many ways. So was she, she hoped, and she wondered if he could see that she had changed equally.

She didn't ask further questions. She simply mounted Patches and followed wherever Jamie and Caruso led. They headed toward the foothills in a breathless run, crossing acres of land as the wind bit their faces and stung their eyes. Patches snorted and sweated. He loved having his head, and his excitement translated through his muscles and into Laramee, who felt a sense of freedom and abandon, inside and out, that she hadn't enjoyed in years. When they reached the foothills, Jamie pulled Caruso up to slow his gait. True to her warning, the gelding fought the bit and twisted, trying to throw his rider off. Laramee gasped, but Jamie squeezed his legs against the animal's body and held on until Caruso came to respect his rider's will, settling into a leisurely jog.

Laramee had ridden with Jamie several times in the past few days, but everything was different today. *He* was different. So was the way he looked at her and the way she felt when he did. The defensiveness he'd arrived with had long since been replaced by humble confidence, but also gone was the stress and frustration that existed between them, replaced by an easy delight. She didn't feel a need to mount an offense or a defense or hide behind a wall. She trusted Jamie. Her feelings ran even deeper than that, and she hoped that by the end of this day she'd be ready to admit it to herself and to him.

Jamie found the trail she and Tyler had cut into the foothills. She hadn't been on that trail since weeks before Tyler died, and judging from the thickness of the scrub pines and brush that surrounded it, neither had anyone else.

He and Caruso took the lead up the hills, slowly picking their way around rocks and brush while occasionally losing the trail.

"Would you like me to lead? I'm very familiar with this area."

Jamie pulled Caruso to the side, tipped his hat to Laramee, and she moved ahead. After another half hour, they reached a stone ledge that overlooked the ranch and its ground. "Is this where you were headed?"

"Yep." He turned to admire the scene spread before him. "I found binoculars in the cupboard, and I carried them up to the bunkhouse roof to scour the hills for a good trail we could ride today. When I saw this, I knew it was the one, except the view is far better than I'd imagined."

Even while sitting high atop Patches, Laramee felt hidden by the brush and branches. With the mountains to her back, her perch provided familiar but still majestic views of land that stretched for more than a hundred miles.

Jamie dismounted and Laramee followed.

"It's nearly noon. Shall we eat?" Jamie asked.

Laramee nodded and pulled the food and drink she'd brought from her saddlebag while Jamie spread a blanket out for their picnic.

They sat close, facing out at the land below. As they nibbled on the sandwiches and fruit, Laramee tried to wriggle information from him about the rest of the day's plans.

"Uh, uh, uh," he scolded playfully. "I'm not giving away more of my surprises."

"Plural?" she yelped, laughing as she smashed against him. "You never really told me how my father reacted to the news that the Brockbanks were putting in an offer on the ranch."

Jamie smiled and pressed a finger to her lips. "No work talk today."

"Then I guess I'm going to have to fire you," she said, adding a chuckle.

He feigned sad resignation. "I feared as much." Then cocking his head to one side, he reached for her sides and tickled her as he teased, "I see a potential labor dispute ahead."

She squealed with laughter until Jamie released her. She felt the mood shift as Jamie took her hand. He ran a finger along her jaw and shook his head slowly as he said, "I don't think you'll have to worry about that. You'll find me quite a pushover where you're concerned."

He encouraged her to move closer and lean back into him. "I loved how you find pictures in the mountain peaks. Today, I want you to look out as far as you can, then close your eyes and imagine one perfect day in your future. A day built around your most secret dreams. Not dreams and hopes based on guilt or responsibility or the needs or wants of others. Try to see a day you can only now imagine wherever, with whatever, and with whomever, you want in it."

The request unnerved her. "Why?"

"I want to know what you dream about when you close those gold-dusted eyes at night."

She laughed and tipped her head to the side. "All right. I share, you share?"

"Absolutely."

She closed her eyes and smiled. "I'd like to see myself standing behind an easel." She opened her eyes and looked at Jamie. "I still want to be an artist of some sort."

"Great. What else?"

"I imagine children playing around me. Maybe on the floor with paper and pencils like me, but they'd be free to pursue their own dreams, whatever they were."

"And where do you see yourself?"

She leaned back until the sun kissed her face. "By a mountain or a city or the sea. No place in particular, and every place. I think I could be happy anywhere if I were with the people I loved most."

His heart leapt that she hadn't confined her dreams to this prairie, perhaps implying that her heart was still open to him.

"Now your turn," she challenged.

"All right." Jamie drew in a deep breath and let it out as he formulated his own vision for the future. "My dream is a simple one— a quieter, slower life. I want family time to be a priority. And I'd want a life centered in God. I'd want to partner with my wife in every way, including spiritually."

"And children?"

"Several. And I'd change my share of diapers."

"Partnering in every way."

"Exactly."

They enjoyed a shared chuckle until the laughter ran out and the mood mellowed again. "And who do you see yourself with, Laramee?"

She shook her head slowly. "Why go there now? Can't we just enjoy being together?"

"No. Because there's something between us. I don't want to ignore it if it could be something wonderful, but I also don't want it to confuse you and cause you to miss out on the life or man you want. So, who do you want in your life, Laramee?"

She folded her arms in front of her and tried to brush the exercise away. "It's not that simple. I don't think we live our lives just for ourselves. We can't selfishly disregard the people who've helped us or those who need us."

"I agree...to a point. We're connected collectively, and we help and support others as we walk our path, but that doesn't mean we abandon our goals every time someone else needs us or thinks they have a better idea for us. We'd end up running around in circles, never moving forward."

"Is that what you think I'm doing?"

"No." She felt his body stiffen as it held her. "It's what *I've* been doing. I realized that this morning when my father showed up."

"I saw you two arguing. What is it between you two? Mike also. I know you love each other, but there's something bitter there."

Jamie began nodding slowly, confirming her assessment. He moved away from her and positioned himself to face her. Then he picked up a stone and said, "You're braver than I am." He dropped his gaze to the dirt and squatted, digging random lines in the hard earth. "You bared the most tender parts of your heart and soul to me, and I should have been brave enough to do the same. Instead, I told you the basic details behind my fall from grace and hopscotched over the worst of it. I really did plan to fill in the gaps. I promise. I just don't even know where to start."

"Just start over, from the beginning, and this time, tell me everything."

CHAPTER 18

*H*e'd shared his story many times after his arrest, first to his lawyer, then to his case manager, and then to his fellow residents at Sipapu when he was asked to face his past clearly and take responsibility for his choices. It had gotten easier to share with each telling when he believed he had nothing else to lose, but this time was different, the hardest telling of all, because he'd found something precious in Laramee, and she'd helped him reclaim a still-missing part of himself. The thought that she might hate him or leave, once she knew the truth, terrified him.

Jamie stood and paced. "Do you know that most kids get their first taste of alcohol from their own parents and that the average age of that first drink is around fourteen years old? That's the *average* age, which means a lot of kids get exposed even younger. The impact of alcohol on a young brain is so powerful and damaging. Children who become dependent on alcohol might not have, if that first drink had been consumed as an adult. My parents knew all that, and they never drank in our home or in front of Mike or me. Never. Not once did I even smell it on their breath. It was part of their vow to protect us, and we grew up with that example, that you didn't need to drink or get drunk to be social."

He scoffed at himself. "And then I turned fifteen and local college scouts were already coming to see me play football or wrestle. I was the number-one guy on the party guest list. Everyone wanted to be my friend, and I don't just mean my peers. Parents I didn't even know would come up to me and put their arms around me as if I was their pal. They'd host these 'team parties,' and 'unity dinners' to build 'team morale.'" He used air quotes to illustrate the irony of the names. "One night, beers were being passed around. I figured some seniors sneaked a few in, and I told myself to be cool, that it was no big deal...just the price of being a sophomore on varsity. And then a parent put his arm around me and shoved one in my hand. I was shocked at first, and I turned it down, and then they teased me." He stopped and threw his arms in the air. "Instead of being embarrassed that a kid had more sense than he had, he teased *me* for not accepting an illegal drink from *his* hand."

Jamie's fists curled in frustration. Every time he revisited the moment of his first drink, he saw the adult who put the first can in his hand. The fact that an adult who should have been a mentor was an enabler still burned him, and he wondered if that parent ever knew the destructive spiral his irresponsibility set in motion. "The seniors egged me on, and I figured, 'hey, it's a parent offering the drink, so it must not be as big a deal as my folks made it out to be,' and I drank it."

He looked at Laramee to see how she was processing all this. He couldn't read her reaction, so he went on. "After that, I was offered beer at every party, but here's the worst part. I started going to parties to *get* booze. Sometimes there were coolers filled with cans, and sometimes there were kegs, and some parents who really wanted to be cool brought out shots and weed for their 'special guests.'"

"Didn't your parents or Mike notice?"

"Mike was at college by then, and my parents trusted me so completely that the idea that I would get drunk at fifteen never crossed their mind. And then things started to go downhill. A girl was throwing a party, and a bunch of us jumped in her mother's new car. We took turns driving, and one kid wrecked it into a brick mailbox holder."

Laramee uttered, "Oh, no," and Jamie stood and paced to get some space as he continued.

He pointed to the scar on his chin and said, "That's where I got this. "The police came. We were all tested, and we all failed. But one of the kids' fathers was an attorney, and he convinced the judge that we were good kids with college scholarships on the line. He pulled strings and got us off on probation with some community service. I can still see the look of disappointment on my father's face, but my mother's tears...that nearly broke me, and I begged their forgiveness and promised I'd never drink again."

"Did you keep that promise?"

"No. Because at that point, I didn't just *want* another buzz or high, I *needed* it, and drugs and alcohol were readily available. My parents controlled every minute of my life after school and on weekends, but they couldn't control what I did or drank at school or practice. I got really good at covering the smell on my breath by gargling with alcohol-based mouthwash or eating peanut butter or mints. My coach shamed my teammates for not having my courage to play through the pain. I wasn't courageous. I couldn't even *feel* the pain."

"Oh, Jamie. How did you stop?"

"I wish I'd had the sense or the will to stop, but I didn't. Not until I hit rock bottom."

He closed his eyes, but he could not stop the devastating images of that evening from returning. "We were doing shots and weed behind the school before a wrestling match. There were five of us, and one of the guys talked trash to a visiting player, luring him over before the game, but they went crazy on this kid. They jumped him and beat him so bad. I freaked and tried to pull them off him and then they turned on me. Someone called a security guard who called the police, and we were all arrested and charged with conspiracy and attempted homicide."

"Laramee folded over and hid her face in her hands. "Are you serious? Was he okay?" she cried.

Jamie fell to his knees in front of her. "Eventually, but he needed surgery to repair damage to his face and eye." Jamie felt the knot grow in his throat again, and he couldn't speak for several seconds. "We were big, strong athletes with four DUIs between us, less than stellar grades, and reputations for being more physical than needed to get the job done in sports. The prosecutor wanted to make an example of us by charging us as adults. Two of the guys were seniors. They were definitely looking at jail time. The rest of our futures were up in the air."

"What happened?"

Jamie rose to his feet. "The injured kid testified that I was the person who tried to stop the assault, but the judge wasn't impressed. Why should he be? I had an arrest record for underage drinking, a DUI, a mark for driving a car without a license, and now this. The DA was talking about pulling that car wreck back and adding it to my list of sins, calling it grand theft auto because the owner of the car didn't give us permission to take it. I thought my parents might literally die right there in the courtroom. I don't know what my defense attorney saw in me, but he spent every last cent of whatever goodwill he'd accumulated with the judge and pled with him to place me in a treatment program called Sipapu, a hardcore, bootcamp-type work program where they throw you into the desert for months. The judge glared at him for suggesting such a thing, and my attorney pleaded for me again. I don't know why I got that break, but the judge allowed it. The defense attorney's faith in me, and being sent to Sipapu, are miracles I give thanks for every day."

He looked at Laramee to assess how she was handling the ugly details of his past, but her head was tipped and he couldn't see her eyes. He tried to resurrect a little of his character by adding, "My attorney believed that in my core, I was a good person."

Laramee lifted her head. Her brow wrinkled as she studied him, and he died inside because he couldn't tell what she was thinking.

"I've tried to honor his trust in me by becoming that man, but the start was rough. We spent a few days in a clinic as gray and cold as a prison. It was manned by counselors and nurses who looked like they'd just as soon eat you as help you. We dried out there and determined the pecking order of our group."

"How did you do that?"

Jamie pointed to his crooked nose and the scars on his forehead and right cheek.

"The leaders let you fight?"

"No. They broke fights up quickly, but things escalate fast when you bunk twelve desperate, detoxing teens together. The counselors explained all the risks to my family up front. A few cuts and bruises were infinitely better than doing time. We thought those first few days were rough, but we didn't know what rough was until we reached Sipapu. We drove all night, and they dropped us off on a pile of nothing in the middle of a barren desert the next morning. All we had was a simple pack that had a few ounces of water, a protein bar, a change of clothes, and a spoon. There was no fight left in us because we'd never been so hot or so afraid. No one said anything to us. The driver just dropped us off and drove the bus away. An old Indian guy appeared off in the desert. He started walking, and we just followed because we didn't know what else to do."

Genuine interest seemed to replace Laramee's earlier disappointment.

"He led us to the base of a bluff and pointed to a tiny patch of shade. Then he walked to a crack between two rock walls and drank from a trickle of water falling there. We became grateful for these seemingly small things—a patch of shade and a trickle of water."

After being silent, Laramee breathed out a long breath. Jamie didn't know if it was a sigh of empathy or just pent-up stress from hearing his story.

"I hated everyone and every minute for the first two weeks, and I made sure they all knew it. That was until I started worrying that they really would let me die in the dirt if I didn't get with the program and pull my weight. We tended a garden basically grown in sand, we hauled our water, cooked our food, cleaned the sand floor of our 'home' as if it were a Persian rug. They raised horses nearby, but we were in charge of hauling water and feed for them and for keeping the fences strong and straight. We attended school in the blazing sun, and we walked or rode out to the mountains to dig and study and collect rocks because they wanted us to stay busy. After a while, we'd be so tired and sore that we wished they'd just bury us there in a rock pit. We began and ended every day with tough love stories and confessionals and firesides, and bit by bit, I began to tolerate the place and the routine, and then I liked it, and then, one day, I realized I also liked myself again."

"How long were you there?"

"Three months. And when my time there was over, I didn't want to leave because the place...that brutal place, felt safer to me than returning home to the life I failed in."

"I know that fear. How did you do when you got home?"

"All right. My parents' entire lives had been upended. They sold our home and moved across town so I could start with a fresh slate at a small private school. They didn't try to hide the fact that they didn't trust me. No sports. No clubs. I was tested every week, and I stayed clean and sober. I worked with my dad after school and during my senior summer, and every other minute I was at home, school, AA meetings, or within line of sight of a family member. I was seventeen, and I'd blown the bright future in front of me. My college years were spent commuting to state college instead of claiming my dream of being a big hero at a top university."

He laughed sadly and dropped back onto his seat. "But my college summers were spent as a counselor at Sipapu." He closed his eyes, savoring the memories. "I loved watching those rough, angry kids turn their lives around. The harsh conditions always took me back to my first experience there, steeling my will to never lose control of myself again."

The seriousness of Laramee's expression worried him, and he tried to lighten the mood with a joke. "Now you know why I was so patient with you at The Alpine. You tested me, all right." He extended his hand to her, but there was a significant delay before she took it, and when she stood, there was a noticeable stiffness to her posture that kept her from leaning into him. He needed her to see the man he had become, not who he once was.

"Being here with you these past few days has pushed me and so many of my buttons—frustration, fatigue." He looked deep into her eyes. "Also desire and caring. It's been good for me to be challenged in new ways. I've felt like the man I was at Sipapu. Strong, capable, in control, until—"

"Your family showed up."

"You saw it."

"You thought they were checking on you, didn't you?"

"I know the price they paid to support me through all that, the least of which is that I humiliated them and broke their hearts. And I cost them a small fortune in legal fees, fines, and reparations to that boy. They had to move, they lost friends, and their standing in business and in the community suffered. I've blamed them for suffocating me and for continuing to see me as I was, instead of giving me the grace to be who I've become. I hated to have you see that exchange between us, and then something clicked inside me, and I realized that I needed to stand up and push back a little. To ask them to treat me as they would any redeemed soul. To show me the forgiveness they said they'd given me. I felt things level out between us, as if they understood what I was asking for—what God had already granted me. They accepted me as an equal."

"That's all I've wanted as well."

"Thank you."

But Laramee's brow pinched, as if he hadn't understood her at all, and then she turned her head away from him and stood. Jamie soon realized she wasn't advocating for him. She was advocating for herself.

"You're upset. What are you thinking?"

"You wouldn't like it."

The words pierced him, but the cold tone left him staggering inside, assuming a full retreat was coming. "If it's how you feel, I want to know."

"I told you *everything*. My most painful things, but you didn't trust me with your story."

He bit his bottom lip and absorbed her anger. "I'm trusting you now."

"I fell apart in your arms and completely opened up my soul to you, and you kept all this locked inside until today, on what might be the last day we're together?"

"I'm sorry. I was afraid of this very outcome. That you would look at me differently."

Laramee's phone rang, but she ignored it. "I'm not upset because of what you *did*. You were a kid. I'm upset because of *why* you didn't tell me. You've done the exact same thing to me you accuse your family of doing to you. I've felt small around you and grateful that someone like you would be kind to some loser like me, and instead of being honest and leveling things out between us, you maintained the high ground and kept silent about your own mistakes. And then you tell me you stayed quiet because you were afraid I couldn't handle your news, as if I lack the character to see you for who you are. *That's* what offends me."

Laramee's phone rang again, followed by a text. She looked down at the screen and shrank. "Sutton's here. He's looking for me."

"Let him wait," Jamie growled. "He doesn't own you."

Laramee's eyes flashed as if to remind him that he had no claim on her either.

"Tell me how I can fix this," he asked.

Another text notification buzzed her phone and Laramee began gathering up the lunch supplies.

"Please," he asked. "Don't rush off. I don't want us to leave things like this."

"I guess you'll just have to *trust me* to figure my way through it all, won't you?"

Jamie helped pack the last few items into Laramee's saddlebags, and when he finished he took her hand and begged for a minute more of her time.

"Not now, Jamie. I can't spin dreams and pretend with you anymore." She mounted Patches, even as Jamie tried to grab her reins.

"Pretend? Is that all this was to you?"

Her lips trembled as she said, "I was the only one who was completely honest, remember? So, tell me. What was all this to *you*?"

Jamie stared at her, dumbfounded. He wished they could take the horses and ride higher and higher into the mountains and never face the storm brewing below, but he was tired of running and hiding. "I need you to know two things before you ride back to the ranch. One, I care deeply for you, Laramee. Your happiness is the most important thing to me. If Sutton is the man you see when you close your eyes at night—the man you picture building your world with—then choose him, and I'll clap and cheer at your wedding. But if you want to explore what's between us, please leave the door open a little, and let's see where this might go."

Her eyes held fast to his, and her lip quivered as she asked, "Is that all you have to say to me?"

"No. And this might be the most important thing I have to tell you. Your father loves you, Laramee. Stubbornness and fear held his tongue. I blasted him for being so stupid and for wasting precious time with you, and then I've gone and done the exact same thing, and I'm so sorry. But no matter what happens between us, promise me you'll head straight in to see your father. He's waiting to talk to you, and it's good news. I promise you."

"You...you spoke with my father about me?"

"Yes. He has so much to tell you."

Tears fell and she brushed them away. "Please tell me everything is all going to be all right."

"Everything is going to work out just fine...for you and your parents. And whatever is best will happen between us. I promise."

CHAPTER 19

*P*rickles rose on Laramee's arms. Jamie's eyes were shining, and when she looked into them, she believed his promise, every bit of it, and armed with that hope, she kicked Patches and flew home with Jamie and Caruso thundering behind her.

When she arrived in the yard, she saw a fury in Sutton that sent a chill up her spine. His eyes were fixed on Jamie as he said, "Head up to the house, Laramee. Your folks are waiting for you."

She stiffened over the way Sutton delivered his news, more as an order than an invitation. She looked back at Jamie, and had it not been for his encouraging nod and his report of a happy reunion awaiting her, she would have pushed back against Sutton's commands. Instead, she tied Patches's lead to the fence and hurried up to the house.

Her mother was waiting for her in the doorway with a smile that erased years of sorrow lines from her middle-aged face. She hugged Laramee tight and said, "I've needed that for so long."

Her mother's love-filled eyes shifted between Laramee and the tension happening by the corral. "Sutton's in a lather. I've never seen him like this."

Laramee·looked back, worried at the way Sutton was approaching Jamie before Caruso even came to a stop.

"Come inside, Laramee. They're reasonable men. They'll work it out."

Laramee looked back at the men and wished she could be as sure as her mother and Jamie that everything would work out, but at the moment, the pull of home and forgiveness was too strong.

"Where's Dad?" she asked.

Her mom's smile was so broad it nearly crinkled her eyes closed. She tipped her head toward the door that led to the deck. "He's out back with a hot funnel cake. He had me wait to fry it until he saw you headed home on Patches."

Funnel cakes were a portal to the days before Tyler died, when her father would buy a few from the last vendor open and the three of them would eat the deep-fried batter sprinkled with powdered sugar in the truck on the way home from a rodeo. The thought that he remembered how much those cakes meant to her caused her hands to tingle.

She headed out the door and found him in his chair, cradling the cakes in his lap. His face lit up like old times as he held the treat forward. "I've owed you one of these for a long time, Lar. I hear I've dumped all my guilt onto your shoulders. I'm told that's why you left. I'm so sorry, Girl. Can you forgive an old fool who loves you?"

Laramee fell into his open arm and felt it tighten around her. Jamie had gotten this news right. It was good. Very good. And she did believe that everything was going to work out just fine.

As much as Jamie hated to admit it, Sutton's fury sent waves of fear through him. He'd fought with his brother, tussled with friends, been slammed into a wrestling mat, and taken hits on the football field, but the highest price those encounters cost were a few bruises and a bloody nose. Sutton was in a rage, and the win he wanted was much more than a number on a scoreboard or bragging rights. He wanted to eliminate his competition for Laramee.

Jamie guided Caruso, the temperamental gelding, through the corral gate and watched Laramee until she was safely inside with her folks. It was now time to face Sutton, who slowly moved away from his vehicle and toward Jamie and the horse.

"For the record, nothing happens in this valley without me knowing about it. The Uber Eats guy you paid $500 to deliver the flowers and that gourmet dinner for two from Denver couldn't find the place on a map so he called the sheriff's office for directions. Naïve me…" He chuckled an ominous laugh. "Believing you when you said your primary concern was Laramee's happiness. But here you are, throwing money around at Laramee faster than most people around here can earn it. And then I drove in and saw the Stone's old film projector and makeshift movie screen set up out back with two chairs, and I knew you weren't just trying to make her happy. You're trying to break us up and turn her head."

"What I told you in the beginning was true. I had no interest in Laramee when I arrived, and she had zero interest in me. Things just changed."

"Liar!"

Sutton's shout set Caruso prancing nervously. Jamie forced himself to stay calm, but the tension he felt transmitted through his legs to Caruso, upsetting the animal further.

"Listen to me. Really listen," he pled. "Laramee isn't the same woman who left here years ago. She doesn't even know who she is anymore, or what she wants. If we both care about her, we each need to give her the time and space to figure that out."

"You've confused her. She's never cared about flowers or fancy dining or silly dates. You act like you know her so well, but you don't know anything about who she really is or what she wants."

"The real shame is that *you* don't."

"I've got years invested in loving Laramee and this family. You're crazy if you think I'm going to let you waltz in here and take her away from me."

"Listen to yourself. You can't *invest* in a woman and assume you're owed a payout. She doesn't owe you anything except her thanks."

Fire flew from Sutton's eyes. "She thinks you're a gentleman. You're not. You're a snake."

Jamie was glad he was on Caruso, four feet above the ground where Sutton couldn't land a good punch. "Just think about what I'm saying. You met Laramee when she was grieving and trying to hold this place together. Of course, she wasn't thinking about fun and dates and her needs. But think back to who she was before Tyler died. What were that young woman's dreams, Sutton? She's got new dreams too, but she won't let herself explore them because of you."

"No. This is all because of you, but we're going to fix that today." Sutton smiled an threatening grin. "Climb down off that horse, pack your things, and get off this ranch before Laramee comes out of that house. I know about your past convictions for drunk driving and possession."

Jamie's anger flared. "How did you learn all that? I was a kid. Those records are sealed."

"Someone owed me a favor."

"You broke the law!"

"I *bent* the law, and I'd do it again to protect Laramee. I also know you were nearly charged as an adult for battery, and I bet Laramee will run you off this ranch herself when she finds that out."

The blood drained from Jamie's face and then rushed back in a furious torrent. Caruso felt his rider's mood change, and the horse pranced nervously and snorted his displeasure while Jamie did his best to rein him in.

"I actually respected you, Sutton, and all you've done for Laramee, but the man I see right now isn't the man Laramee described. All I see is a bully and a tyrant. I already told Laramee the truth about me, except for one thing. I held off telling her exactly how I feel about her, out of respect for you. But not anymore. I'm falling in love with her, and I'm not going anywhere if she'll have me."

"Don't say that! Get off this ranch. I want you to leave now."

Sutton rushed through the corral gate, slamming it in anger as he flew toward Jamie and Caruso with his hands extended as if ready to pull Jamie off the horse. Caruso reared on his hind legs and stepped sideways, drawing closer to the fence. Jamie leaned into Caruso's neck, tightening his legs against the horse as he struggled to hold the reins. From the corner of his eye, he saw a flash of red in the distance, just before Caruso landed back on all fours and reared wildly again. Panic registered on Sutton's face as he scrambled for the reins to calm Caruso, but Jamie already felt himself slipping. He glanced at the ground to find a safe landing spot, but the fence was to his left, so he leaned right, catching a glance of open dirt and a glimpse of Laramee running his way from the house screaming, "Jamie!"

The horse twisted again, whipping Jamie around and off the saddle. All he saw was wood before his head exploded in pain and light. The pain…the pain…like swimming through nails that pierced his head and eyes and neck. He was vaguely aware of voices calling his name and of hands on him, but his primary fight was against the frightening relief the blackness offered.

One voice brought images to his mind, vast fields of brown brush and pictures formed by mountain peaks. He remembered *The Old Grey Mule* and a woman's laughter, and he saw his sienna image sitting by the falls, sketched on paper as it faded into white.

&

*H*ums and beeps. Warm hands. So many voices. Worried familiar voices. Soft logical voices. More hands, and voices calling, "Jamie…Jamie…Jamie."

A smiling face hovering above him in blue scrubs said, "Hello, Jamie. I'll tell your family you're awake. They're in the family waiting area, napping. Only two guests are allowed at a time. I'll send your folks in first." She made clicks on her device and then rose and moved to the door.

He recognized his parents, who arrived and entered. His mother took his left hand, his father, his right. Tears were in their eyes as they smiled and chattered, "I love you." Peace flowed through him as they stroked his hair and patted his shoulder and cheek. When he closed his eyes he saw a panorama of a hundred images of windswept prairie and a skinny woman with long brown waves.

"Where's Laramee?" he asked, but his father quickly hushed him, casting a quick, worried glance toward the doorway. "We'll talk about all that later, okay?" Instead, he began sharing the details of the accident and his injuries, barely mentioning Laramee in the tale. When he finished, Jamie asked about Laramee again and his father replied, "For now, just rest."

Doctors and nurses scurried in and out, wearing contented smiles and offering congratulations on the positive turn in his recovery.

"How would you like us to treat your pain?" asked a nurse. "Your parents told us you're in recovery with over ten years sobriety. They asked us to treat your pain without reviving your craving for the drugs. We opted to use local anesthetics until you could speak for yourself."

He was grateful for the news and thought how blessed he was to have wise parents. "The risks?"

"Local anesthetics pose the least risk of your cravings returning for alcohol and other substances. We can keep doing what we already are if you're comfortable."

"I'd rather bear the pain than get hooked on oxy or worse."

"Okay. It's your call." The medical staff made note of his wishes and whisked him out for more tests. Through all the tubes, and in the lights, he saw Laramee.

Mike was waiting in his room when he returned. He was dressed in a wrinkled suit and tie as if he'd rushed to the hospital straight from the board room. Jamie knew that was probably the case. He leaned over Jamie and pressed his forehead to Jamie's thickly bandaged one. "So glad to have you back, brother."

Jamie was sweating from the pain. "Glad to be back...I think."

"Despite your being the world's worst cowboy, I give you an A for effort."

"Gee...thanks," Jamie said in response.

"I'm heading back now that we know you're out of the woods. Someone in this family has to work." He shot Jamie a wink. "Before I go, I wanted you to know we placed the contract in Sterling Stone's hands this morning. He said he'd give the offer some thought but judging from the sparkle in that rancher's eye when he saw the figures, I suspect he'll accept it gladly."

The effort required to formulate a complete thought and speak was too great, so Jamie offered a thumbs-up in reply.

"Harrison Brockbank thinks the company will be mining turquoise there for a long time, buddy, and it is beautiful stone. Sterling Stone was so especially pleased to hear that The Silver Buckle Mining Corporation is known for being very respectful of the land."

Jamie realized that Mike was holding his other hand, so he squeezed it. "Details."

"Don't worry. We've included a provision to give the Stones a share in all future profits."

That was the news he most wanted to hear, and upon hearing it, he slipped back into sleep.

He lost track of the passage of time. Minutes and hours, nights and days passed without much notice. The morning sun poured through his window, and he found himself in a new room with fewer machines and less beeps and hums. His parents were asleep on two lounge chairs on his right. Once again, guilt swept over him for putting them through another crisis, but this one wasn't his doing...or was it? He recalled what he could of the moments before his fall and realized he had egged Sutton on. He laid his arm across his eyes, hoping for sleep to take him again.

His mother woke him up by stroking his hair and calling his name. "Jamie, your tray is here. You need to eat, son."

He swam through the pain and found his headache less grievous and his shoulder pain more tolerable at rest now, so he tried to stay awake. Eating with his left hand was a trip, but he preferred it to being fed by his mother. Conversation ran thin, and they were all grateful for the television in the room, but when a topic worth discussing did come up it always circled back to Laramee.

"Has she been in, Dad?" he asked.

"Yes. Twice. With her father. Sterling asked about you. He seemed like a different man today. It might please you to know that Laramee was holding his hand when they left. I suspect that you not only helped save that family's livelihood, but you also somehow saved the family itself."

The mention of Laramee's name sent Jamie scurrying to sit more upright. "Why didn't you wake me?"

"We tried, but not very hard, I admit. A very contrite Sutton was also here."

"Was he here or was he here *with* her?"

"I wasn't sure, and I didn't know if the news was going to be something you'd want to hear."

Jamie fell back into the bed. "Do you think they're engaged?"

"I didn't see a ring, but he was circling around her like a lion guarding his den. He's not going away, but I think he's terrified you're going to bring charges against him, so if you want to play it that way, I think you have some leverage to ask him to back off."

Jamie sank back into the mattress. "I would never treat Laramee like a negotiation. I'll respect her choice. Either way, I don't blame Sutton for my fall. I should never have ridden Caruso."

"For what it's worth," his mother said, "I'm proud of you for how you're handling all this. Sutton may have saved your life. Laramee said you two were arguing and the horse reared and then you fell and hit the fence. Luckily, your shoulder took the brunt of the fall, but your head took a nasty hit too. That's the reason you have that gash in back. Sutton jumped into action. He stabilized your neck and back and applied pressure to your wound during that long drive here. You could have died if he hadn't been there."

Jamie wanted to add that he also wouldn't have fallen if Sutton hadn't been there, but he didn't. "So, he was a hero again." The last thing Jamie wanted was to be beholdin' to Sutton. "It's my own fault if Laramee accepts his proposal. I waited to tell her about my past and I've made a mess of things."

His mother wriggled her head in partial agreement. "You may not believe we old folks can remember what it was like to first fall in love, but we do, and it was messy for us as well."

The news shocked Jamie. "You two?"

She chuckled and looked at her husband. "I was quite young, and I needed some convincing."

Jamie looked at his father. "What did you say to win her over, Dad?"

William looked back at his wife. "What *did* I say to win you over?"

She rolled her eyes. "See? Love is still not as easy as it seems. It wasn't so much what he said as what he did. He trusted me to figure out my own mind, but he made sure I always knew he was there, not like a stalker, but offering me little glimpses into the man he was, and the life we could share."

His father shook his head. "I'm afraid I did better for myself than I did for you."

"You're not responsible for this mess with Laramee."

"Maybe not, but I may have initiated that random meeting between you and Victoria. I thought she'd be good for you. She was successful, pretty, she didn't drink. I guess I didn't do a very good job at playing matchmaker."

"You did great, Dad. Victoria wasn't my perfect match, but I don't regret the time I shared with her."

"Thank you for relieving my guilt on that. You changed to fit her. I do regret that. We wish we could tell our children who would be great for them and spare them all the heartache of figuring things out for themselves."

His mother took his hand. "The only ones who can make those choices are the ones who'll have to live with the consequences of their decisions. I will give you one bit of advice, though. No matter who you choose to pursue, don't sit back and *hope* love finds a way. Sometimes, we must *open* a way for love to work."

Jamie gave that idea some thought.

His father stood. "So, if all goes well, you're going to be released tomorrow. Laramee and her father drove your Range Rover up here this last trip. We could all drive it home. How does that sound?"

"Sounds good."

"All right then."

"Dad, what do the Brockbanks plan to do with the Stone's ranch?"

William leaned back and sighed. "They bought it for the turquoise. The land can't support development. Once the Stones agreed to let the turquoise be mined the land became nothing more than a means to an end."

"And Laramee understands that?"

"Yes. I made sure of it when she stopped by the other day. In fact, she was practically luminous with joy when she told your mom and me that Sterling is giving both her and her brother their share of the selling price now so they can launch their own dreams."

"What if I had an idea for that land. Would you be willing to let me propose a project to the Brockbanks?"

"Of course. What did you have in mind?"

"Let me give it some thought tonight. We can talk about it on the long ride home."

His father and mother stood. "We'll see you tomorrow," his mother said as she hugged him goodbye."

His father squeezed his hand. "We'll be here around noon. I can't wait to get us all back home."

After they were gone, Jamie found a little notepad and pen in his utility table. He started making a list of all the tasks he'd need to attend to in order to get his proposal ready for the board. This was one thing he could do for Laramee, no matter who she chose to love.

The door squeaked. Jamie opened one eye and saw Sutton standing in the doorway, looking sheepish, like the mild-mannered person Jamie had first met. He had his hat in one hand, and he rubbed the other across his mouth and coughed to clear his throat. When he had collected himself, he said, "I'm sorry about the other day."

Jamie still found it hard to dislike the guy. "I hear you may have saved my life."

Sutton clasped his hands in front and nodded. "Yeah, well...I sort of caused the whole thing. How's your pain?"

"Not great, but I'm managing."

"Are they giving you the good stuff?"

"No." The question caused Jamie's defenses to rise.

"That makes sense considering your past. And I'm sorry for digging into your juvenile record. I'm normally not that guy. I love being a cop and helping people. I let this jealousy thing eat at me until I lost my way for a while. It was a terrible thing to do, and I'm sorry."

"Thank you for saying that."

"Did you ever tell her you love her?"

Jamie ran every missed opportunity through his mind and bit his lip. "Not in so many words."

"Do you ever ask yourself why?"

"Did you really come here to play twenty questions? What do you want, Sutton?"

Sutton looked down and watched as he moved his hands around the brim of his hat. After a few moments, he looked up and said, "I've thought a lot about what you said...about how our first priority should be Laramee's happiness. Do you still believe that?"

"Of course, I do."

"Have you considered that perhaps that's why you couldn't admit you love her."

Jamie sat up straighter in the bed. "What are you talking about?"

"I should never have read your juvenile record, but now that I have, I can't unsee it, you know? And seriously, you've got to recognize that you're kind of a high-risk guy. Who's to say you won't fall off the wagon again or go on a bender or leave her someday."

Jamie bolted forward and cried out as a stabbing pain bit into his shoulder and neck. "I'm not that person anymore."

"Hopefully not, but then, why aren't you taking painkillers? You don't trust yourself, do you?"

The tension in Jamie's jaws made his teeth hurt, but he couldn't think of a convincing rebuttal to shut Sutton's inquisition down.

"I'm glad you're doing well," Sutton said. "I really am. I drove up here with Laramee. She thinks I'm in the ER talking to my paramedic friends while she's in the gift shop choosing a card for you, but I had to have a word with you before you see her and ask you to consider whether you are the best person to make her happy. I don't doubt that you love her but ask yourself if there's the slightest chance you could relapse and break her heart. I think you're a good man, Jamie, but if you're not absolutely certain about the answer to that question, you should probably bow out, don't you think?"

There was a smug deliberateness to the way Sutton positioned his hat back on his head. Gone was that earlier humility he showed when he arrived. This man was all business, and his business was making Jamie feel unworthy of Laramee.

Jamie saw Laramee before she saw him. She was heading down the hall, focused on checking room numbers, and when she entered the room, Sutton broke into a broad, friendly smile and tapped Jamie on the foot. "Great talking to you, Jamie. I'll leave so you and Laramee have a little time to say goodbye."

Laramee appeared to buy his deceptive generosity. She smiled proudly at him and touched his arm as she said, "Thank you, Sutton."

"Of course. I'll meet you downstairs in the lobby in...say...thirty minutes?"

"That'll be perfect. Thanks."

Could Laramee not see past Sutton's performance? Jamie asked himself. The answer was evidently not, because the beaming smile she showed to Sutton now beamed on Jamie without any interruption. "The nurse said it was okay for me to pop in."

"Of course, it is," Jamie said, noticing that his hands were shaking. She was dressed in a blue denim skirt and her pink blouse, and her hair was elegantly swept up in a bun. "Thanks for coming all this way."

"I've been here before, but you were out the entire time. I had an errand in the city today anyway, but I wanted to stop by and tell you my father accepted the Brockbank's offer. I'll stop by the library and fax our confirmation over before we mail the signed contract."

Jamie's eyes slipped to her ringless hand before locking with hers. A thousand silent words passed between them. He let his eyes shift to hers again before asking, "Are you and Sutton..."

"No," she filled in quickly, rubbing her fingers. "But he asked me out to lunch, and I couldn't say no." The words hung there like a feather on a breeze as she drilled her gaze into Jamie like a laser. "But we never know where one special date can lead."

"I guess we don't."

The obscure comments summed up his final missed opportunity to tell Laramee he loved her, and he replayed that day over and over—the plans he'd made for their special date together and all the unanswered questions left hanging between them. Still, her comment opened a challenge, begging him to put up or shut up.

"I hear you're already a wealthy heiress."

"I guess I already am to some extent. My parents set aside a million dollars each for Max and me."

"That's wonderful," he said though he hated the idea of her new wealth and the life she and Sutton could now launch with it. "What do you plan to do with your share?" He hoped she wasn't about to announce that she and Sutton were planning to use it to buy a ranch of their own.

"I've already spent it."

"On what?" he asked in a panic.

"Well...I haven't actually spent it, but I've got a plan for how I want to spend it." She pulled the chair closer to his bedside. "First, I need to thank you. You've already done so much for me. I know you're the one who cleared the way for my father and me to finally talk. Thank you for doing that. He told me about his own guilt, and he took all that blame and guilt I've been carrying around away from me."

He took her hand. "Good. I'm so glad for both of you."

"You gave me back my father, and in so many ways, you've given me back my own life too. That's why I feel so bad asking you for another favor."

His voice grew husky. "You can ask anything of me. You know that."

The mood turned intimate and tender. "I saw you fall," she began. "I ran over and you were lying in a pool of blood, and once again, I felt utterly helpless."

"I hear Sutton saved me."

"It was only right since he was the reason Caruso threw you." Laramee's voice was low, and she paused often as if saying the words still pained her. "I thought...I thought you were gone, and just like Tyler...and little Knox...I could do nothing. I just stood...and watched...and hurt. I was tired of feeling helpless and weak, so I spoke with my parents, and they support my decision."

He leaned in toward her, anxious to hear what this decision was about. "What did you do, Laramee?"

"I can't afford to build a trauma center, but with my inheritance, I can afford to get people to one faster. I put a deposit on a helicopter, and I put a pilot on retainer with the stipulation that he live in my parents' house. That is, if you can convince the Brockbanks to sell me my family home and a small plot of land for us to build a hangar."

Her selfless generosity left him in awe, and yet it seemed so typical of Laramee. "I'm sure they'll agree to that. In fact, I feel sure they'll gift the house and land to you for such a noble cause."

Her face melted in gratitude. "Thank you, Jamie. All those feelings of failure and helplessness were the last bits of guilt I was holding on to, and this plan erases them. I can finally let them go."

She stood and pulled a manilla envelope from her purse. "I also wanted to give this to you, just in case you ever forget who you are again."

Inside was the sketch she'd made of him back at the ranch.

His throat felt thick, and his eyes began to sting. She really was saying goodbye. He didn't trust his faltering voice to speak, so he simply nodded and mouthed the words, "Thank you. Laramee, I should have said this earlier, but I—"

He wanted so much to tell her he loved her, but Sutton's words stole his own. He'd effectively neutered Jamie's self-worth in minutes, leaving him wondering whether he was as Sutton had said—a high-risk man that could destroy Laramee's happiness. Sutton had played both the hero and Devil cards, ingratiating himself yet again to Laramee while also cutting Jamie's legs out from under him. All he needed now was to wait downstairs to collect Laramee—his prize for yet another heroic rescue.

Laramee stood by the edge of his bed. "Was there something you wanted to tell me?"

She smelled like lavender, and her eyes were filled with expectation. Jamie wanted to pull her to him for a kiss and tell her the things he'd left unsaid up on the ridge, but Sutton had done his work well, sowing doubts about Jamie's steadiness and worth, and whether he was the better man for Laramee. "I'm getting discharged tomorrow."

"Oh. So, I hear. I caught up with your father in the lobby."

Jamie thought that seemed odd since his father and mother supposedly left over an hour ago.

"What will you do next, now that the farm is sold?" He prayed Sutton's name wouldn't come up as her answer.

She took his hand and squeezed it. "Mom is already starting to pack. I guess I'll help with that for a few weeks and see what opportunities present themselves."

An awkward silence settled in. He wanted to fill that emptiness with promises and professions of love, to tell her about the grand dream he was working on, but all he could do was look away.

"Well..." She too dipped her gaze. "I guess I should be going. Thank you, Jamie, for everything. You'll never know how deeply you've impacted my life."

She bent over and kissed him. The kiss was soft and sweet, and it lingered far longer than a simple goodbye. Jamie wondered if she was waiting for him to say more, or if she was taunting him, but that would have been so unlike her.

She wiped a tear from her eye and pulled away, but Jamie held on to her hand until the distance grew too great. He felt utterly empty as their fingers slipped apart, and he fought to convince himself that he was a good man, a man who would make her happy. What had she said to him up on the ridge? *I trusted you...*Something changed between them after he shared his revelations. She didn't trust him anymore. He wasn't sure he could either, and whatever hope he'd clung to died in his heart.

She turned for the door and then turned back again. Jamie thought his heart would stop. His mouth was dry, and his throat felt tight as he asked, "Is there something else you wanted to say?"

"There is one other item." She sniffed and straightened. "It's the matter of a bet?"

Jamie remembered the deal they'd struck over whether he could last an entire week on the ranch. "I think a medical emergency releases me from my wager."

"Oh, no." She smiled through her tears and shook her head. "I don't remember any such contingencies being included in the plan."

Jamie struggled to sit. "Then I believe, Miss Stone, that I owe you two dozen ginger cookies."

"I believe you're right, Mr. Cannon, but what I'm more interested in knowing is what compensation you would have asked for if you had won. You said you'd expect a very good prize. What would it have been?"

Jamie remembered when they'd made the bet, and the way the light played off her eyes as he first realized how badly he wanted to kiss her. He'd made a game of teasing her, and the sweet memory cut him as it replayed in his mind.

"Well...the way I see it, you win either way. If I'm still here at the end of a full week, you've enjoyed seven days of free labor, and if I die or wear out, you get cookies. So, it seems to me that if I win, I should be able to claim a very good prize."

Laramee raised one eyebrow and rested her chin in her cupped hand. "Such as...?"

Jamie lowered his voice to a whisper and said, "I have an idea of what I want but give me a few days. I'm sure I'll be certain by the end of the week."

"It sounds suspicious."

"Good. It's my turn to drive you a little crazy."

"No hints?"

"Oh, I'm sure there'll be a few hints if you're perceptive."

He remembered every word and look and feeling surrounding that moment, and every one that happened after, and he knew exactly what prize he hoped to ask for—a chance to love her—but as Laramee stood in the doorway awaiting his reply, all he could now hear were Sutton's questions—

"You said our first priority should be Laramee's happiness. Do you still believe that?"

"Of course, I do."

"Have you considered that perhaps that's why you couldn't admit you love her?"

He wanted to push those concerns aside and tell Laramee what he wanted, that what he'd wanted from almost the first day they'd spent together was to be with her. To love her and be loved by her. To kiss her and make her happy every day for the rest of his life, but Sutton's other words stole his will—

"You don't trust yourself, do you...If there's even the slightest chance you

could relapse and break her heart, you should probably bow out, don't you think?"

Jamie didn't know how long he had been caught up in his own thoughts, but it was long enough for worry to seize Laramee's face. She took a step forward, calling out to him. "Jamie? Jamie?"

He pulled himself back into the moment, knowing what he had to do. "I'm sorry. I-I-I don't remember what I was going to ask from you if I won."

The coloring of her face paled, as if whatever final hope or expectation she had been clinging to simply drained from her. "Then I guess it doesn't matter after all." She smiled back at him as she opened the door. "You're a ruined man now, you know, Mr. Cannon. A man who loves pork and beans and canned chili."

"And you, Laramee. I love you," he whispered after she slipped through the doorway and away from him forever.

§♣

*L*aramee fought back tears as she left Jamie's room. A woman on the elevator rightfully assumed she'd suffered some terrible loss, and she placed her hand on Laramee's arm, saying "God Bless," before she exited at her floor. Laramee *had* suffered a terrible loss. She felt sure Jamie's love was hers before the accident, and now it was gone. She'd gotten flippant and angry on the ridge because Jamie had withheld his secrets from her for so long. His misstep hadn't changed how she felt. She was simply trying to make a point about being honest and open with her, but had she gone too far? Was that why he seemed so nervous and why he had withdrawn from her?

She thought about turning around and returning to Jamie's room, to apologize for being so foolish. To let him know that she loved and trusted him, but she argued herself out of it, knowing she'd die if she confessed her feelings, and he rejected her again.

She found Sutton leafing through a magazine in the lobby, but she turned down another hall, as planned, and headed for the cafeteria.

William Cannon was nursing a soda and watching the door. As soon as she walked to him, he stood and smiled.

"How'd it go?" he asked with wide hopeful eyes.

Laramee rushed to his table and sat, dropping her head into her hands. "We were both wrong, Mr. Cannon. Jamie doesn't love me."

"What? Are you certain?" William dropped into a chair, as shocked as Laramee. "He as much as told me so this afternoon."

"I gave him every opportunity to say something, but he didn't. It was awkward between us. It's never been that way."

William leaned into his chair. "When he and Victoria broke up the last time, I promised myself I'd never meddle in his love life again, but I was so certain this afternoon when I called you. I'm sorry, Laramee. I'm truly sorry."

CHAPTER 20

*E*arly April, 2023

*L*aramee added a garbage bag filled with random linens to the moving container and locked it for the night. It was after nine p.m., and all she wanted was a long hot bath. She took a final look at the homestead before going up to the house. She'd be back from time to time to visit the pilot she'd hired, but the ranch would never again be home.

She'd received an email from Mike, confirming that Jamie had struck the deal with the Brockbanks to allow the pilot to live in the family home. He promised to keep her apprised of the progress of the mining operation. Jamie negotiated the sale, but that agreement was struck when she and he were still living on daydreams. And then the accident occurred, and they each returned to their former lives. Since dealing with Jamie would cause her too much pain, she asked Mike to be her contact, and he'd agreed.

She looked at the old bunkhouse and realized cleaning it out was another item on the packing list. The building would serve as quarters for the mining crew, so games and puzzles and movies and books could stay. Only the personal items and the trash needed to be removed.

She sighed and carried two boxes down, one for things to keep and one for trash. She gave the bathroom and kitchen a quick scrub and tossed the food from the fridge in the trash box. The quarters where Jamie had stayed were empty except for furnishings. Laramee closed that door and moved to the women's side where she slept.

She'd grabbed her belongings the day after the accident. After a quick sweep, that room was also closed, and she moved on to the family room. Dread filled her as she opened the old cupboard that contained her rodeo pictures and pads of art paper filled with her sketches. She grabbed things and sorted them into two piles, stacking the memories in the "keep" box without looking at them. Those old dreams and memories would only stir more discontent, and that was the last thing she needed.

She decided to leave the empty drawing pads and art supplies for the miners as well, but not before checking everything to be sure she wasn't leaving used pages and dried out paint.

She riffled through the first tablet and declared it clean. The second and third ones also. But the fourth tablet held a love letter written in a hand she didn't recognize. She assumed at first that it had been written by a former client on the dude ranch, and she almost considered closing the tablet and avoiding the pain the tender words about love and being loved harrowed up. A sliver of her heart held on to the hope that it was written for her, and knowing she'd wonder and agonize over that forever, she read on.

You're hurting tonight, and I wasn't able to comfort you. We're both confused and a little lost right now. Why is it so hard to tell you I love you when loving you is so easy? I'm in and out. Up and down. I can't sort things out. So, I made five lists, trying to analyze us, but they didn't clear my mind, so now I'm going to write my thoughts out, hoping that seeing my feelings on paper will help me sort through my confusion.

I think you're partly to blame for my dilemma. I always thought the one selfish choice we get to make in this life should be who one chooses to love, but you've messed with my head and changed my heart on that point, Laramee..."

Laramee gasped. *Jamie wrote the letter for me! He loves me!*

You always think of others, seeing their needs and putting their concerns ahead of your own. You can't even give your heart to anyone without first deciding who needs it most. Loving you has made me more aware of this concept. I don't know if I agree, but I agree that if it's important to you, then I need to consider it too.

I don't know if it was you or this place or this strange time, or if it's possible to separate the three, but I will never be the same person after our time together. And neither will you, I suspect. You've helped me find the missing pieces of myself. You've made me want to be a builder of something more important than a portfolio. I love the land again and the joy of working up an honest sweat. You've restored good principles in me—to work until I'm ready to drop, and to lie under a cloud and stare at a sunset until it disappears. Thank you for that and so much more.

I love you, but who am I to tell you what your life should look like or who you should love? You deserve the sky and the earth and the moon. What do you want, Laramee Stone? Am I the better man? And...am I enough for you?

⌘

*L*aramee was exhausted and empty, making the task of packing seem even more monumental. There'd been no sleep after reading the letter. Jamie loved her, but he never said the words. Maybe he loved her as she loved Sutton, with a friendly, grateful, comfortable kind of love that never met the high bar of being *in* love. But what good was there in defining it now? Jamie never said the words, and he was gone. It was time for her to move on.

She stood in front of a three-inch stack of newsprint and a table filled with glassware. One hand held two sheets of paper and the other held a mug, and neither one was moving. Her eyes were set elsewhere, on the bunkhouse where she felt sure she had spent the most magical days of her life.

Cathy Stone walked over and placed a kiss on her daughter's cheek. "Thank you for helping me pack. You're welcome to take whatever you'd like to set up your own apartment, but don't feel you need to keep any of my old stuff."

Her mother's words felt like an intrusion, forcing reality into her memories of hours spent in that dilapidated old bunkhouse with Jamie. She missed the simple hours of sharing time together, like doing dishes and putting puzzles together with him. They laughed and joked over those ancient puzzles with so many pieces missing that the picture remained a mystery, even after the last available piece was placed. She missed cooking with him, more because of their honest talks than because of the food. She closed her eyes to recall the look on his face when she revealed the sketch she'd made of him. She never wanted to forget what he'd said about her talent—that she didn't just sketch people, she sketched who they were, as if sketching their souls. And then he'd said, *God is in your gift, and He is in you.* After that, forgiveness came, and her healing began.

The memory that left her eyes burning was of the day spent in Jamie's arms as he warmed her in front of the fireplace. It haunted her and left her feeling guilty because she couldn't pack it away like an old dish. It was part of her, a moment she would carry into any future she chose.

Her mother called to her again, and Laramee couldn't ignore her sweet voice. "I'm sorry. What?"

"You don't need to apologize for daydreaming." Cathy Stone laughed and hugged her girl.

"Are you happy, Mama?"

"So very happy, sweet girl."

"Tell me why."

"Well…" Cathy said as she dropped into a chair. "I feared we'd never actually get to retire, and here we are, heading to a retirement condo in Florida. Better yet, your father and I are speaking in a way we haven't in a long time, Laramee. About personal and important things. I've missed that, and now I have it again. And whatever years we have ahead of us will be gentle and sweet." She covered her mouth as a girlish giggle escaped. "I won't even know what to do with myself after so many years of mucking and feeding and tending things. But it's even more than all that. There's a saying that goes, 'You're only as happy as your least happy child.' I suppose I'm happy because good things are happening for each of my children. Max is using his inheritance to buy a house for his family close by on the Florida shore. And he dreams of us all coming down to vacation together. I just love the thought of all of my future grandchildren splashing and playing together. And you're spearheading this plan to make something good come from Tyler's death. I know that would make him happy. And you're following your dreams again. What more could I possibly want out of life?"

Laramee savored the feel of her mother's arms as they slid around her and pulled her close. A moment later, her mother was off to pack another room. Laramee tried to picture her mom's sweet vision of the future. With her folks settling in Florida, near where Max planned to settle, she could imagine trips south where they'd all be together. She imagined her future children splashing with Max's and the close family bonds they'd all build together.

She raised the volume on her phone's playback list and got to work in earnest, wrapping and packing her mother's dishes and loading boxes into the second moving POD. The inside of the POD was like an echo chamber, and as she slid and dropped boxes, arranging them as tightly as possible, she missed the sound of Sutton's car coming up the driveway. She had no idea how long he stood there before she turned and saw him, shrieking a little at the fright of seeing an unexpected man in the doorway.

"How's it going?" he asked as he leaned into the wall.

"We're making slow progress," she said with a forced smile as she spread her arms wide across the chaos overtaking the yard. "Mom has everything divided into three piles—throw away, giveaway, and anything she wants to cram into a two-thousand-square-foot condo."

Sutton huffed out a sad laugh. "Your father called. He asked me to take Shakespeare, Nugget, Caruso, and that old mare. They'll be a great addition to my hunting business. And I'll board Patches for you until you decide what you want to do next."

The finality of the move and the ripple effects on the animals hit Laramee hard. She tried not to cry knowing that Sutton's first reaction would be to comfort her, and that would just complicate the heck out of an already agonizing situation.

She was grateful he hadn't raised the topic of marriage again since the accident, but the anticipation of it being raised was almost as painful as declining would be.

"Thanks, Sutton. You're doing us a favor by taking them. We know they'll be somewhere where they'll be loved.

"That's all I ever wanted for *you*. For you to be somewhere *you* knew you were loved."

She stepped back and leaned into the POD, needing the support to face this conversation again. "I know that, and I'm grateful for your love and help, but I-I…"

"I figured all I had to do was get Cannon out of here and things would work out between us, and now he's gone but we're no better than we were when he was here."

She closed her eyes and said, "I'm sorry."

"I never noticed it before. Not until Cannon came. And then I couldn't stop seeing it, that light of love in your eyes when you looked at him, and I faced the realization that it never happens when you look at me."

She pulled a ragged breath and asked, "What do you want me to say?"

"There's nothing more you *can* say. I didn't want to accept it until it was too obvious to deny. I saw it when he fell off Caruso, but I told myself that was understandable. The guy was your hire, your friend, and he was hurt, so of course you'd worry and care for him. But it was unmistakable when we went to the hospital to see him. It was like electricity ran through you as soon as you stepped inside the hospital door. It hurt me so much that I didn't just leave the room, I left the floor so I wouldn't have to see your expression when you left his side, and still I hoped you'd finally choose me."

Her mouth fell open, but no sound escaped.

"I always knew you didn't love me as much as I loved you," he continued, "but I convinced myself that if I loved you enough, if I poured everything I was into our marriage, I could make you happy."

She moved to him, barely touching her hands to his chest. "You have made me happy."

He smiled, but there was no pleasure in it. Only sad acceptance. "Did you ever love me, Laramee? Not friendly, grateful appreciation. Did you ever really love me?"

She walked a carefully choreographed line between truth and deception, saying, "I do love you, Sutton." It came out like an apology.

He hung his head. "I know. You're just not *in love* with me." He stared at her for several seconds, weighing, measuring her answer. "Are you in love with Jamie Cannon?"

She felt as if her legs were failing her. "Please, Sutton. Please just take the animals and go." She wanted to drop onto the ground, curl into a ball, and cry out the last drop of love left in her broken heart.

"Are you here because he turned you away?"

The voice was caring but the words were too bitter to hear. Laramee turned on Sutton and threw them back at him. "Yes. He turned me away. I was an idiot to fall in love with a man in four days, but I did, and he turned me away. Is that what you wanted to hear? Does that make you happy?"

He dropped onto a packed box and lowered his chin to his chest. "I love you too much to enjoy watching you ache. It only adds to my guilt."

"What guilt? What are you saying?"

"Jamie Cannon loves you, Laramee."

Chills coursed through her at the hope the words brought. "How do you know that? Did he tell you he loves me?"

"Yes."

"When?"

"That last day in the hospital. We struck a deal of sorts when he first arrived. I wanted you, and he wanted you to be happy, no matter what that meant. I used that against him...and against you."

Laramee moved to him and pushed him upright until he was facing her. "What are you talking about?"

"I did something shameful. I convinced myself that it was the right thing to do, the best thing for you and for me, but—"

"What did you do, Sutton?"

"I turned his love for you against him. I opened his sealed juvenile record and read about his past drug and alcohol abuse. The last time we went to the hospital, I went to his room while you were buying him a card. I told him he was a high-risk suitor. That statistically, he could revert back to his old addictions, and that if he loved you and wanted you to be happy, he'd let you go and not risk ruining your life."

Laramee pressed her hands to her head as the ugly pieces came together, explaining why Jamie had withdrawn from her. His letter made so much sense now. He wanted what was best for her, even if it meant giving her up. She turned on Sutton. "How dare you?"

He stood, and the rest of the story spilled out in a wild ramble. "I know how bad it sounds. I was desperate. I convinced myself that I could make you happy. That you'd eventually love me, but I finally realized that I was cheating all three of us out of ever having what you two had already found."

"Jamie loves me."

"Yes. Now you've got to find a way to make him feel worthy of you."

CHAPTER 21

*E*arly May, 2023

*F*rom the corner of his eye, Jamie caught Mike peeking in his office. "Can I help you?" he said without taking his eyes off his computer screen.

"I'm headed out. Wanna grab some lunch?"

Again, without making eye contact, Jamie lifted a paper sack in the air. "No thanks. I packed today."

Intrigued, Mike walked in and took a glance at what his brother had packed. "Canned stew?"

An aggravated sigh and eye roll preceded Jamie's push back from his computer. "What do you want, Mike? You're all about work. I'm trying to work and you're interrupting me."

"Personally, I commend you for your commitment, but some members of the family are worried about you."

Jamie grunted and returned to his keyboard. "Tell everyone I'm fine."

"Funny how no one worries when *I* pull eighty-hour weeks."

"Is there something I can do for you? I'm trying to finish this proposal before the closing today."

Mike took a seat. "The Stones Throw Ranch closing?"

"Something attached to it. Something I've worked on for Laramee."

"So, talk to me for real. How're you doing since things didn't work out between you two?"

Jamie leaned back in his chair until he was nearly horizontal. He stretched his tight arms over his head and behind until he groaned aloud. "I'm miserable, angry at myself, and feeling a little hopeless. Is that what you wanted to hear?"

"I never want to hear that you're unhappy, Jamie."

He rubbed his fingers across his eyes. "I know that. I'm just doing what I do best—being morose."

Mike's brow wrinkled like a Shar Pei's. "Because you love Laramee."

"A moot point, Brother. I'm not the best man for her."

Mike placed his forearms on Jamie's desk and leaned over them. "So, you love a woman you can't have, and all you can do is hurt over her."

"An almost perfect summation of my misery. Except for one thing." He spun his computer screen around so Mike could see it.

"What's this?" Mike asked as he leaned closer to read all the columns on the chart.

"The fulfillment of a promise I made to Laramee, and one Reese Brockbank helped me sell to The Silver Buckle Mining Corporation Board."

"Explain."

"You know her brother Tyler died because the care he needed was too far away."

"Sadly, yes, which is why Laramee bought a helicopter—to move the patients to those centers more quickly. And, by the way, she found a pilot with his own helicopter who was willing to be her on-call flyer for five hundred grand and a fifty-year lease on the house."

"That's great news. She'll still have a nice sum left to launch a new life wherever she wants. How did you know about the chopper deal?"

Mike skirted the issue and then admitted, "We've been emailing documents back and forth. She tucked that good news in to the last one."

"She can't even bear to email me." Jamie blew out a rush of air. "All that matters is that she's really making this dream of hers happen. I made two promises to her: that I'd get the Brockbanks to agree to allow the pilot to live in the Stone's home, near the chopper and that they'd build a hangar there to protect the bird."

"Which all parties are already on board with and making plans for. So, what's this other deal?"

"To include a special provision in the dividend calendar—to give the Stones a share in all future profits."

"We've already discussed that as well," Mike said, drawing out the comment as if he were still confused and fishing for more details.

"The Brockbanks generously promised Sterling Stone eight percent on all the turquoise pulled from the land, but Reese negotiated an extra two percent for community development."

"Good will."

"Exactly, but a particular good will project."

Mike sat back and gave his brother a sideways stare. "You hope to build the hospital Laramee dreamed of."

"Much smaller. A medical center on the Stones' land, but one with cutting-edge equipment so life and death isn't determined by where you live."

Mike fell back into the chair. "Over time, that's going to cost a lot more than two-percent of the turquoise revenues."

"I've put the company's needs first, but all those early mornings and late nights? I spent those hours pulling in favors and donations from some of my new favorite people. The Brockbanks have been amazing. All of them. They want to be a partner in the community where many of their new workers will live, and that means they want a safe medical facility there as much as Laramee does." Jamie pointed to the charts on the screen. "Harrison Brockbank estimated the projected turquoise revenue and handed that data off to his brother Lucas Brockbank who is the Silver Buckle's CFO. He calculated what the two-percent revenue share for community development will bring in, and you're right. It's far too little to even pay the interest on a building loan. So, Reynolds Brockbank, the other business-savvy brother whose girlfriend and he just happen to run in the same circles as Victoria, are arranging a Denver fund-raising gala they hope will bring in ten million dollars, which is enough to get this project started."

Mike looked as if his head would explode. "You're kidding me."

Jamie smiled. "Nope. And there's more. Barrett Brockbank works for a big New York City Law Firm. He's agreed to handle all the contract work and apply for permits and grants. His younger brother, Finn Brockbank, is an artist with a marketing degree. He's going to handle all the marketing for the gala, plus, his alma mater includes an architectural school who encourages their students to submit plans for a goodwill project as part of a scholarship competition. The school chose the medical center as the project this year, so we'll have plans for a beautiful, efficient medical center for free."

"Unbelievable."

"It gets better. Finn contacted the New York ad agency he interned for. One of their biggest clients is Merit Medical Network. He asked the ad agency to present our clinic plan to Merit, and they loved the idea of placing remote trauma centers in rural areas so much that they're providing us with a grant, and if the program runs well, it could become a model across the Midwest."

Mike grew quiet. "The Brockbanks are an amazing family, but you, little brother, you've done a remarkable job as well. I'm so proud of you, Jamie, but what do you hope to accomplish by fulfilling Laramee's dream?"

"It's not like that. I know we're never going to be together, but I can't help that I still love her. And part of loving someone is helping make their dreams come true, isn't it?"

"You're a good man, Jamie. She loves you and you love her. How did things not work out?"

"What did I have to offer a woman who's perfectly happy picking up an axe to chop wood or mend a fence, all while living on canned chili in a dusty bunkhouse, dreaming of how she could make everyone else's life better? I began to wonder if practical, deer-hunting, soapmaking, hide-curing Sutton really was the better man for her than a spoiled, privileged, entitled man with a habit and a record."

"You forgot about that man being equally kind and gentle and loving. And the rest of that stuff is behind you."

"I couldn't risk it. Not with Laramee. She deserves better."

᠁

*a*n hour before the meeting was set to begin, Jamie began reconsidering his decision to attend the closing. He entered the conference room and looked at the seating. No matter where Laramee sat, they'd be near one another, a situation he feared would break his resolve.

He walked to Mike's office and peeked inside.

"What's up?" Mike asked.

"I need a favor." He put the proposal on his brother's desk. "Can you present this for me at the closing?"

Mike studied him for several seconds before nodding. "Are you sure this is how you want to handle this? It's your gift to Laramee."

"I don't need any credit. All that matters is that Laramee knows these plans are going to happen. They're very clear and straightforward. You should be able to explain it all easily. Besides, Reese and Lucas will be at today's meeting, and they can answer any questions."

"You did something amazing here, but okay. Of course, I'll handle this."

Jamie pressed his lips tightly and nodded. "Thanks. Did you send a driver for the Stones?"

"Sterling wouldn't hear of it. They're all driving in so Sterling can head straight to a bank in the city to deposit his check. He didn't trust having his money deposited electronically."

Jamie chuckled as he pictured Sterling's reaction to the idea. "Has Laramee said anything about her future plans?"

"Art school, I think. She didn't say where. Only that she wasn't going to let imperfection take something else she loved away from her."

Jamie knew the statement directly related to her time at ASU when she wasn't awarded a scholarship for her art, but he wondered whether her statement might also be aimed at him. His doubts about whether or not he was good enough for her caused him to pull back from her, but how would she have known that? The question picked at his peace as he left Mike's office and headed for his own.

Reese Brockbank arrived with another man who slightly resembled Reese. Jamie assumed the other man was Reese's brother, The Silver Buckle Mining Corporation's heralded CFO, Lucas Brockbank. After all the phone calls and exciting chats about the medical center, Jamie considered Reese and all the Brockbanks, dear friends. Back pats and handshakes ensued as Reese introduced Lucas to the Cannon brothers. Jamie discreetly excused himself after explaining that Mike and his father would be handling the closing.

He slipped into his office and stood at the window that overlooked the company's parking lot as Sterling Stone's truck arrived. He held his breath, waiting to catch a glimpse of Laramee. When he saw her, he felt his heart stop at the changes he saw. Her brown hair hung straight and free, and her clothes were new and sophisticated. Instead of wearing her signature jeans and button-front shirts, she arrived in a pair of slim black slacks and a scoop-necked, coral-colored sweater that hugged every curve. Dark sunglasses hid her eyes, but when she pulled them off, Jamie was pleased to see the same gentle features and soft caring glances pass between her and her parents.

He followed her with his eyes until she disappeared into the building, second-guessing his decision to avoid the meeting. He sat at his desk and leaned back, repeatedly clicking a pen as he argued with himself over whether or not to attend the meeting. He heard voices outside in the reception area offering greetings before the meeting. He homed in on Laramee's.

"Where's Jamie?" she asked.

He heard his father ask the receptionist to page his youngest son, and then he heard Mike offer up an explanation. "He's not going to be joining us today. Something came up on his schedule."

Jamie could tell by his father's response that he understood, and now both men in his family were attempting to cover up for his absence. Laramee, however, was having none of it.

"Then we can't close today."

Panic hit first, followed quickly by guilt as Jamie backed away from the door and paced across the room.

Mike rushed in to save the deal. "You and I have been handling all the back and forth, Laramee. We don't need Jamie to close this deal."

"I have a few concerns that I need to have resolved before I can advise my parents to sign."

"Concerns that only *Jamie* can resolve?" asked his father with a curious, almost playful tone.

"Exactly," Laramee answered with the same curious tone.

Jamie half expected his father to barge in and yank him out, and to avoid that spectacle, he opened the door and set his gaze on Laramee. His resolve melted as soon as their eyes met, but Laramee stood firm and resolute.

"Would you like to come in and discuss this privately?" he asked, gesturing for her to come into the room. She slipped through the door, and Jamie closed it behind her. Once the two were alone, they spent a moment studying the changes in one another.

"You...look...wonderful," Jamie began. "Very sophisticated."

"You looked great in my brother's jeans, but this look is...it's you. I see that now."

She blinked rapidly and turned away from him. Her eyes fixed immediately on the artwork hanging behind his desk, beside his diploma. It was the sketch she'd drawn of him, and he knew he'd exposed his heart.

"It's good to see you," he began, not knowing whether to hug her or to simply offer her a seat. "Would you like to sit down so we can discuss this calmly?"

"Not particularly."

He was unsure if she was referring to the sitting or the calm discussion part, but he had a good idea. She wasn't angry or lost, uncomfortable or shy. She knew what she'd come for, and she got to the point.

"You were trying to avoid me, weren't you?"

He sat on the edge of the desk, facing her and confessed, "I thought it would be easier."

"For whom? For you?"

Her answer caught him off guard. He could imagine four sets of ears, pressed to the outside of his door, listening to every word.

"Mike is authorized to handle the closing," he said. "What do you need me to do for you today?"

"I need to go over a document with you."

The answer was a brutal one. Despite having done his best to avoid her, he had seen her, he'd heard her voice, and he'd watched the caring way she watched over her parents. His feelings surfaced again, even stronger now after having spent the last two weeks thinking about her, wondering how she was spending her hours, and if he ever crossed her mind. He'd issued himself enough emotional and mental flogging to wise up considerably since they'd said goodbye, but he'd evidently done a fine sales job convincing her that he was not the man she deserved because she appeared to be all business today, with some document in hand.

She pulled a piece of paper from her bag and set it on the table. He didn't recognize it at first, and then he realized that it was his letter, the one he'd used to write out his feelings for Laramee. He hadn't thought about it since the night he wrote it, and seeing it struck him with a sense of regret he wouldn't have expected.

"Did you write this?" Her voice was softer now.

"I did." His body slumped, and then he straightened, figuring he owed it to her to look her in the eye. "It was the night your father was taken to the hospital. You were so sad, and I was trying to sort out my feelings because I didn't want to risk making a mistake."

"You say you love me in this letter."

He sighed and held her in his gaze. "Surely you didn't need a letter to know that."

Her eyes glistened and the hard set of her face eased. "Then why did you push me away?"

He'd argued with himself over this very question a hundred times in the ensuing weeks, and none of his well-rehearsed, sensible answers came to him. Except one. "If it came down to choosing me or

Sutton, I wanted you to end up with the better man. I wasn't sure that was me."

Laramee stepped to him and clasped his arms. "Then tell me who is, and don't say Sutton. I love him like a brother, but I'm not in love with him. He understands that now, and I didn't have to tell him. He saw it whenever we were together."

"He was the one who said—"

"I know what he said. He told me everything about the conversation you two had in the hospital. He asked me to fix the damage he caused." She moved a hand to his cheek, and he leaned into it. "James Cannon, you're not just the better man. You're the perfect man for me."

Jamie struggled to process Laramee's words because every other faculty was entirely focused on her face that grew softer and more love-filled as she spoke. He caught her up in his arms and pressed his cheek to hers. "I have so much baggage, Laramee. I'd die if I ever disappointed you."

She pulled back and smiled. "We'll disappoint each other from time to time, but who else will see divinity in my sketches or find my cooking unique? Who else would you suggest I tell my secrets to or ask to hold me while I dream my dreams."

"I'm more concerned about who will make those dreams come true."

"Are you volunteering?"

He closed his eyes and searched his heart. Could he keep a promise to never relapse back into the foolish patterns of his youth? He would fight these addictive tendencies for the rest of his life. Could he dedicate himself to being the better man? He had his answer. "I love you, Laramee. Choose me, and I'll always do my best to be the man you deserve."

He pulled her to him and kissed her, soaking in the way she filled his arms. He whispered, "When I first saw you today...you looked so different than you did on the ranch."

"I was always in there, somewhere. I couldn't find me until I was able to forgive myself. You made that possible by helping my father and me find our way back to each other."

"And what about now? I hear you're in art school?"

"It's my plan, but I'm sure I can find one nearby. Would that be agreeable to you?"

"Very." He kissed her again and asked, "Can I assume we have a deal?"

"There is one other item. The matter of that bet?"

"I still owe you cookies."

"More than that." She smiled and winked his way. "I'm still waiting to hear what compensation you were seeking if you won."

He brushed his lips over hers until she sighed. He pulled back and smiled. "At least one of these every day."

Laramee sighed again and said, "Corporate accepts your offer."

He pulled her to him, enfolding her in his arms. His mouth moved across hers in small teasing circles and then their kiss went deep and sweet.

Mike opened the door and whooped. "Ladies and gentlemen, it appears our closing has turned into a merger."

Applause and happy laughter broke out in the office, and then Laramee stepped back and crossed her arms, giving Jamie a devilish smile.

"And I hear you have a surprise for me. Something about a trauma center?"

"I can't wait to show you the plans." Jamie pulled her back into his arms.

"It's the best surprise you could have ever given me. You kept your promise to always put my happiness first."

He kissed her again and rubbed his thumb along her cheek. "I'll always keep my promises."

"Then promise to love me forever."

"Forever and beyond."

"What's beyond forever?"

"Just hold on to me and we'll find out together."

And they knew the best was yet to come.

THE END

ABOUT THE AUTHOR

Laurie (L.C.) Lewis is an award-winning LDS author and weather-whining lover of Tom, their wonderful kids by birth and by marriage, their thirteen perfect grandkids, and God. She's also crazy about seafood, nesting boxes, twinkle lights, sappy movies, and the sea.

Born in Baltimore, Laurie raised her family within the exciting and history-rich corridor between Philadelphia, Baltimore, and D.C., which made her a politics and history junkie, but a recent move to a house overlooking Utah Lake makes Utah her new love.

Laurie has written sixteen published novels in multiple genres, penning her women's fiction and romance novels as Laurie Lewis, and her historical fiction novels as L.C. Lewis.

Her WWII novel, "The Letter Carrier," won two 2023 Whitney Awards—for Novel of the Year and Best Historical/General Fiction—and the 2023 Readers Favorite Gold Medal for Inspirational Fiction. She's also a RONE Award Winner (*The Dragons of Alsace Farm*) and was twice named a New Apple Literary Award winner in 2017 (*The Dragons of Alsace Farm*) and in 2018, winning Best New Fiction (*Love on a Limb*). She is also a BRAGG Medallion honoree, and she was twice named a Whitney Awards and USA Best Books Awards finalist.

Laurie loves to hear from readers, and hopes you'll contact her at any of these locations:

VIP Readers' Club
https://www.laurielclewis.com/newsletter
Website http://www.laurielclewis.com
Amazon:
https://www.amazon.com/stores/Laurie-Lewis/author/B001JPC6XY
Goodreads
https://www.goodreads.com/author/show/1743696.Laurie_L_C_Lewis
Facebook
https://www.facebook.com/LaurieLCLewis/
Instagram
https://www.instagram.com/laurielclewis/
BookBub
https://www.bookbub.com/profile/laurie-lewis

www.ingramcontent.com/pod-product-compliance
Lightning Source LLC
Chambersburg PA
CBHW070739180626
46818CB00007B/2915